RESOLUTIONS

Recent Titles by Jane A. Adams from Severn House

The Naomi Blake Mysteries

MOURNING THE LITTLE DEAD
TOUCHING THE DARK
HEATWAVE
KILLING A STRANGER
LEGACY OF LIES

The Rina Martin Mysteries

A REASON TO KILL
FRAGILE LIVES
THE POWER OF ONE
RESOLUTIONS

RESOLUTIONS

A Rina Martin Novel

Jane A. Adams

This first world edition published 2010
in Great Britain and in the USA by
SEVERN HOUSE PUBLISHERS LTD of
9–15 High Street, Sutton, Surrey, England, SM1 1DF.
Trade paperback edition published
in Great Britain and the USA 2010 by
SEVERN HOUSE PUBLISHERS LTD

British Library Cataloguing in Publication Data

Adams, Jane, 1960-
Resolutions. – (A Rina Martin mystery)
1. Martin, Rina (Fictitious character)–Fiction.
2. McGregor, Sebastian (Fictitious character)–Fiction.
3. Retired women–Fiction. 4. Police–Great Britain–
Fiction. 5. Detective and mystery stories.
I. Title II. Series
823.9'14-dc22

ISBN-13: 978-0-7278-6896-1 (cased)
ISBN-13: 978-1-84751-242-0 (trade paper)

All Severn House titles are printed on acid-free paper.

Severn House Publishers support The Forest Stewardship Council [FSC], the leading international forest certification organisation. All our titles that are printed on Greenpeace-approved FSC-certified paper carry the FSC logo.

Typeset by Palimpsest Book Production Ltd.,
Grangemouth, Stirlingshire, Scotland.
Printed and bound in Great Britain by
MPG Books Ltd., Bodmin, Cornwall.

PROLOGUE

She'd just come in from shopping when the phone rang, struggling through the front door with three overloaded bags and trying to fend off the tail-wagging adulation of Frankie as he greeted her in the hall.

It had been raining and she was dripping wet.

Emily dropped her bags and grabbed the phone.

'We've found your father,' Mac's voice said.

The world slid sideways at that moment and Emily just managed to sit down on the bottom step before it swung a complete three-sixty degrees.

'You've what? Mac?'

'Look, Emily, I'm sorry to give you the news like this, but I've been trying to reach you since first thing and it'll be on the evening news. I wanted to get to you first; sorry it's over the phone.'

The receiver fell from nerveless fingers and dropped on to the tiled floor of her hall. She could hear his voice. 'Em, are you there? Em, are you OK?' She couldn't seem to respond.

Frankie yapped excitedly and then again, this time with an edge of concern. He snuffled at the fallen receiver and barked enquiringly. Emily leaned forward, wrapping her arms around her knees and crushing her breasts close against her thighs. She began to cry, the sobs dragged out reluctantly as though they'd been lodged in her throat so long they were now reluctant to leave. *Are you sure?* she wanted to ask him. *How can you possibly be sure?* But of course he must be sure: why else would he have called? He . . . they . . . must be sure. They had found her dad, after all this time. Not once did it occur to her that he might not be dead.

ONE

More than two hundred miles from home and Alec was feeling the effects not just of the early start but of the tension that had accompanied it. He had insisted on coming down to talk to Mac rather than just sending the news by official channels. The last time Alec had seen his friend and one-time close colleague had been at Alec's wedding earlier in the year. Mac had been a mess back then, just getting back to work after a six-month enforced spell of sick leave.

Sick leave and a hell of a lot of therapy.

Mac was back at work now, here in this little south-coast backwater, and, at first sight, looked as though the peace and quiet was suiting him.

'How did she take it?' Alec asked, fingering his still steaming cup of coffee, impatient for it to cool enough for him to drink. An enticing scent of vanilla accompanied the aroma of fresh ground beans.

'I'll call in to talk to her properly on my way up to Pinsent,' Mac said. It had taken several minutes for him to persuade Emily Peel to pick up the phone and respond to him again. Frankie, the dog, had filled the absence with snuffling and puzzled barks, but the canine conversation had not been loud enough to drown out the sound of Emily sobbing in the background.

'She thought he was dead,' he added. 'That letter she received a few weeks after . . . after Cara died.' It was still so hard to say. 'After Cara was murdered, Emily was convinced that her father must have committed suicide.'

'But you never were.' Alec was curious. He sipped cautiously at the coffee, found it tasted as good as the aroma had been.

'No. A man like that doesn't kill himself. Suicide would have implied remorse, something like humanity. A man who did what he did to that child, I can't believe he would be capable of anything like human feeling. Not for anyone.'

'He appears to have cared for his daughter.' Alec found himself playing devil's advocate.

'Appeared,' Mac repeated flatly. '*Just* appeared. Remember,

I worked that case from the very beginning; I was there when . . .' *There when Peel killed Cara Evans.* 'Which is why I'm accepting the secondment.'

Alec was silent for a moment, then he said, 'You know the offer's being made purely out of professional courtesy. No one expects you to take it up.'

'Poor old DI McGregor. Got to be seen to play nice by him.' Mac grimaced. 'I can't blame them, Alec, but they're wrong. I've always known he'd resurface, and now he has, I'm ready.'

Alec said nothing and the two men sipped in silence, Alec listening to the quiet sounds from the front office as the two other officers who made up this tiny rural team sorted through their day. 'You like it here?'

'A lot, yes.'

'It seems to be suiting you.' Alec was still cautious, unsure of how to ask.

'You want to know if I'm still in la-la land. I've had regular psych assessments, Alec.'

'True, but we all know what answers the shrinks want to hear. I want to hear it from you, Mac. I want to know how you are. How you really are.'

Mac considered the question. It was less than a year since he had seen Alec, but life had changed beyond all recognition. *He* had changed. He had come to Frantham, this funny little town with its Victorian B & Bs and short promenade, as a broken, fragmented near-suicide – though he'd been taking the slow, alcoholic route to that end. It had been winter then, February winds driving in from across the bay, freezing exposed skin. Now, it was winter again – November. The town once more cold, grey, empty of tourists, but Mac had mended. True, the repairs to his psyche were still not complete – the 'glue' still tacky and yet to fully harden – but mended none the less.

'I'm in a relationship,' he said, aware as the words came out just how oddly formal they sounded.

'Really?'

'You don't need to sound so surprised.' Mac managed a laugh. 'You're not the only one that can attract a beautiful woman.'

'Beautiful, eh?' Alec's eyes shone and Mac knew he was

thinking of his own wife, Naomi. Love of his life and a woman Mac too had once held a torch for.

He dug his wallet out of his pocket and showed Alec the picture of Miriam Hastings he carried there. 'We're . . . we're thinking of moving in together, probably after Christmas, when the contract on her flat comes up for renewal.'

Alec nodded approvingly at the picture of Miriam, admiring the long, dark hair and bright, startlingly blue eyes. He looked from the picture to Mac, as though appraising his suitability. Mac laughed, put the picture away, knowing what he was seeing. Unlike Alec, with his square jaw, wavy hair, 1950s Hollywood looks, Mac classified himself as ordinary. His own eyes were grey, usually the rather washed-out, cloudy grey of a day that can't quite be bothered to rain. His chin was a little too pointed, face a bit too thin and nose a little too broad and just a tad crooked – he had played rugby in his teens and the nose had suffered for it. He knew he wasn't handsome, but Miriam said that she loved his smile and the way his eyes changed their tone almost in sympathy with the weather, and he found, much to his own surprise, that he had almost come to believe her.

'I'm OK, Alec,' Mac said quietly. 'No, not one hundred per cent. I'm not sure I'll ever be that, but I'm ready. Alec, I couldn't bear not to be a part of this. You understand that?'

Alec nodded. 'I suppose I'd feel the same,' he admitted. 'But, Mac, be warned. They'll be watching, looking for the cracks to appear.'

Alec left soon after, and Mac called the two other members of his team into the office, brought them up to speed. There had been sightings of Cara Evans's killer; the net was closing. Mac wanted to be there.

Sergeant Frank Baker nodded his greying head. 'We'll hold the fort,' he said. 'Andy and me can cope, and we can call on our colleagues in Exeter if anything exciting happens.'

'Nothing exciting happens in the winter,' Andy Nevins complained. His bright red hair seemed to have brought its own illumination into Mac's rather dark office and his pale, freckled face emerged almost ghostlike from the gloom. Mac thought about turning on the lights, but found he didn't really want the additional luminance. It seemed oddly inappropriate.

'*I* arrived in winter,' he reminded Andy.

'True,' Frank Baker chuckled. 'And you've got to admit, Andy, we've had a fair bit of excitement since. Something of a crime wave this year, by local standards. More murders than Exeter.'

'Yeah,' Andy agreed. 'But he won't be here, will he? With Mac gone, everything'll settle down again. Back to boring.'

'To be honest, boy, I could do with a bit of boring,' Frank said with feeling. Mac was inclined to agree.

The sound of the outer door opening and releasing gale force wind into the front office brought Frank Baker to his feet just before the desk bell rang. Andy rose too.

'Hang on a minute, will you, Andy.'

The young man sat back down and looked nervously at his boss. 'Something wrong?'

'Not so far as I know. Andy, you're coming up to the end of your probationary year. I'd half expected you to have applied for a transfer by now?'

The young man shuffled in his seat.

'I just wanted you to know that I'll back up whatever you want to do.'

Andy looked awkwardly at his boss. 'Even if I want to stay here?'

Mac was momentarily caught off balance by the unexpected reply.

'I like it here,' Andy went on. 'Oh, I know I'll have to move on some time, get urban experience and all that, but I've had more hands-on this year on some really big cases than I'd be likely to have got in five years up the coast. I'd have been bottom of the pile there. Here, you've treated me like I'm an important part of the team. You know?' He finished lamely. 'I'd like to stop here, if it's all right with you.'

Mac found that he was smiling; grinning so much his cheeks hurt. 'It's fine by me,' he said. 'More than fine.'

The young man rose to go, and Mac started to think what needed doing before he left for Pinsent. Andy had paused in the doorway.

'Mind if I ask something, boss?'

'Ask away.'

'The guy that killed that little girl. That Cara Evans. I know his name was Thomas Peel 'cos I looked it up in the file, but you never call him by his name. I just wondered: why is that?'

Mac stared at him, totally floored by the question. He wanted to deny it, to say that of course he used the man's name. Not to would have been . . . Then he realized that, of course, Andy was right. He avoided voicing Thomas Peel's name. Avoided even thinking it.

'I just started thinking,' Andy went on, carefully avoiding his boss's eye, 'about something Mrs Martin once said. She was talking to me mam about someone they knew what had cancer, I think. Anyway, this woman didn't want to talk about it. Wouldn't say *that* word.'

Mac was uncomfortable with the direction this was taking and taken aback by the fact that Andy Nevins should be quoting Rina Martin. 'Andy, where are we going with this?'

Andy shrugged. 'Only that Mrs Martin reckoned that you'd not faced up to something if you couldn't call it by its name. She said if you give a thing a name, you start to cut it down to size. That's all.' Cheeks flaming almost as red as his hair, he retreated into the front office, leaving Mac slightly stunned.

Mac closed his eyes. So now Andy Nevins too had fallen under the Rina Martin spell. But he was right and so was she, Mac acknowledged. Name a thing, have power over it. Wasn't that a kind of ancient magic?

'Thomas Peel,' he said softly. 'His name was Thomas Peel and he killed Cara Evans while I watched and could do nothing, and then I let him go.'

He closed his eyes. Not that he needed to. The image of that night on the beach was so strong, so vivid, he had no need to conjure it up.

Bright stars in a heavy, black sky, pressing down so hard the world seemed compressed. The sea, oily and calm, lapping at the killer's feet as he held the child in front of him, a knife at her throat. Mac could no longer recall the words he'd used as he tried to talk the man into dropping the knife, his ears straining for the sounds of the promised backup arriving. He had just said anything: *keep talking, keep him looking at you, keep the child alive.*

And then the stray siren, despite Mac's demand that the approach be silent, and the shriek of sound broke the spell that Mac had been weaving. Seconds, less than seconds later, the child lay on the sand and her killer had fled and Mac – Mac went to the child and not after the man, despite the fact that reason and his own horrified gaze told him that Thomas

Peel had cut her throat so deeply he had severed blood vessels, severed her trachea: there was nothing he could do.

And that was how his colleagues had found him. Kneeling in the shallow water, the body of Cara Evans cradled in his arms, his hand on her throat, trying to stem the flow of blood that had already spilled out on to the sand.

'Thomas Peel.' Mac said it with more conviction this time, knowing that he'd be hearing that name repeated numberless times in the coming days and that Andy – and Rina – were right: you had to name your fears if you were to have any hope of controlling them. 'His name was Thomas Peel.'

TWO

Emily Peel could not settle anywhere. She had managed to unpack the shopping, even to make herself a cup of tea – though not to remember to drink it. It sat, reproachful and cold, with that sort of cloudy scum on top that forms when too much milk has been added to the mug, like when Calum made it. She'd made *Calum* tea. She *never* made *Calum* tea.

Emily took a deep breath, trying to get a grip on the stupid, random thoughts that were racing through her brain as she tried to block those memories that her mind didn't want to deal with. She ought to take Frankie for a walk, she thought. She ought to get the washing done. She should at least tidy the kitchen.

In the end, she did none of those things – and had done none of those things by the time Calum came home and she realized the day was ended and she had not even been aware of its passing.

'Em?' The front door slammed shut and from the hall came the dull thud that signalled the dropping of Calum's work bag on to the tiled floor. 'You home, love? Why is it so dark in here? Hello, Frankie, boy; where is she, then?'

Calum bustled into the living room, Frankie in tow. 'Emily? What is it, baby?'

He knelt down beside her, taking her hands. 'Emily?'

She stared at him, uncomprehending. 'He's not dead,' she whispered. 'He's not dead. Calum, it isn't over and now I don't know what to do.'

He didn't need to ask who she meant. Instead, he pulled her off the chair and down beside him on the floor, gathering her as close to his body as he could, Frankie joining the group embrace and whimpering softly.

'He doesn't know where you are, Em; you don't need to be scared. He's not part of our lives, not part of you any more. Emmy, he's not here.'

She was trembling, shaking so violently that he too was

truly scared, as though her fear was somehow contagious. 'We'll go away for a while. I'll phone work and tell them I need time off. It isn't a busy time of year; Jim will understand.'

He felt her shake her head.

'Hey.' Gently, he eased her body away from his just enough for him to look down into her eyes. A thought occurred to him. 'How did you find out?'

'Mac called, this morning. He said he didn't want me to hear it from anyone else. He's coming up tomorrow. He's . . .' She buried her head in his chest once more and wept painful, noisy tears. Calum stroked her back and, somehow, welcomed the tears. Tears were kind of normal, after all. That terrible stricken silence was something he didn't know how to handle. 'I'll take the day off, be with you when he comes.'

He felt her nod. 'Then we'll think what to do next. Like I said, I can take some time.'

This time the head was shaken. 'I'm not going to run.' She sounded angry now and Calum saw that as another good sign. She pulled away, wiping at reddened eyes with the heels of her hands. 'Not unless you want me to go.'

'Oh, hey, now don't start that again. I already told you more times than I can count: whatever comes, we face it together. I told you that when you told me who you were and what your dad had done. We'll get through this, Em. You and me. You understand that?'

She nodded, but didn't seem convinced. 'What if he comes here?'

'Why would he? Look at it logically. How could he even know where you were? And if he did know . . . Well, love, if he's not dead now, then he's not been dead for all that time you thought he was. He could have turned up any time over the past year plus, and he hasn't, has he? So what makes you think he will now?'

She tried to agree, tried to smile, to admit that what he said was right, but it was as though Mac's phone call had once more made her father real, solid. She had managed to believe the letter the police had shown her. Managed to convince herself that he was dead, even though suicide was something she would never have associated with her father. Now, however, all of that reality, all of those thoughts she'd managed *not* to have since then, seemed to crowd in on her, waiting in the shadows at the edges of the room, at the periphery of her vision. Waiting for her to acknowledge them. Waiting to drown her.

Mac and Miriam arrived unannounced at Peverill Lodge just after seven o'clock. The evening meal was in the process of being cleared away, but leftover dessert was offered and accepted. The food in the Rina Martin household was always worth sampling and Miriam had become a major fan of Steven Montmorency's cooking. Mac left Miriam ensconced at the kitchen table, digging into sticky toffee pudding and catching up on news with Bethany and Eliza, two more members of the extended family. He followed Rina into the little room at the front of the house that she reserved as her own personal space. Tim Brandon, the youngest member of the Martin household, joined them a moment later with a loaded tray of tea and more toffee pudding.

Love, in the Martin household, seemed, Mac thought, to be doled out in deep blue bowls and drenched in cream. It was also delivered freely in terms of conversation and sound advice, and Mac felt deeply in need of both.

He waited to speak until Tim had settled the tea tray on to the low table set between the two fireside chairs and brought a third chair from the recess of the bay window and he had accepted a cup from Rina, putting off the moment.

'Not working tonight?' he asked Tim.

'No, it's Monday.'

'Oh, of course it is. Sorry, Tim, my brain is elsewhere. I'm glad you're here, though.'

'Trouble?' Tim's dark eyes filled with sympathy.

'Yes . . . no. I mean . . .' He took a deep breath. 'I heard this morning. There's been a break in the Cara Evans case. It's been upgraded to active and I've been offered the opportunity to be part of the investigation.'

Silence seemed to drop upon the room from some point above the ceiling. Mac saw Tim and Rina exchange a glance and knew what was going through their minds. They had known him since his first days here at Frantham and would be thinking . . .

'I'm ready to deal with it,' Mac said softly. 'I know you'll be worried, I know it won't be easy, but, Rina, I have to do this.'

She sighed. 'Of course you do, Mac, but the selfish part of me wishes you'd had a bit longer to prepare.'

'Would that have made it any better?' Tim wondered. 'Sometimes, having time to stand on the edge is harder than making the leap.'

Rina nodded. 'Sometimes,' she agreed. 'Mac, when do you leave?'

'In the morning, first thing. Miriam's going to keep an eye on the boathouse. I expect she'll be staying there as much as she usually does, so no worries about that.'

'And we'll keep an eye on Miriam,' Rina assured him. 'I don't suppose you've any idea . . .'

'How long this will take? No, none at all. But it's the first movement we've had in the case for months; everyone will be eager to push things on as fast as possible.'

'I imagine they will.'

Mac caught the odd tone in Rina's voice and realized what she had heard in his. He had already removed himself from Frantham and therefore from them. He was already thinking and behaving as though he had gone, become part of this other world in which they did not figure.

'I'll be coming back,' he said firmly. 'Rina, I'm under no illusions about what this is going to do to me. I'm going to need my family when this is over.'

Somewhat mollified and reassured, she reached out and took his hand. 'We'll be here,' she said. 'But, Mac, I want you to promise me something. I can understand that you have to see this thing through, to see an end to it, but remember, Mac, you are not invincible and, much as I regret having to say it, you are not indispensable, not to the police. There are other officers. You *are* indispensable to us. Irreplaceable. Promise me you will remember that?'

He had rarely seen her look more concerned or more earnest and he responded in kind. 'I promise,' he said solemnly. 'If I find I can't cope, I will take myself off the case.' He smiled wryly. 'You can be sure I'm going to be under the tightest of scrutiny, you know. They'll be looking for poor old DI McGregor to fall apart on the job.'

* * *

A few miles away, a young woman got off the late train at Honiton Station and checked into the George Hotel on the High Street. She asked about hire cars, said she'd be staying for two days, maybe more, smiled and flirted with the young man at reception. Her blonde hair shone brightly in the strong lights in the lobby, skilfully highlighted and the cut expensive and as tailored as the black wool coat she wore. She had one bag with her and she said it was fine, she could carry it up herself.

The young man at reception watched hungrily as she recrossed the lobby and headed for the stairs.

'Put your eyes back in,' his manager joked, coming from the small office behind reception. He glanced at the registration sheet she had just filled in. 'Carolyn Johnson,' he said. 'Out of your league, mate. Way out.'

The receptionist, blushing furiously, attempted to laugh it off. 'I can dream, can't I?'

'Oh, dream on,' his manager said and retreated to the office, still laughing.

THREE

Mac left early, kissing Miriam goodbye and watching regretfully as she rolled over and snuggled back down beneath the duvet. Outside, the morning was chill and grey and a stiff breeze blew off the sea as he completed the short walk round the headland to collect his car from behind the police station. Old Frantham Town, where his boathouse flat was located, had no vehicular access, a fact which had helped keep it free of the second-homes brigade. It also had a population of rather determined and conservative locals who resisted change with a tenacity that Mac had at first viewed as eccentric, but which, less than a year into his tenure, he now understood completely.

Frantham was fine for the tourists – the locals needed the tourists – but Frantham Old Town was theirs, pure and simple, and he was fortunate enough that they had accepted him as an honorary local after so short a time.

The weather seemed to be reflecting his morning mood: cold and bleak and totally lacking in view. Still dark when he left the boathouse, the slight lifting from black to grey that announced predawn this time of year was immediately blurred again by a thickening sea mist, the fog rolling in as the cold breeze suddenly subsided. His brain seemed full of that selfsame fogginess. What on earth did he think he was doing, heading north to participate in an investigation, the first round of which had damn near finished him off both mentally and physically? He really wasn't up to this; Alec had as good as told him so the previous day, and Rina had tacitly agreed, he was sure of that.

He could call Alec now: tell them that he'd changed his mind, made a mistake, really wasn't ready. No one would hold that against him. Like Alec said, the invitation to rejoin the investigation had been extended out of courtesy. No one had expected him to say yes. They'd all be relieved if he took himself out of the equation.

Yes, he could call Alec, then turn around and rejoin Miriam

in that warm bed. No need to get up again for at least another hour. His brain nagged at him, inner voices yammering and pleading, but his feet seemed to have other ideas and continued with their steady tramp, tramp, along the wooden walkway and then on to the solid if shabby concrete of the promenade.

Too late now. Moments later he was in his car, manoeuvring out of the tiny space at the back of the police station, and on his way. Too late now for second thoughts. For good sense or good advice.

'Thomas Peel,' he said aloud, remembering his conversation with Andy the day before. The name had become a mantra now, a focus and reminder. 'Thomas Peel. And this time I'm going to get the bastard.'

Heading north-east, back to that other coast, that other sea, but first to see the other victim of all this. Peel's child.

Calum met him at the front door. Mac had met Emily's boyfriend once before, spoken to him on the phone a couple of times, but not recently. He was shocked by the young man's pallor, by the dark circles beneath his eyes.

'We didn't get any sleep,' Calum said. 'She just couldn't manage to close her eyes. Every time she tried, she dreamed about him, even before she fell asleep.'

Mac nodded, remembering a time when Thomas Peel had walked through his every dream, sleeping and then, as time went on, waking too.

'I'm sorry.' It seemed such an inadequate thing to say, but Calum nodded, looked grateful for the sympathy.

'I told her we should take some time away. I can get holiday.'

'You should be at work today?'

'I phoned in. Boss was OK; we're not exactly busy.'

Mac recalled that Calum worked for a little company that designed and installed high-end kitchens. He didn't imagine that the current economics were healthy. He followed the younger man through to the back of the house and into the kitchen. Emily stood by the sink, kettle in hand, but a look on her face that suggested she couldn't think what to do with it.

Calum took it from her, kicked a chair out from under the table and sat her down, gestured to Mac to do the same. He ran the tap and plugged the kettle in.

'So,' he said, 'what's happening? Where is he, then? And how come the bastard didn't have the guts to kill himself like we thought he had?' He shrugged, as though realizing he'd answered his own question.

'I knew he wasn't dead,' Emily said slowly. 'I just wanted to believe he was. Just really, really wanted to.'

Mac reached out and took her hand. Back then, when they had hunted Thomas Peel the first time, he had sat for hours, or it had seemed like hours, holding her hand, drinking tea, not knowing what to say or how to stop the tears, though the silence after the tears had been worse. She clasped his hand now and managed a brief smile, and he knew she was remembering that time too, and that, like him, she could no longer have told anyone who was comforting whom.

Emily had that kind of skin that was always milk pale, Mac thought. Mousy brown hair that was shot through with blonde in summer, and the darkest blue, almost violet, eyes. She wasn't conventionally pretty, though her oval face was delicately proportioned and her hair was surprisingly thick and soft. It was the eyes that stopped her from being plain, that captured the attention and held it long enough for the viewer to realize that she also had a lovely, sweet smile. He could fully understand the almost worshipful look that Calum cast in her direction, the slight jealousy with which he regarded Mac's hand on hers.

'I don't have all the details,' he said. 'But there's been a sighting, one that checked out. Someone saw him who knew him from before, a man called John Bennet?'

Emily nodded. 'They worked together.'

'He saw . . .' That problem with naming again, but this time the word Mac had trouble with was . . .

'My father,' Emily said. 'He saw my dad. It's all right, Mac. I can cope with you saying it. I can't change the fact I'm related to him.'

'He saw him and followed him, watched when he went into a little boarding house, then called the police.'

'Where?' Calum demanded.

'He'd come back to Pinsent,' Mac said.

'He'd come back? Why? How come no one else saw him?' Calum looked away. The kettle had boiled and he made tea. Coffee for himself. Mac noted that his hand was shaking.

'Why go back to Pinsent?' Emily was astonished. 'He'd know someone would be sure to see him. The boarding house. The police . . .'

'Went there, but he'd gone. According to the landlady, he'd checked out earlier that day, just "popped back in", she said, to see if he'd left his scarf.' He paused. 'Mr Bennet was on his lunch break. He still works the same job as he did when your father knew him; still gets his lunch from the same corner shop . . .'

'He wanted to be seen.' Emily nodded emphatically, as though that made perfect sense, which, given what Mac knew about her father, it probably did. The man was an exhibitionist, a walking ego. He loved to play games. 'He knew when Mr Bennet would go for lunch and where he'd go. He showed himself.'

'That's what we think,' Mac confirmed. 'They put out an alert and got two more sightings for the same day, another the morning after. That was three days ago and there's been nothing since, but it's the best lead we've had in a long time and it's confirmation that he's still alive.'

'Why is he doing this?' Calum shook his head. 'I don't get it. The bloke was free and clear. Why come back?'

'Money,' Mac said. 'We know he was owed money. My colleagues think he's come to collect.'

'Owed? By who?'

Mac took a deep breath. 'Thomas Peel is a killer,' he said. 'And we know Cara Evans wasn't the first child he abducted. What we also know is—'

'That he got kids for men who . . . who like that sort of thing.' When it came to it, Emily couldn't say it either.

'Paedophiles?' This was new to Calum. 'Em, you never told me that, I mean . . .'

'He never touched me if that's what you're worried about.' Her voice was harsh. 'I never told you that part because it was all bad enough already. Because that bit of it didn't make it into the newspapers. Because it was just one more thing to chuck at you, to make you want to say . . .'

'To say I love you,' Calum interrupted her. 'Em, I'm still here, I ain't about to run away. I'm not living with your dad.'

Silence gathered itself in the tiny kitchen; silence that shouted at them that living with her father was precisely what they'd all been doing. Calum shook himself, handed mugs of tea to Mac and Emily. 'So, what now?' he said. 'All that other stuff, you kept it back from the media?'

Mac nodded. 'We had names, no proof. We had one case of blackmail, knew there were more. Calum, it was all such a tangle, such a bloody mess, it was decided we would keep that side of things under wraps until something broke. Nothing did, not until now.'

'He's contacted someone?'

Mac nodded. 'I'm sorry, I can't tell you much, largely because I don't know much, but we had permission to monitor certain phones calls. He made a call to one of those men.'

Silence again. Nothing to say. Far more questions than could be fitted into that small space filled by a little wooden table, two school chairs and three bodies.

Calum finally broke the spell. 'So, what now?' he asked again. 'Do you think he'll come here?'

'You think he knows where I am?' Emily had confronted that question already, but to hear Calum ask Mac thrust it at her with renewed intensity.

'I think he might,' Calum said. 'Look, Em, your dad is a lot of things, but we know he's clever and we know he likes everyone to know it.' He looked at Mac for confirmation. Mac, gaze fixed on Emily, just nodded.

Emily took a deep breath, released it slowly. 'I'm not running,' she said at last. 'If he comes here, Mac, then we can let you know. You can arrange for someone to watch out, can't you? Maybe even tap the phone?'

Mac frowned. This was not the response he had expected. He'd been all set to offer the option of a safe house until this was all over, but it seemed he was not the only one set on facing his demons.

'We're sure,' Calum said, pulling his rather skinny body up to full height and squaring what, considering his frame, were surprisingly powerful shoulders. He would need them, Mac thought. Need all the breadth he could muster.

'OK, then.' He took a business card from his pocket and wrote his mobile number on the back. 'Any time, just call me. I'll arrange for a family liaison officer to get in touch today and they'll coordinate with me and the rest of the team.' He drained his mug and stood, feeling overlarge in the small space.

'You'll ring me later?' Emily asked. It seemed that some stranger in family liaison would not be enough.

'I'll ring you later,' Mac confirmed. Calum saw him to the door. 'If you change your mind,' Mac said, 'we can arrange for somewhere to stay.'

'She's decided,' Calum said. 'Take a team of horses to shift her now, and if Em's decided, then I have too. We can do this, Mac.' He shook Mac's hand, an oddly formal gesture. It was, thought Mac, as though Calum was sealing a deal, and it occurred to Mac that Calum expected him to keep his side of it.

FOUR

Mac had not been back to the place he had once called home in eighteen months. He had spent most of his sick leave away, staying with friends and then, when the strain of their sympathy grew too much to bear, in a remote cottage loaned to him by a colleague. The cottage had been a legacy left by some distant relative. It had been up for sale, but there had been few potential takers. Some things are too remote even to appeal to the most enthusiastic of second-homers and the price bracket just too high for the locals. Mac had been caretaker, occasional viewings officer and increasingly morose guest, until both he and the owner had decided the property was too remote even for him. He'd sunk even deeper into despair: so deep that he was suspected of frightening off at least a couple of sets of possible buyers and his colleague became concerned that another set might turn up one day and find him drunk or dead.

That had been a low point in six months of low points, and he'd woken up one morning to find himself in a monastery of all places. He had no memory of having arrived or of the past six days, but apparently his new place of residence had been courtesy of Alec who had friends in some very unexpected places. He was, he was told, officially on spiritual retreat.

'Retreat?' Mac had asked.

'It's better than running away.'

Mac smiled, remembering Alec's comment. 'Better than running away.'

Very true. Peace, quiet, someone to talk to or not to talk to . . . Mac had shifted tack, retreated rather than tried to run, and eventually returned to work. He had not, though, completely returned, not until now. Now, it seemed, he was running hard in the opposite direction and he had drawn others back with him. He was certain that Emily would have lacked the courage to make her own stand had anyone but Mac been the one to bring her the news, and he was as yet undecided if that was a good or a bad thing.

He made the final turn off the main road, second left at the roundabout and into Pinsent. This little seaside town, very much like his now beloved Frantham, with its promenade and rows of tall, Edwardian houses now converted to flats and B & Bs. Here, though, it was possible to drive along the road next to the promenade, unlike Frantham promenade which was now a paved pedestrian zone. In summer he'd have had to ease along slowly, avoiding the holidaymakers who determinedly ignored the crossings. Now, in the depths of winter, though the cars still moved with habitual slowness, the road was clear and dreary. He glanced out towards the sea, grey and cold-looking in the winter sun of the early afternoon. He glanced at the clock on the dashboard and noted that it was nearly two, that he was hungry, that he was not expected until the planned briefing at four. Not quite ready to run headlong after all, he pulled into a side road and walked back to a once familiar café facing the sea and ordered tea and bacon rolls, sat in the window and watched the world go by, thinking how much of it had gone by since he had last been here.

'Well, hello, stranger!'

Mac's heart sank. He wasn't ready yet to face outsiders. His colleagues would be bad enough. He managed to compose his face into some semblance of welcome as the woman drew out a chair opposite and sat down, uninvited.

'Ginny!' Mac laughed with relief and genuine pleasure. 'How the devil are you?'

'I'm good, really good. You?' She tilted her head and studied him thoughtfully. 'You don't look too bad at all, considering.' She wagged her finger, mockingly, schoolteacherish. 'You had a lot of people worried, young man.'

Mac laughed again. *Young man*. He was at least a dozen years older than Ginny.

'Still married, I hope?'

Her eyes softened. 'Oh yeah, it's all still good. Kids are in school now, you know. Both of them.'

'Never. I can't believe that.'

She laughed. 'A lot can happen when you're not watching,' she said. She reached across and patted his hand in an almost maternal gesture, then glanced at her watch. 'Speaking of which, time to pick them up. I'd best get a move on. I saw you through the window, thought I ought to say hello, you know. I'm glad you're OK, you were always well . . . you know. You were all right.'

She left, allowing the door to clang behind her. Mac ordered another cup of tea. Ginny hadn't changed, he thought. No reason why she should have; it hadn't been that long. He wondered if she was still working, if her husband really didn't know. What secrets families keep . . .

Carolyn Johnson had ordered a taxi to take her to Frantham and then hired a car from the DeBarr garage-cum-filling-station-cum-car-hire just outside the seaside town. Once, the DeBarrs had owned half of Frantham-on-Sea and their name still graced the Hotel up on Marlborough Head, but the mini-empire had long since shrunk down to what Ray DeBarr considered a satisfyingly manageable size.

'How long will you want it for?' he asked the attractive blonde as she lay her documentation on the desk in front of him.

'Oh, three, four days maybe. Can I extend if I need to?'

Ray checked through her licence and insurance details. 'Of course; not much call this time of year. I'll give you a card; you give me a call and you can renew over the phone. Now, how would you like to pay?'

He watched her appreciatively as she left, sashaying out across the forecourt towards the waiting hatchback, and half-heartedly wished himself twenty years younger, correcting that to thirty and conceding that he probably couldn't have afforded her anyway. She wore jeans and a black, three-quarter length coat, but he'd have made a bet that both bore labels his wife would have drooled over and even he may have heard of.

'Back in the day,' he mused to himself, filing the copies of Carolyn Johnson's paperwork. Back when being a DeBarr actually meant something. He chuckled at his own fantasies. Having money wasn't the same thing as having class, and the young woman he had just encountered seemed well in possession of both.

Ten minutes later, the little hatchback pulled up in front of Peverill Lodge. The blonde-haired woman calling herself

Carolyn Johnson took a moment or two to compose herself before getting out, suddenly taken by surprise at the attack of nerves. Rina was the one person in the world who still daunted her, but, even had someone put a gun to her head and demanded the reason, she could not have explained why. Would she be home? Knowledge of the routine in the Martin household told her that lunch would be over, that the Peters sisters would most likely be having their afternoon nap, and that Rina would be busying herself with something or other that probably involved sticking her nose into someone else's business.

Which, after all, was precisely why 'Carolyn' had come back to see her.

Hooking her black leather bag off the passenger seat, she got out of the car, crossed the road to Peverill Lodge and rang the bell. Somewhat to her surprise, it was Rina who opened the door, and to her great satisfaction it was several seconds before the older woman recognized her.

Then understanding dawned. 'Hello, Karen,' Rina said. 'I had an odd feeling you might turn up some time soon. You'd better come in.'

Mac was at the same time back on home ground and also feeling the trepidation and strangeness of being an outsider. Somehow he had expected things to have changed, but the front desk was still scuffed and in need of a polish, and still scarred with rings left from hot mugs. The green lino still looked as if Noah might have made use of it for bedding down something with sharp claws, and he would have sworn the same youths still waited on the uncomfortable benches.

The desk sergeant, a man Mac did not recognize, glanced up with an enquiring smile as Mac entered the reception area. Behind the man, through a frosted glass screen, Mac could see silhouettes moving as officers assembled for the briefing. Alec must have been looking out for him because he appeared just as Mac was about to introduce himself to the desk sergeant. Alec buzzed him through the half-glazed door.

'Everything all right?' he asked quietly.

'Everything's fine,' Mac assured him and surprised himself by finding this was almost the truth.

*   *   *

'What is it you want?' Rina asked.

'Direct as ever.' Karen was amused.

'Of course. I see little point in prevaricating. Do you take sugar?'

'One, please. Thank you.' Karen took the china cup and saucer from Rina, aware as she did so that the cup rattled gently against its rest. She lowered it on to her knees, wondering if this use of china was a Rina Martin ploy to test her nerve. Who needs lie detectors when you have bone china? 'I came back to see George,' she said. 'He's my brother. I want to know he's OK.'

'You could have phoned if that was all. You have my number. I promised to keep an eye on him and I have.'

'I want to see him.'

'Why?'

'Why not? I have a right to come and see him.'

Rina shook her head. 'No, my dear, you don't. Your rights ended when you left. George's rights are paramount now, and he has a right to get on with his life.'

'He'd know I'd not abandon him.'

'He never felt you had. Karen, George understood completely why you had to leave in such a hurry. He's not a fool and he knows you far better that you give him credit for. George loves you, is grateful to you, but is under no illusions. He knows what you are.'

'And what am I, Rina?'

'I believe the technical term is sociopath.'

'Really. Not a psycho, then?'

Rina smiled, chuckled softly. 'You know better than that, sweetheart. What were you studying? Psychology, wasn't it? No, a true psychopath has no ability to empathize, and I know, Karen dear, that your problem in some ways is that you have empathized too much.'

'You have to defend your own.' Karen shrugged lightly. The cup and saucer rattled.

'There are ways and ways of defending.'

'Are there? Rina, I know you mean well; you always do. I know you believe every word you're saying, but I want to see George and I want to take him with me. He belongs with what's left of his family. I should never have left him behind, but I can put that right now.'

'And if he doesn't want to go?'

Karen's laughter was genuinely disbelieving. 'Of course he'll want to go,' she said. 'What is there to keep him here?'

'Oh, you'd be surprised,' Rina said. 'I really think you would.'

As it happened, there was a great deal to keep George in Frantham. While Hill House might not exactly be most people's first choice of home, events had conspired to make sure George felt it was his. He'd made friends there, he'd earned kudos by defending both his home and his carer, saving her life when she'd been brutally attacked, and, more than all of that, he'd now spent more time there than he'd spent in any place for a very long time.

He had a room of his own. He had stuff of his own that he could be fairly certain would not have to be abandoned when the family did another night-time flit, and he had a best friend who might actually, tentatively, delicately, be thought of as his girlfriend. Not that he'd yet risked calling Ursula that, but everyone else at Hill House and at school thought of them as an item, even if he'd not yet had the nerve to own the phrase himself.

He certainly didn't want to be going anywhere.

Damn, even his school work was OK these days, largely due to Ursula, of course, but also down to the fact that he was settled and calm and actually enjoying school – most of the time at least.

Rina's call came just a few minutes after the minibus had dropped them all after school. It wasn't unusual for Rina to ring Hill House for either himself or Ursula, but her timing *was* unusual. She usually waited until he'd been home for a while, knowing that they'd then have time for a proper chat.

George knew at once that something must be wrong.

'What's up?' he asked, his absence of preamble a habit picked up from his older mentor.

'Does anything have to be up?'

'Doesn't have to be, but it is. I can hear it in your voice.'

Rina sighed. 'It's Karen,' she said.

'Karen? Nothing happened to her, did it?' It occurred to him to wonder how Rina would know.

'She's fine, George. In fact, I suspect she's more than fine.

It's just . . . George, she turned up here. This afternoon. She wants to see you. No, more than that, she wants you to go with her. She wants you to leave, George.'

There was silence on both ends of the line. George found that his chest had tightened. He held his breath, as though waiting for the next blow to fall.

'George?' Rina sounded concerned, well aware that on occasion she lacked finesse. 'I'm sorry, love. Are you all right?'

'She's here?' George felt he could only take in so much of what Rina said. 'No, Rina, she can't be here. What if Mac sees her?'

'Mac left this morning. He's gone up north for a while.'

'And she's come back.' It occurred to George that this was no coincidence. Though with the next thought he wondered how Karen could possibly have known. *He* hadn't been told that Mac was going away. But, then, that was what Karen did. What she had always done: *known* things. Known things and then done something about them, and Mac, George suspected, comprehended exactly what she'd done the last time she'd been in Frantham and that someone was dead as a result of that.

'What does she want, Rina? Is she coming here?'

'She wants to see you, George. She wants you to go away with her.'

'Away with her? No, I don't want to, Rina. I want to stay here. Is she coming here?'

'I didn't tell her where you were, love, but I don't think it'll take her long to find out. George, don't you worry: you aren't going to go anywhere, but I didn't want her suddenly appearing on the doorstep and you being taken by surprise.'

'No, no, thanks.' George chewed his lower lip, a habit he'd been trying hard to break. Just turned fourteen, he'd started to think of himself as one step from an adult; now, suddenly, he seemed to have been plunged back into the uncertainties and insecurities of childhood. It wasn't that he was scared of his sister. Not really. The two of them had been so close before their mum had died . . . 'I'll have to see her,' he said. 'Talk to her and tell her I want to stay here. She'll be OK with that, I know she will.'

He could hear the doubt in Rina's voice as she replied. 'If

that's what you want to do, George, then how about you meet her here?'

George breathed a sigh of relief. He did want to see Karen, really he did. He loved his sister, but . . . 'Thanks, Rina,' he said. 'Thanks for that.'

'No problem,' Rina told him, though it sounded like a lie. 'I've got her number and I'll give her a call, then phone you back.'

George lowered the receiver as carefully as if it might explode.

Mac followed Alec through to the briefing room, struck by the familiarity of it. That same slightly dusty smell, overlaid with a faint scent of lavender polish and pine disinfectant. He could recall the time when the briefing room would have been thick and acrid with the smoke from a dozen cigarettes, but that era was long gone.

The furnishing was basic here. Long tables stacked with paperwork and computer equipment, set against the wall so that the rats' nest of cables from all the electronic equipment could be tucked away enough to satisfy health and safety – provided they didn't look too closely and see the doubled-up plugs in inadequate sockets. Plastic chairs on tubular frames, the red seats old enough to be faded to a dull orange and stained by years of handling, were tucked under desks and occupied the central space. Incongruously, in the corner set aside for mugs and kettle, an old, faux-leather fireside chair half-blocked the door to a tall cupboard. The chair had just appeared one day and had stayed ever since. Ten years or so, to Mac's knowledge. It had become convention that anyone sitting there should be left well alone, their residence there an indication that the day had been a bad one.

Against the long wall, facing the main door, a trestle had been set up and was now bowed beneath the weight of storage boxes. Mac recognized the Cara Evans case files. Above that, on hessian pinboards, a uniformed officer was adding to the current images, reports and contact details. A picture of Cara Evans, taken a few weeks before she had died, smiled across at him.

Mac caught his breath. He remembered the picture painfully

well: it was the one Cara's mother had given to the police on the day her daughter had first been reported missing.

'Find her for me. Please find her for me.'

'I will,' Mac had promised her. Then, immediately regretting the certainty of that, he had amended it. 'I'll do all I can.'

But he had found her. Trouble was, he had been too late.

Officers had begun to wander in. Some talking, laughing, catching up on the day. All glanced in Mac's direction. Some nodding, newer officers looking askance at this stranger. A few coming over to say a word or two, clasp his arm, a quick pat on the back. Mac responded, smiled, returned the greetings, but none of it felt real. It was as though he stood a foot or so to one side of himself, watching, observing, hearing and feeling, but not fully there. He could feel Alec's scrutiny, his anxiety, and when someone handed him a copy of the current case file, he did his best to look casual and competent, perching against the edge of one of the side tables and flicking through a file he could not seem to see, his eyes refusing to focus, mind refusing to make sense of the words.

I shouldn't have come back, he thought. *I should have swallowed my pride and told Alec I couldn't deal with this. I should have let well alone.*

But it was too late for that. His decision had been made, and already others had built their plans upon the foundations of his return.

FIVE

Alec had arranged accommodation for Mac: one of the holiday lets that, in season, would have been occupied by families so determinedly set on enjoyment that they would have taken little notice of their surroundings.

'It's only temporary,' Alec said as he led Mac inside. 'We'll fix up something better.' He hesitated. 'I remembered you didn't like hotels . . .' He trailed off and Mac nodded. Alec had obviously sorted this out in a hurry, further proof he had not been expected.

'It's fine,' he said. 'Don't worry about it.'

Alec left, having arranged to collect Mac the following morning and checking he knew where to find the local shops. Being Alec, he had brought essential supplies: bread, milk, tea, a couple of ready meals and a handful of leaflets advertising the local takeaways. Mac was grateful and almost overwhelmingly homesick. He tried to call Miriam, but got no answer on the boathouse phone. He tried her mobile, got the voicemail, guessed she'd be out on a job. He thought about trying her work mobile, but abandoned the idea almost immediately. If she was out working, then the last thing she'd need at a crime scene was him phoning her just to have a good whinge, especially, as had happened several times lately, she'd been appointed lead CSI.

Mac sighed, flopped down on the saggy couch and took a look around the open-plan living, dining, kitchen that made up the main area of the holiday flat. It reminded him of the place he had rented for his first month or so in Frantham. That too had been an apartment resting during the winter off-season and it had been very similar in layout to this, though that one had a better view, directly out over the ocean. Getting up, he twitched the curtain aside, confirming his suspicion that the only thing to be seen here was a row of slightly rundown shops.

He checked out the bedrooms: bunk beds in one, a double bed in the next. Sheets, blankets and a duvet had been left folded on top of the bare mattress. He dumped his bag on a chair set beside yet another uninspiring window and noted that, thankfully, everything at least looked clean.

Back in the main room, he tried Miriam's phone again and again got the voicemail. He missed her. Missed the little hideaway above the boathouse that Rina had found for him. True, it was tiny, but it was neat and clean and full of his own belongings and, more often than not, Miriam was there.

Desperate now to hear a friendly voice, he found Rina's number and called Peverill Lodge, glancing at the clock and hoping he would catch her just after their evening meal. She picked up on the second ring.

'Hello, Mac, how are you holding up?'

'I'm . . . well, I'm managing. Be better tomorrow when I'm busy.'

'Have you eaten?'

'Not yet, no. But I will, I promise; that will be my next call.'

Rina harrumphed her disapproval. 'Make sure it's something decent, then. Mac, we had something odd happen today. Karen came back, demanding to see George.'

'Karen? Are you sure? No, of course you are. You saw her?'

'She came here. She wants George to go away with her. He, of course, wants to stay. There's far too much holding him in Frantham now for him to want to be uprooted again, but—'

'But you don't think Karen will see that. Rina, it looks as though I've picked a bad time to leave. Tell Frank Baker and Andy. Give them a heads up, just in case there's trouble.'

'I will,' Rina promised, 'though I don't know there's a lot they can do. Nothing wrong with a girl coming back to visit her brother.'

'Everything wrong if that girl is trouble. Rina, you know what she did as well as I do.'

'But can you prove it, Mac?'

Prove it? Probably, but he needed to be there and then he needed to explain why he had not presented his evidence before, and that might prove, well, something of a problem. 'Let's just hope she takes herself off again before it becomes an issue,' Mac said. 'I'll try and get back for the weekend, depending on what happens here.'

'Is much happening there?' Rina wanted to know.

Mac had to smile at Rina's obvious curiosity. 'So far, not a lot,' he said. 'Enough for me to know that I was right to come back, I think. But also enough to know I don't belong here any more. Rina, it's the strangest feeling, coming back and wondering how the hell I could ever have thought of this place as home.'

'And is Frantham home?' she asked softly.

'You know it is, Rina, love,' he said. 'I'll be back as soon as I can. Count on it. And, meantime, tell George not to worry; we'll sort it out.' He just hoped, as he hung up, that sorting it out did not involve arresting George's sister.

He was unexpectedly hungry now. Not hungry enough to eat one of Alec's ready meals; he'd vowed after his first weeks in Frantham, when he'd lived on anything that could be prepared in five minutes' use of the microwave, that he'd never touch such things again. He flicked through the leaflets Alec had left, remembering some of the names from his time in Pinsent. Found an Indian restaurant that did deliveries and phoned through an order for the set meal for one without really paying much attention to what it was. Remembered then that he had promised to call Emily.

She must have been waiting for his call because she picked up on the second ring.

'I've got your number set up on the caller display,' she said. 'So I knew it was you.'

He asked if the police liaison officer had been in touch.

'She has,' Emily told him. 'Lydia. She's nice, I've got her numbers and she's arranged for the community support officers to keep an extra lookout. She said she could stay if I wanted, but I've got Calum and I'm sure there's other people need her more. I can get in touch any time, she said. And she's going to sort out about having our calls monitored and all that. She says she doesn't think he'll show up here, but I've been thinking and I think Calum is right and he might.'

'Oh?' Mac queried. 'Why is that, Em?'

'Because he's already shown himself once. There's no reason not to now. He's getting ready for something else. He's showing off, telling you, and me too, just how untouchable he is.'

'I doubt he's thinking about what *I* might think,' Mac mused. 'You may be right about him turning up at your place, but I don't think I'm that relevant to him, Emily.'

'Mac, it became personal. The night . . . the night he killed that little girl, he stood there and made you watch while he killed her. He knew there was nothing you could do, that you'd never expect him to actually go through with it. I mean, who would? No one expects to see a threat like that carried out, but he did: he killed her and you watched. You were there. It was personal, you and him. Mac, he'll know you'd have to come back and finish things. He knows you. He knows you were nearly destroyed by what he did; you couldn't let it go, not being you . . .' She trailed off, running out of words. Mac didn't quite know how to respond, but he knew in his heart of hearts that she was right. It was personal. It had gone beyond job and duty and justice.

'You're right, of course,' Mac said quietly. 'I had to come back, see this through.' For a moment, there was silence between them. Mac was aware of his own breathing, how loud it sounded, how tense and tight his lungs felt as he drew each breath in. He wondered if it sounded loud to Emily or if she too was listening to her own strangled breaths, in, out, in, out, tight in the throat and loud in the ears. In the end, he heard her move, heard Calum's quiet voice in the background.

'I'd better go,' she said. 'Calum's cooked tonight. He's better at it than me. Make sure you eat, won't you, Mac? It's easy to forget the ordinary things, but sometimes they're all you've got left to hang on to.'

Mac smiled. 'You're starting to sound like Rina,' he told her.

'Rina?'

'Ah. I forgot you didn't know Rina. She's a friend. A really good friend. She lectures me about eating right and all that.'

'You be careful, Mac,' Emily said. 'Remember, he thought he'd killed you too that night. He won't like the fact that we got away from him, you and I.'

'I will,' he promised. 'And you too.'

A knock on the door told him that his food had arrived and he rang off, found his wallet, paid the man with the quilted bag and the red shirt and big smile who waited at the door. He no longer felt like eating, but, noting wryly that he'd promised two women that night that he would, he went through the motions of finding a plate and cutlery, set the kettle on to boil and, because he could no longer bear the silence and the harshness of his too-loud breath, he turned the television on and stared at the screen while he ate, not tasting any of it. Afterwards, he reflected that this evening was so like those first lonely evenings in Frantham, that the only thing missing was the bottle and glass he had habitually left on the kitchen counter. For a moment he almost felt that same terrible level of despair.

Mac took a deep breath and found his mobile phone. This time Miriam answered. She had just arrived home, she told him, and Mac was warmed by the knowledge that home, tonight, was his little flat above the boathouse.

'I love you so much,' he told her as they said goodbye. 'You just take good care of yourself.'

'I will,' she promised. 'You come home soon, Mac, and remember, any time you like, you can just walk away. No one who matters will think any less of you if you do – you know that, don't you?'

'I know,' he said. 'But I'll be fine.' He hoped with that he wasn't telling her lies.

SIX

Next morning was bracing, the wind coming in off the sea and harsh enough to take the breath away.

'I'd forgotten just how bloody cold this place was,' Mac commented ruefully as he got into Alec's car.

'Oh, you're turning into a soft southerner, that's your problem,' Alec laughed, blowing on his hands to warm them before he started the engine. 'No, the weather's turned mean this morning and they reckon it's in for the week. Naomi sends her love, by the way, and you're invited to dinner on Sunday.'

'Give mine to her,' Mac said. 'And thanks, but if I can get back home at the weekend, I'm going to.'

Alec nodded. 'Don't count on it,' he said. 'Things start moving, we'll be lucky if we get lunch anywhere.'

Mac looked at his friend, who was now concentrating on pulling out into the traffic and not looking his way. It seemed to be taking a lot of concentration considering the lack of other vehicles.

'Alec?'

'Yes.'

'What's happened since last night?'

Alec grimaced. 'DCI Wildman,' he said. 'As of this morning, he and his team are leading the investigation. Rest of us are now other ranks.'

'Wildman.' Mac closed his eyes. 'Someone up there doesn't like me and I don't think I mean God.'

Alec managed a laugh. 'Look,' he said, 'we knew there'd be someone from the taskforce coming in. That was inevitable. We just don't have the resources, never did; that was the problem last time.'

'Oh, I know, but whatever spin you try and put on it, any scenario that includes Wildman is a bad one. I thought the man was an arse and he thought I was an idiot long before the Cara Evans case, and we neither of us took the trouble to, well, to hide that.'

'No, I remember. Look, Mac, we just do our jobs, let him do his, and, well, keep it zipped.'

'I will if he does.' Mac subsided into silence for a moment or two, but it couldn't last. 'He's more than an arse, Alec, he's . . . Does he know I'm here?'

'Oh yes,' Alec nodded, 'and he's waiting for any excuse, Mac, remember that. Don't give him one. Right,' he interrupted as Mac began to object again, 'glove compartment, two files. Our assignments for this morning, well away from you know who. Get yourself up to speed.'

Reluctant but glad to have the distraction, Mac fished the folders out. One was familiar to him, one was not. Philip Rains had been in prison since before Mac had left for Frantham. Thomas Peel had blackmailed him for years and, when his usefulness as a distraction had become greater than his usefulness as a source of income, he had thrown him to the proverbial lions via an anonymous phone call to one of the crime hotlines and a brown envelope containing some particularly nasty pictures of Rains and two young boys.

Alec glanced over. 'Got a ten o'clock appointment,' he said. 'Prison governor reckons he's been a model inmate, but, of course, he's getting all that personal attention, isn't he?'

Mac nodded, understanding what Alec meant. Rains could never be part of the general prison population. He'd have been dead within the month. Less, probably. Someone would have known who he was and what he'd done and taken it upon themselves to do something about it. Mac had a sneaking suspicion that Alec thought that was exactly as it should be, though unlike some of their colleagues – Wildman included – he'd never voiced the opinion out loud.

He turned back to the file, noting that Rains was due for a parole hearing in six months and would have every reason to be behaving himself. 'Have his family stayed in contact?'

Alec shook his head. 'There was never a suggestion he'd touched his own kids, but the wife took the children and left the country. She's Canadian, I think. Not British, anyway, and I understand she's gone back to her parents. Rains always reckoned Peel threatened his family. Maybe he did. Either way, I think she did the right thing. Finally.'

Mac glanced sharply in his direction. 'You think the wife knew what Rains was into?'

'How can a woman not know? I mean . . .' Alec shrugged and trailed off.

'People keep secrets, even within families,' Mac argued. He thought of Ginny, the woman he had bumped into so unexpectedly in the café and wondered again if her husband really didn't know how she came by the extra money. Surely, by now, he'd realize she didn't actually have a cleaning job? 'People see what they expect and want to see,' he said. 'Some things feel so unbelievable or so unacceptable that they *really* don't see them. The human brain is nothing if not flexible.'

Alec snorted. 'Look, I can fully understand not *wanting* to see, not *wanting* to know, but there must be something at the back of your mind tells you this isn't right or that doesn't add up. The way I see it is that she put her own kids at risk too.'

'I thought Rains didn't touch his own children.'

'Well, no, he didn't, but you're not telling me he wasn't tempted and you're not telling me there wouldn't have come a time when his friends didn't get access to them.'

'Maybe,' Mac said. 'Most people do have their line in the sand, even if it's a pretty wavy one.' He found himself thinking about George and Karen and what they'd gone through with their violent father, and their mother too battered and beaten by years with him to be capable of fighting back. Karen had drawn her own line and it had been a pretty decisive one. She'd realized she could do nothing to change or save her mother, do very little, when her dad was around and she was so young, to protect herself, but when Parker had come back from a spell in prison and started hurting George, he'd crossed Karen's line and she'd made him pay for it.

Mac found himself excusing her attack on Edward Parker, her father. The world would not be a worse place for his loss, but it seemed that once she had crossed her line, set herself up as protector of her little brother, there was nothing she was incapable of in pursuit of that. He had once told Rina that he thought such love would become a terrible burden for George to bear, and he had seen nothing that disabused him of that view. Worse, his attempts to protect George from knowledge of what his sister had done and why had come to nothing. George was *not* someone who refused to see. Loyalty and love might prevent him from speaking of it, even with Rina or Mac, but he had said enough for Mac to understand the depth of George's comprehension. George, young as he was, looked life in the face and dealt with it.

Karen was capable of everything, up to and including murder – up to and including such obsessive love that Mac feared for anyone who might stand in the way of it, and that, bizarrely, included George himself.

'Penny for them,' Alec said.

'Oh, I was thinking about home. Frantham.'

Alec smiled. 'About Miriam?'

'Actually, no. Not at that particular moment, but now you've brought her to mind . . .'

Alec laughed at that. 'I'm happy for you, I really am. We all thought . . .'

'That poor old McGregor was a lost cause. Hey, don't bother to argue, I thought it too. But I've been lucky.'

Lucky that new friends had chosen him, taken it upon themselves to make him whole again. And what a bizarre selection of people they were, Mac thought.

Further thought was interrupted by their arrival at the prison gatehouse, and Mac turned the focus of his thoughts back to the man they had come to see. 'I never interviewed Rains,' he said. 'What should I expect?'

Alec reached through the window to present their ID and permission to visit. 'Banality,' he said, and Mac got the distinct impression that in Alec's eyes that made it worse.

It was another fifteen minutes before they'd dealt with the formalities and Rains was brought out to them. They had been put in the visitors' room, a space occupied by a dozen small, melamine-topped tables surrounded by blue plastic chairs and with a coffee machine wedged into a corner close beside the door. Off this main area was a viewing room, glass-panelled and equipped with telephones, alarms and a large wooden table stacked with paperwork and currently occupied by two prison officers who seemed to be trying to work out some kind of shift rota. They had glanced up as Alec and Mac passed by the open door, assured them that Rains would be no trouble and gone back to their work.

Rains was brought in through another door at the far end of the visiting area. Dressed in blue jeans and a white T-shirt, Rains approached them cautiously, pulling out a chair and settling himself uneasily at their table. He was a tall man, matching Mac for height but not quite reaching Alec's. Pale, with tired eyes and hands that shook slightly as he accepted the coffee they had bought for him from the machine. He'd once been a powerful, well-built individual, Mac guessed; there was a squareness to the shoulders and a tightness to the shirt sleeves that spoke of someone who once played around with weights, though now a layer of flab covered once-flat abs and his face sagged at jawline and chin.

'Thomas Peel,' Alec said.

'What about him?'

'Been in touch, has he?'

Rains sighed. 'And why should he have been? We've got nothing to say to one another. Not now.'

'But at one time? No, don't bother answering that: we know you had a lot to say to one another. Regular correspondents, weren't you? Email and little postcards and the telephone conversations. Oh, and the blackmail, of course.'

Rains looked away. 'I told you: that was then. He's the reason I'm here, nothing more to say.'

'Oh,' Alec said. 'Peel is the reason you're here, is he? I thought it was the children you abused, the ones you photographed.'

Rains's attention snapped back in Alec's direction. 'Photographed, yes. I never touched them though.'

'But you watched while others did more.' It was the first time Mac had spoken, and Rains turned his head slowly to regard him with a surprisingly steady gaze.

'I know about you,' Rains said. 'You were the cop that got that girl killed. Peel told me so. He said he'd never have cut her throat if you hadn't been there. He said your face was an absolute picture.'

Mac drew a deep breath and then held it, releasing it slowly before he spoke. He was relieved beyond measure that his voice was almost steady. 'I don't doubt it was,' he said. 'I would count myself a much lesser man if I hadn't reacted to the death of a child. Would you have taken a picture of that too, Mr Rains?'

Rains took a swallow of his coffee but did not speak.

Mac was aware of Alec's anxious glance, knew he had to maintain his control. Test number one had been accepting the offer of return to the case; here was test number two. 'So,' Mac asked, 'has your erstwhile colleague been back in touch?'

'Erstwhile,' Rains savoured the word. 'Use big words like that in here and you'd get a shiv in your back just for being a ponce. No, my erstwhile friend has not been in touch. Not since he came to watch me being sentenced.'

Alec and Mac exchanged a glance, and Mac saw Rains smile. He knew the man felt he had scored a point. Rains had been sentenced months after Cara Evans had been killed, and the hunt for Peel had still been intense.

'Came to gloat, did he?' Alec asked innocently, and Mac was encouraged to see the transient look of disappointment that fled across Rains's face.

'I'm surprised you said nothing,' Mac added. 'After all, you seem to blame Thomas Peel for, shall we say, drawing attention to you in the first place. Without his help, we might never have caught up with you. But, I suppose, you already know that?'

Rains flinched, the satisfaction now completely wiped from his face. Mac drove the point home. 'A simple word would have done, I'd have thought. A little note to your barrister, telling him that one of the most wanted men in the country was sitting in the courtroom. Where was he, Rains – sitting in the public gallery? Did he smile and wave when the sentence was handed down? Or did he cheer like all the rest? Did he spit at you when they led you out, Rains? After all, he'd have to blend in, wouldn't he?'

Rains was on his feet, the plastic coffee cup falling to the floor as he knocked the table in his haste to get up. Out of the corner of his eye, Mac could see the two men in the observation room start to move towards the door and he saw Alec gesture that it was all right.

'You must be very frightened of him,' Mac said softly. 'Very loyal or very much afraid and, well, given that Peel showed you so little loyalty, I'd have to draw the second conclusion.'

'I've nothing more to say,' Rains said, and Mac could see that he was badly shaken, though he was unsure of what exactly he had said to have disturbed the man's composure.

'What would happen if he thought you had?' Mac asked. 'Had more to say, I mean.'

'And why tell us now that Peel was in the courtroom?' Alec

mused. 'Did he tell you to?' He sighed. 'That's the one big weakness he has, in my book. This tendency to showboat. The need for the world to know how clever he is, getting one over on a court full of judges and reporters and police like that. It must have really frustrated him that no one noticed, but, I suppose, like everything else, he knew that it was a bit of information that might come in useful one day. He must have felt that time was now.'

'I don't know what you mean,' Rains said.

Mac could almost see Rains's mind working as Alec pressed the point home, Rains trying to figure out who was the fool here. 'So, he knew we'd be bound to come and talk to you some time soon, seeing as how the Cara Evans case has been upgraded to active again, and how you and he were once so close and all. So, the way I see it is this: he's been in touch, time to time, maybe telling you he's sorry to have dropped you in it, maybe even telling you to hang tight, say what you know the parole board will want to hear, wait it all out, and then the two of you, when you get out, well, it'll be just like old times. Is that what he's been telling you, Rains?'

A sharp look told Mac they'd hit home somewhere. 'And then he tells you, Rains, old friend, play that ace. Tell them I was there in the courtroom. Tell the pigs when they come to talk to you that I was there, within reach, and that I was still too clever for the bastards. Is that what he told you to say?' Alec waited for a response, but Rains, fists clenched at his side, gaze fixed firmly on the floor, said nothing.

Mac stood and Alec followed his lead, signalling to the officers that they had done with the prisoner.

'Pity we weren't impressed,' Alec said. 'Like my friend here said, Peel is an exhibitionist, can't resist the urge to show off.' He shook his head sadly at Rains. 'You can't hope to compete, not even vicariously.'

He dug in his pocket for change and crossed to the coffee machine, deliberately ignoring Rains. 'You want anything?' he asked Mac.

Mac shook his head. 'I'm not a big fan of machine coffee,' he said.

'Prefer the coffee shop on the promenade, don't you? That Italian stuff with the syrup,' Rains said.

Mac stiffened. He turned to look at Rains, schooling his

expression to maintain some semblance of neutrality. 'Peel tell you that, did he?'

Rains was exultant now. 'He knows all about you, McGregor. He knows just how much he hurt you, just how much of a problem you had with the booze – and you know what? He's going to finish what he started, grind you into the dust.'

'That what he did to you, is it?' Alec asked casually. He took a swallow of his coffee and grimaced. 'Think I'm with you,' he said to Mac. 'This is truly bad.'

The prison officers were ready now to escort Rains back to his cell, and Mac followed Alec through to the observation room. His heart thumped and his chest tightened so rigidly he thought he might run out of breath. Already he could hear the blood pounding in his ears and a red mist blurred his vision.

Alec pulled out two chairs. 'Sit,' he said quietly. 'Take a minute, Mac.'

Dimly, Mac heard him leave the room and go and speak with someone outside. Then he was back. 'I've requested the visitor book and the phone records for the past three months,' he said. 'We'll go back further if we have to, but Peel only floated to the surface again this past month or two; I'd make a bet on him being in those records. Oh, and they're bringing in some tea.'

Mac took a deep breath and nodded. 'If Peel's been watching me . . .'

'Then you need to let your people know. Exeter too. See if they can put any extra support in while you're gone.'

'I'll get on to DI Kendal,' Mac said. 'I've worked several cases with him since I've been down there. Frank and Andy need to be given the heads up and so do—'

'Anyone who knows you down there, Mac. Look, if Peel is taking that much of an interest, maybe you should get yourself back down there. You'll be splitting yourself in two, worrying about your friends and trying to keep on top of what's happening this end.'

'You don't think I'm up to it?' Mac asked harshly.

Alec shrugged. 'Damn sure I wouldn't be,' he said frankly. He groaned, suddenly thinking of something.

'What?'

'Oh, nothing. I'm just visualizing the moment we have to brief DCI Wildman, that's all.'

Mac managed to laugh. 'He will, no doubt, be delighted,' he said. 'Probably leave me tethered out in a field somewhere as bait.'

'Not funny, Mac,' Alec said, and Mac nodded as the realization hit them both that this was exactly what Mac was, and for that reason, if no other, he had to stay.

For the next hour or so they went through the records of visits and phone calls. On the visitors front there was little enough to look at. None of Rains's family came to see him and his friends seemed to have melted away. He'd had a local vicar, one Reverend Tom Longdon, come to see him twice, and a woman called Sara Curtis who was on the list of official prison visitors. During the past month he had made only two phone calls, both to his legal representative, and received only three. Two of those had been regarding his parole hearing and the third was from the same Reverend Longdon. Other than that, Rains seemed to have had little or no contact with the outside world for at least the past three months.

'You fancy the Reverend Longdon for being Peel in disguise?' Alec joked as they drove away, heading – late – to their second appointment of the day.

'Or maybe this Sara Curtis,' Mac suggested. 'Thomas Peel in drag.'

He closed his eyes, leaning his head back against the rest and striving for composure, or at least the surface veneer of it. He had, he reckoned, spoken Thomas Peel's name more times in the past twenty-four hours than he had in the past year and, he was almost relieved to discover, Rina and Andy Nevins were right: the name did not fill him with so much dread. He had taken possession of it, used it, exposed it for what it was: just two words, just sounds, just letters, strung together in a particular configuration.

'Why would he want to stalk me?' Mac ventured. 'I mean, that's what it amounts to, isn't it?'

'Unless, of course, that was just one random fact Peel managed to acquire and happened to mention to Rains, knowing he'd pass it on to us.'

'Which sounds really likely, I don't think,' Mac said. 'But why now?'

'We don't know that it is just now,' Alec pointed out. 'You may well have been the object of his attention ever since he killed Cara Evans.'

Mac shook his head, closing his eyes again. He could feel Alec's scrutiny. 'No, it has to be more recent. Before DI Eden retired, I hardly used the place. Eden made the most foul coffee imaginable, strong enough to stand a spoon up in – that's if it didn't eat its way through the metal first. Eden went in July and I started to buy my coffee regularly at the coffee shop on the promenade just after that.' He opened his eyes, stared out through the front windscreen. 'I can't believe I didn't see him.'

'He may not have been there.'

'What do you mean?'

'I mean, it would have been simple enough for Peel to hire someone to keep an eye on you. I'm guessing Frantham is like Pinsent in the tourist season. Incomers everywhere. It's only this time of year that strangers get themselves noticed.'

Mac nodded, accepting that, feeling a little better at the thought that Thomas Peel may have been doing his spying at second hand. The thought that Peel might have been so close, and Mac not known or acted, was an unbearable one. 'Right, so what's next on our "to do" list?'

'Ricky Marlow – the man Thomas Peel went to visit when he surfaced three weeks ago. And then to have another chat with John Bennet, Peel's work colleague.'

'The one who alerted us to the fact that Peel was back,' Mac nodded. 'Emily, Peel's daughter, she said she remembered Bennet. She's of the opinion that her father wanted to be seen, that he showed himself to Bennet.'

'We came to the same conclusion. He stood around on the street corner until Bennet left work at lunch time. The cob shop Bennet used was just across the road. Bennet admits to being something of a creature of habit. Peel would have known that; the two of them worked in the same office for five years. Peel went back to the B & B to collect a scarf he'd left behind.'

'Strange to think about Peel working for a living.'

'But he did and apparently was very good at what he did. Bennet is another draughtsman; they both work, or rather worked, for the same architects' office. Bennet has three kids, and Peel visited his house on a number of occasions. He must have wondered . . .'

'Any evidence he did?'

'Thankfully, no. Peel was never alone with the Bennet children.' Alec indicated, turned off the main road and down an increasingly narrow lane. 'Peel went to see his old friend Ricky Marlow at work. We're visiting the great man at home.'

'Great man?' Mac queried.

'Ricky – Richard Marlow – owns the Ramolt Hotel in town, part-owns three pubs and two car dealerships, and has an extensive buy-to-let "portfolio" or whatever it's called. Supports a dozen local charities and yada yada.'

'Oh, *that* Richard Marlow.' Mac frowned. 'And the connection with Peel?'

'Well, on the surface, it's that the architects that Peel used to work for did the extension on Marlow's house and other bits and pieces on his pubs or something. Anyway, Peel did the drawings, generated the computer models or whatever they do now, liaised with Marlow on the changes. According to Marlow, that was the extent of their involvement, but . . .'

They were turning now into a set of double gates at the end of a long drive. The house up ahead was modern but obviously not off the peg. Painted white and with an odd, green pantiled roof that Mac was not sure he actually liked, it spread expansively either side of a massive front door. Single-storey wings extended the frontage even further, and glancing through the tall windows as they parked up, Mac realized that one wing housed a large indoor pool.

'All right for some,' he said. 'Second pool on the other side?'

Alec laughed. 'Apparently, he collects orchids or something,' he said. 'I believe that's where he keeps them.'

'Orchids. Right.'

'You don't like orchids?'

'Actually, no. They're sticks with fancy bits stuck on the ends. You can't tell me that's attractive. And we have nothing on Marlow except that Peel contacted him?'

'So far, no. Usual rumours about dodgy dealings and backhanders, but nothing more concrete or more unusual. He's cooperated with the investigation, claims he was as shocked as anyone could be when Peel turned up, but he failed to report their meeting and it was only after John Bennet reported seeing Peel that Marlow admitted to having his own encounter.'

'He came forward, then?'

'No, we managed to track Peel's movements on CCTV, saw him coming out of one of Marlow's pubs. We confronted Marlow and he admitted Peel had been to see him.'

'And? What did Peel want?'

'That's what we don't know. Marlow insists Peel just bought himself a drink and sat at the bar nursing it. Marlow says he saw him, recognized him and realized he was maybe the last person he wanted around, told him to leave. Marlow says Peel left without comment, but I find that hard to believe.'

'Witness statements?'

'Indicate a brief conversation between the two of them. Marlow just insists that Peel took a bit of convincing, that Marlow threatened to call the police, a threat which he did not carry out either at the time or retrospectively. He claims just to have been glad to see Peel go, to have been worried about what Peel might do if Marlow crossed him.'

'Which may be true.'

'Which may be true, but . . .' Alec opened his car door and had to grab the handle as a gust of wind caught it and wrenched it back. Mac was more cautious, holding on to the door as he got out of the car, and looked around, noting the depth of gravel on the drive and the measured manicure of the lawns.

Money, he thought. And lots of it.

The front door opened as they crossed the drive, and Mac realized that Marlow must have been watching them, waiting for them to get out of the car. He stood on the top of the short flight of steps, holding the door half-closed behind him as the wind pushed hard against it, as though intent on fighting its way inside.

'Bitter day,' Marlow said, stepping back and gesturing for them to go in. 'A truly bitter day.'

Mac could not help but wonder if he meant the wind or purely that the police had come to call.

Marlow's study was book-lined and so thickly carpeted that small children could be lost in the pile. The hall floor, Marlow told them, was reclaimed parquet from an old manor house that had been demolished when his was being built. He said it was two hundred odd years old. The carpet in the study, Mac thought, certainly did not have that age or pedigree, but probably, he considered, a similar cost.

An orchid sat on the heavy oak desk, long stems strapped tightly to green canes, and did nothing to rectify Mac's opinion of the plant, though he had to admit that the flowers were interesting. Deep orange with freckled faces and very different from the ones he was used to seeing in the local supermarkets trapped in their plastic bags.

Marlow gestured them to twinned captain's chairs, preparing to seat himself in a somewhat more opulent example behind the desk.

'Would you like something to drink?'

Both declined. The tea at the prison had been no better than the machine coffee, but both Mac and Alec had downed two mugs of the stuff while working their way through the visitation records. Mac felt he was already swimming.

Ricky Marlow sat down, steepling his fingers and regarding the two of them with a degree of impatience. 'I've agreed to see you,' he said, 'but I really don't see what more I can say. Peel came into the Eagle and Dove, and I just happened to be there. Had I not been there, I would have been none the wiser regarding his presence in Pinsent. That being the case, I could have told you nothing; having happened to be there, I can still tell you nothing.'

'But you failed to report him,' Mac said. 'I find that a little hard to understand, Mr Marlow. You knew that he had committed murder. Mr Marlow, he killed a child.'

Marlow gestured impatiently. 'And you're right, of course. I should have called the police the moment I saw him. Recognized him. The truth was I was taken aback. I could only think how angry I was that he'd put me in that position, come into one of my premises and sat there, sipping a drink, bold as brass. It was the sheer effrontery of it. I'm sorry to say that put everything else out of my mind. I just wanted him gone.'

'What did he say to you?' Mac asked.

'I've already been over this so many—'

'Please, Mr Marlow,' Mac said. 'Go over it for me.'

Marlow sighed, slumped back against the heavy leather,

button back of his chair. 'He said, "Hello, Richard." I said, "What the hell are you doing here?" and he said he was having a drink. I told him he should go; he said he hadn't finished his drink yet. I told him he could have a refund, that he should leave immediately. That went back and forth for a minute or so, and then he left. Nothing more.'

Mac considered. 'You say the exchange went back and forth?'

'Yes. It was boring. It was tedious. It meant nothing.'

'It *meant* nothing?' Mac queried.

'I'm sorry?' Marlow looked confused.

'You said it meant nothing. Not "we said nothing else" or "nothing more interesting". You said the conversation, the exchange, *meant* nothing. That implies that something more was said than your simple request that he leave and his simple refusal to do the same.'

Alec had raised an eyebrow, his expression quizzical. He too turned to look expectantly at Ricky Marlow.

'I didn't mean . . . I didn't think anything. I . . .' Marlow frowned and began again. 'He said he hadn't finished his drink. I told him he could have a refund and he laughed. He said he wanted more than a refund and I told him he'd better think again.'

'Any reason he might think you owed him something?'

Marlow shook his head impatiently. 'None,' he said. 'Marstons – the architects Peel worked for – they did quite a lot of work for me. Designed the two wings on the house, the courtyard extension out back that we built so we could have a separate guest annex, and a few other bits on other properties. They did good work. Peel was a first-class designer and troubleshooter. It was standard practice to send him out with the first drafts of the architect's designs to do any snagging. I've got to admit that's partly why I kept going back to them. Most architects are so tied in to their so-called visions that they don't see the practical snags until it's too late. Marstons like to iron out the problems early on and Peel had a good eye. I admit, I requested him after the first job they did for me. I knew we were on the same wavelength where the building work was concerned.'

'And on other matters?'

'I don't recall that we discussed any other matters,' Marlow said coldly. 'He was there to do a job.'

'And you don't waste time in small talk with the hired help,' Alec suggested.

'I wouldn't have phrased it like that, but no, I don't. If Peel disliked my attitude, he never gave any indication. It was nothing personal. I'm just a very busy man.' Stating that seemed to remind Marlow that he might be wasting time at that very moment. He got up – an indication that the interview was at an end. 'I've really nothing more to say,' he said. 'And I have to say that this is coming very close to harassment.'

Alec rose, but Mac waited for a moment. 'Mr Marlow,' he said quietly, 'I think that you and Peel have something in common after all – both busy people, both direct and to the point – but remember, Mr Marlow, the last time Thomas Peel wanted to make a point, he killed a child. He didn't have to kill her – he could have released her unharmed, even injured her but left her alive. He knew that it was just one man between him and freedom, that backup was a long way off arriving and that, whatever he did, that man would run to the child first instead of chasing after him. Peel could have simply left the scene, left Cara Evans standing on the beach. The outcome for Peel would have been the same, but, instead, he decided to make a point, to tell the world that here was a man who did not go in for half measures or incomplete actions, and so he killed that child.'

Marlow's eyes narrowed. 'You're the one, are you? The one that let him get away?'

'He read me right,' Mac said quietly, unable totally to keep the bitterness from his voice. 'He read me right. He knew that Cara Evans would be my priority, not him. He knew he didn't have to kill her or harm her; he could still have run away and I'd still have gone to the child first. Yes, I'm the one that let him get away and I let him run because I still had that tiny, ridiculous little fragment of hope that I might be able to stop her bleeding to death. I've got *my* excuse, *my* reason for letting him get away. It may not be a good one, but it's there. What do you have, Mr Marlow? How will you feel when Thomas Peel kills again?'

Silence. Mac was suddenly aware of the ticking of a clock, of Alec's feet shifting against the thick pile of the carpet.

'I'm not afraid of much,' Richard Marlow said at last. 'I'd

certainly never had any reason to fear the likes of Thomas Peel, not before – I'd not even taken notice of the man, truth to be told. He did his job; I didn't even think of him unless he was there, doing it. But that day, there he was, sitting on a stool in my bar, drinking gin and tonic, large as life and making no attempt to hide himself. I knew he'd come *because* I was there. Most of the regulars would expect me to be there on a Wednesday lunchtime, so it would have been no great stretch to assume I'd be there that Wednesday.'

'Was he a regular?'

'Had been, yes. He'd call in for a drink and lunch one day a week. I never gave it a thought. Suddenly, he was there again and he was bold, blatant. The bar staff didn't know him – they were both new to the job – but I don't think he'd have cared anyway. He said I owed him – more than a refund for the drink – and I asked him what the hell he meant. He just smiled, said I'd remember in time, but if you ask me, he was just trying to wind me up.'

'And did he manage it?'

Marlow sat down again. 'Damn right he did. But I still don't know what he meant.'

'So . . . you think it was more than a wind-up?'

Marlow glared. 'No, I don't. Don't you go putting words in my mouth.'

'But suddenly you were afraid of him,' Alec said. He sounded, frankly, disbelieving.

Marlow flared, leaping back to his feet and pointing to the door. 'Go, now,' he shouted. 'I've got nothing more to say. Not to you, not now, not any more.'

Mac stood this time, but he took his time crossing the silent, almost quilted floor. He could feel Marlow's frustration and building anger as they left, footsteps loud on the precious parquet floor and then crunching on gravel as they returned to their car.

'You rattled his cage,' Alec said.

Mac nodded. 'Yes,' he said, 'but I still don't know what about.'

SEVEN

Rina had never been one to let a spot of weather stop her and she was out on the promenade mid-morning, breathing in the chill, damp morning air. The storm had raged all night, suiting her moiling thoughts perfectly, and now, having had little sleep, she was at least close to some kind of plan.

Out at sea, the first glimpse of a clearing day lightened the horizon, though grey clouds still sat low over Frantham as the night storm swept on inland.

'It's going to be a lovely day,' Rina announced.

'When?' Her companion was less impressed by a bit of white space in clouds that were still far out at sea. Tim pulled his scarf more tightly around his neck and tugged his hat down over his ears. It was, Rina thought, a measure of his discomfort that he'd agreed to wear not only the bright blue scarf that Bethany had knitted for him, but also the purple tea-cosy hat that Eliza had provided. The Peters sisters were inveterate knitters, though to Rina's knowledge they had, between them, only mastered two stitches and their choice of colours sometimes left a little to be desired.

'When's it going to improve, then?' Tim demanded again. He did not like the cold or the wind, or being up this early in the morning when he'd been working the night before, his mentalist act at the Pallisades Hotel a few miles up the coast having been reprised at a very late private party after closing time.

'Oh, by this afternoon, I expect,' Rina said. She smiled at the tall man shivering beside her. 'You need to get a bit of meat on those bones,' she told him. 'Then you'd feel the cold less. Lord knows how you eat as much as you do and never gain an ounce.'

'Can we at least walk?' Tim asked plaintively. 'Or even go and have a coffee. I'm freezing, Rina.'

She took pity on him and began to stride along the promenade, avoiding the coffee shop, much to Tim's disappointment.

'Rina, this isn't going to turn into one of your yomps, is it?' He looked anxiously towards the end of the promenade and the cliff path that rose precipitously beyond that, leading out of town and into very exposed country.

'I don't yomp, Tim. Only the SAS yomp, so far as I'm aware, and that is one role I never played, even in my extensive career. In fact, I was never much of a male impersonator.'

'You actually like this weather, don't you?' Tim complained. '*You* had a good night's sleep. *I* didn't get in until nearly four. *I* shouldn't even be aware of the state of the weather yet. Why do you have to come out here to think when you've got a perfectly nice sitting room at home?'

Rina took his arm. 'It will clear your head,' Rina told him, 'and, Tim dear, I really do need you to have a clear head.'

'This is about Karen, isn't it?'

'It is indeed. Tim, I think I've been guilty of a grave misjudgement and I really don't know yet what the consequences will be.'

'For George? Surely she can't do anything about George. Isn't he a ward of court or something?'

'I don't think legal legitimacy will bother her, do you? But no, not just for George. I have this dreadful feeling that George is only one of her concerns.'

Tim paused, turned his mentor to face him and stared intently into her face. 'You really are worried,' he said. 'Rina, I've been through a lot with you these last few years; why should Karen coming back spook you so much now?'

Rina sighed. She patted Tim's hand and retrieved his arm, unable to look at him and still order her thoughts. To see Tim's concern somehow unnerved her, but she could feel it anyway. Rina was never unable to meet his eye; Rina never dissembled with him and, he was right, they had shared some really frightening times.

'Tim, I'm afraid because I underestimated what Karen could become, I'm sure of it. Oh, she's done nothing yet, not here anyway. It's more . . . more the look of her, the way she has become so much her own person.'

'I thought she always was,' Tim objected. 'She always struck me as being very strong, very determined. The way she'd held the family together, protected her mother and brother. Rina, that took some doing.'

'It did indeed and that, Tim, is what I saw in her back last winter when she and George came into our lives. I admired her spirit, I admired her courage. I saw, I suppose, a little of myself in Karen's tenacity and drive, and I wanted so much for her to have the chance to reach her potential. To be free to live her life and not have it blighted because she made what I thought at the time was a decision driven by desperation. So I did a very wrong thing, Tim: I let her leave when Mac knew she should be made to stay, face the consequences of what she had done.'

'Rina, dear, you've lost me. I know Karen tried to kill her father, but after what he'd put them through I'm not sure anyone could blame her for that.' He paused. 'That's not what you're talking about, is it?'

'No, Tim, it's not. I'm talking about the death of Mark Dowling. The as yet unsolved murder of Mark Dowling.'

'Ah,' Tim said.

'Ah, indeed.'

'You think Karen . . . why would Karen kill Mark Dowling? Rina, the list of people who wanted that nasty little . . . well, Mark Dowling out of the way – it would include half of Frantham, and I dare say the other half would have been pretty light on the objections. But you're not just speculating, are you?'

Rina shook her head and once more paused to lean on the promenade railing and stare out to sea. Sighing, Tim turned up the collar of his coat and shoved his gloved hands deep into his pockets, resigned now to being cold again, though glad they had not carried on past the end of the promenade and up the cliff. At least the yomp seemed to have been called off.

'Rina, why haven't you told me this before? Does Mac know all of this?'

'Oh, Tim. Look, this is what we think happened, though you've got to understand, as far as I know, Mac had no proof, not concrete proof at least, not then.' She took a deep breath and began. 'Mark Dowling had been threatening George and his friend Paul. He found out about that stupid prank they played on Mrs Freer. In fact, it's quite possible that fear of Dowling was what put them up to it in the first place. Anyway, as everyone now knows, Mark Dowling killed Mrs Freer, for which act may he burn in whichever hell people like him are consigned to.'

'Rina!' Tim was genuinely shocked. 'Anyway, you don't believe in hell.'

'For some people I'm prepared to waive my disbelief. Tim, Mac and I were both pretty sure that Karen killed Mark Dowling. Whether she did it purely to protect her brother from Dowling's bullying or whether it was also vengeance for his murder of the old lady is a moot point, but Mac was going to bring her in for questioning. He was fairly certain he could build a case.'

'Does George know this?'

'George knows, though we've not really talked about it. I don't think George has ever been under any illusions regarding his sister; he left that folly to the rest of us. Anyway, the morning Mac went to arrest Karen, I called her.'

'You warned her? Rina that's . . . Does Mac know that too?'

'I suspect that he suspects, but, again, some things are better left unsaid, even between friends. Maybe *especially* between friends. Anyway, Karen was gone when he arrived, and George, bless him, had put two and two together and figured out what she'd done.'

'But why did you warn her?'

'Oh, Tim, like I said, I made the most appalling error. Ironically, I acted out of the same concerns that led Karen to do such dreadful things. I wanted to protect young George. I felt he'd gone through enough.'

'And you made the judgement that Mark Dowling got what he deserved,' Tim said flatly. 'Oh, Rina, darling, sometimes we can't make those judgements, we really can't. Those decisions are just not ours to make.'

'There was more, Tim.' Rina seemed set on maximum self-castigation. 'To be truthful, I suppose I admired Karen. Her tenacity, her courage, her commitment to her mother and brother. I was wrong, terribly wrong, and, yes, I suspected that one day she'd come back; I just didn't think it would be so soon and, to be honest, Tim, I didn't think I'd be the one having to deal with her. I thought Mac would be here. I thought Mac would know what to do.'

'If Mac had been here, she'd probably have just sneaked a quick meeting with George and been gone again,' Tim suggested. 'But the fact is, she's here and Mac is gone and . . .'

'And I've got to deal with the mess I've made,' Rina finished.

'I didn't say that.' Tim reached out and touched her hand. 'Rina, it's not entirely your mess. Circumstances created Karen. George too, for that matter. This mess started long before you interfered and the only misjudgement you made was due to some misplaced compassion. No one can think the worse of you for that.'

'Can't they? Oh Tim, I'm not worried about it coming out that I warned Karen. Mac will be mad as hell, but he already suspects as much. I'm worried about . . . how can I explain this? It's that Karen has changed. Oh, the seeds of this new Karen were already there, and you're right, of course: circumstance created her, and maybe genetic factors as well – I really couldn't say. But it's the woman she's become that worries me. She's had time to harden her attitudes, to become vengeful.'

'Vengeful?' Tim laughed, then stopped when he caught sight of her expression. 'Rina, I think . . .'

'That maybe I'm getting ahead of myself? Maybe I am, Tim, but she's changed. When we knew the old Karen, there was still something of the lost child hiding in there. With the right input, I believe that Karen could have been salvaged. But she's changed, Tim. I saw her, remember, and the young woman who came to Peverill Lodge yesterday was not the Karen that left here all those months ago. She's had time to find herself. Whereas before she was all the people her brother and her mother needed, now she's just Karen. Confident, purposeful. Her own woman, Tim, and I can't put my finger on what troubles me so much, but it does. Deeply.'

While Rina and Tim walked on the promenade, Karen was sitting in her hire car, staring at a most unpromising and unrevealing entrance. A sign – wooden, painted green with rather stylish black lettering edged in gold – told her that the driveway led to Hill House, but she could see nothing more. The driveway led from the main road, uphill on to the cliff top and then curved back on itself. The grounds of the house were edged with trees which, even at this wintry season when all leaves had fallen, were planted densely enough as to give no clue as to what lay beyond. Karen scowled her frustration. She didn't actually want to go to the house, not today; to go there and declare that she was George's sister and wanted to see him would open up all sorts of complications. Karen was all too aware of what happened when the authorities got involved. No, she just wanted a glimpse of the place where George was now housed – she could not believe that he could call it home.

Rina hadn't told her where he was, but that had been easy enough to find out. A simple question, directions to the children's home – Karen had assumed there would only be one close by – had given her directions to Hill House.

She started the engine and drove a little further along the quiet road, hoping that the trees would thin and provide the view she wanted, but she was disappointed. Only a few hundred yards further on, the road turned away. She saw a sign pointing the way towards the cliff path that would lead back to Frantham and which, she assumed, passed at the rear of the children's home. She considered getting out of the car and walking the path, but the day was cold and damp and she was hardly dressed for hiking.

How, she wondered, was he doing at school these days? She had a new school all picked out for him. One that would push him just that bit harder. George was a bright kid, but he tended towards laziness if left to his own devices. She'd make certain he made the best of his talents, help him with his homework again, just like old times. It had shocked and appalled her just how much she had missed her little brother: their closeness, their talks. For so many years it had just been George and Karen, the two of them against the world. Their mother had seemed so much like just another child – a slow and often rather awkward child – that Karen barely even considered her, beyond her being just someone else who needed looking after. It was George who had been her co-conspirator, her friend, her confidant, the one she had planned for and supported and who was going to have the brightest of futures under Karen's guidance. Far better than any sodding kids' home could ever provide.

Rina had said that George wouldn't want to leave, but Karen had no room for doubt, not a moment of it. George would jump at the chance to leave with his big sister, to be back with the only family he had, and he'd enjoy the life Karen had planned for him. It would all be just as it had always been – only better. No violent father, no weak and ineffectual mother. Just George and Karen and whatever opportunities the world might bring, and if there was one thing Karen had learnt these past months, it was that opportunity was everywhere for the person who had the courage, the nerve, the intelligence to grasp it.

Alec and Mac rejoined their colleagues for the three o'clock briefing. DCI Wildman was already holding court. A big man, tall and portly, dressed in what Mac was sure was the same dog-tooth check jacket he'd been wearing the first time Mac had met him ten years before and a pair of dark brown slacks – worn below the belly – Wildman was a figure destined to draw attention for all sorts of reasons. His red hair was thin on top now, Mac noted, shocked at how much that fact pleased him, and the round face was now just a little jowly and somewhat more podgy in the cheek than Mac recalled.

Wildman, chatting to a group of officers at the far end of the room, noted Alec and Mac as they arrived, jerked his head in acknowledgement and then beckoned them over.

Alec groaned, then fixed a welcoming smile and led the way through the mess of desks and orange plastic chairs. 'Chief Inspector, good to see you again. You remember DI McGregor?'

'I remember.' Wildman shook hands with Alec and then with Mac. 'You up to this?' he asked bluntly.

'I'm up to it.'

'I bloody hope so. Last thing we need is a weak link.' The implied 'this time' hung between them like a threat.

One thing Mac was certain of: Wildman would not have rushed to the child. Wildman would have chased Peel down and flattened the bastard. He looked at Mac and found him lacking, and the painful fact was that Mac looked at himself and saw that selfsame thing, even though he could not have promised to react differently should that choice be presented again.

'Right.' Wildman clapped his hands and silence did not so much fall as land. 'Let's make a start, shall we? Gather round, children, and I'll choose someone to kick off the show-and-tell.'

Polite laughter, the odd groan, a muttered insult from Alec

that Mac didn't quite catch but thought might well be sexual. The collective scraping of chairs and settling down that did, indeed, remind Mac of a classroom. And then it all began: the results of the house-to-house enquiries carried out around the B & B where Peel had stayed, the officers tasked with reviving the original case making their recommendations as to which of Peel's former associates should be approached again. Mac was unsurprised to learn that several were now serving at Her Majesty's pleasure; slightly more surprised to discover that three of Peel's closest friends were now deceased.

'How?' Wildman demanded.

'One, Kevin Hill, had a heart condition, collapsed at home. Wife found him when she came back from shopping. DOA, never regained consciousness. Been under the doc for several years, so . . .'

'So no PM,' Alec mused. 'What's on his sheet?'

'Oh, mostly small beer. In his younger days he was known for being handy with his fists and light on his feet. Enforcer for a couple of the local loan sharks. Later he seems to have gone a bit upmarket, stealing cars to order. Nothing recent, as in the past five, six years. No job, living on disability benefit of one sort or another. Wife works a part-time job in a local hairdresser's.'

'Nothing sexual?'

'Not on record.'

'Check him out again,' Wildman said. 'Find out who came to see him the days before he popped his clogs.'

Mac, resentfully, found he couldn't argue with that. 'And the other two exes?' he asked.

'Car crash, part of a multi-vehicle pile-up on the M5, that did for Henry Clark. He was on the sex offenders' register and facing arrest. We raided his flat but came up empty.'

'Saved the cost of a trial, then,' Wildman said.

'Evidence came from Peel's computer. Emails sent between Peel, Clark and a woman who has yet to be identified. They exchanged images.'

Mac remembered the images; he pushed them aside before they broke his concentration.

'A woman?' Wildman questioned.

'Called herself Sophia,' Mac said. 'Used a series of disposable email addresses. So we handed it over to the techies.'

Wildman nodded acknowledgement.

They didn't even know if 'Sophia' was female, Mac thought; only that she, or he, had a library of images that could be requested by some kind of catalogue number, though how users had received those numbers or accessed the catalogue no one had been able to ascertain.

'And the third death?' Alec asked.

'Suicide. Stuart Evans. Hanged himself. He was—'

'Cara Evans's uncle.' Mac nodded. 'He was the link between Cara and Peel.' Evans had taken Cara from her parents' home, given her to Peel: that much had come out previously, though not *why*. He had never really told them why, and Mac had sat through hours and hours of interrogation with Stuart Evans. Dimly, he recalled hearing about Stuart Evans's suicide in the days that followed Cara's death. Those few days before Mac had finally imploded and been removed from the case and from the scene altogether, been given compassionate leave which turned out to be neither compassionate – too much time to think, to blame, to despair – nor leave. Some things just can't be departed from.

'Someone will have to go back and talk to the parents,' Wildman said. 'Tell them the case is live, that we have new leads. Best do it soon, eh, before the media get wind and pre-empt us. Best talk to Peel's kid too.'

His gaze had been wandering about the room, flitting from face to face, but came to rest finally, inevitably, on Mac.

'I've already spoken to Emily,' Mac said. 'There's a local liaison officer in place, and she's given permission for her phone to be monitored. She's pretty sure her father will show up there sooner or later.'

'Right, then,' Wildman said. 'So just the parents of the dead child to deal with. Best get on to that today, don't you reckon?'

Mac nodded, shifting his attention to his notes and hoping Wildman would look away before he raised his gaze again. Alec rustled papers and cleared his throat before delivering their report. Mac listened as Alec outlined the day's interviews, putting flesh on the bones of swiftly compiled observations and contemporary annotations.

'We think there's little doubt that Rains and Peel had recent contact,' Alec summarized, 'and, more disturbingly—'

'It looks like our Mac has picked up a stalker,' Wildman finished. He seemed amused by the prospect. 'And what about this Richard Marlow? From what I understand, he's already made a formal complaint.'

This was news to Mac and Alec. 'Very prompt of him,' Mac said. 'We only saw him a couple of hours ago.'

'Well, it looks like he didn't appreciate your techniques,' Wildman said. 'To which, I say, bollocks to him. Sounds to me as if he's hiding something, so I want to know what. Anything else?'

Small points, quickly cleared up. Other contributions to the briefing, but nothing of great significance, and then they were dismissed to prepare for the next step, to drink coffee and create an action plan. To go and speak with parents whose grief was still so fresh that Mac dreaded being in the presence of it.

'He's testing you,' Alec said.

'I figured that one out, thanks.'

Alec half smiled. 'You want to drive?'

'No, I'll let you do the honours. I'm a lousy driver when I'm distracted.'

'You want me to go on my own?'

'And fail Wildman's bloody test? No. No way I'd forgive myself, anyway.'

'Isn't that the whole problem?' Alec said.

A message was waiting for Karen, alias Carolyn Johnson, when she got back to the hotel. 'A lady called Rina Martin phoned for you,' the receptionist told her. 'She suggests four o'clock on Saturday. She said you'd understand.'

'Carolyn' thanked him and made her way up to her room. Tomorrow, then. Tomorrow she would see George and tell him what she had planned for them both.

EIGHT

It had been a day for confessions and explanations, Rina thought as she made her way back home. Tim had left her mid-afternoon for a meeting with a local computer games company he was now consulting for. Rina had made her reluctant way to see Sergeant Baker and PC Andy Nevins, to ask for any news of Mac and to tell them, as she had promised Mac, that Karen Parker was now back in town and that Rina was very anxious about her intentions.

To her relief, Mac had already spoken with Sergeant Baker and Rina found herself to be presenting old news. Sergeant Baker seemed happy with the simple knowledge that Karen 'was trouble' and that 'Young George is the only concern here', and Rina had left it at that, not confessing either her part in Karen's sudden departure or that she suspected Karen to have been guilty of far more than mere troublemaking.

Walking home, she was wryly amused but also oddly concerned to realize that Mac was also part of this silent conspiracy. Frank Baker knew that Mac had been bringing Karen in for questioning, knew that Mac was seriously concerned about something, but it had not crossed his generous mind that the cause of concern was the death of Mark Dowling.

'I think Mac was worried about the lass, see. Her dad was heavily involved in some really dodgy areas. I think the boss felt that there was the worry Karen might have been involved too, might have had some gen on what her dad had been up to. Turned out he was part of a much bigger problem, didn't it, Mrs Martin?'

It had indeed, Rina thought. The repercussions of Edward Parker's death and Edward Parker's associates had, shortly afterwards, rippled out through the quiet backwater that was Frantham and linked it all too painfully with the wider, crueller world.

Getting home, Rina came to a decision. Mac was absent, Tim too preoccupied with getting on with his own life – as was right and proper; he'd spent far too much of his life hiding away with a group of oldies, and it was time he stood on his own feet – but she did need help from somewhere.

In the privacy of her little room, Rina made two phone calls. One to a man called Fitch and another to one Abe Jackson, a man Rina had once suspected of being anything but a good guy. That done and help promised, she felt better, able to face the remainder of her mad little household and the welcome ritual of dinner and dominoes – and the feeling that she could put Karen aside, just for a little while.

Mac and Alec arrived at the Evans house a little after six. Lights shone through half-closed curtains and the car was in the drive. Mac had not been to their new house, but he had heard that Cara's parents had moved about the time that he left for Frantham. Somewhere, he recalled, he even had a change-of-address card, the strange and strained bond that had formed between them adding him to the list of those who should be personally informed that they had moved.

'They don't blame you, you know that,' Alec said as he pulled up in front of their house.

'I know it, but I don't understand why they don't. I was there, Alec. How can they accept I could do nothing?'

'Because they know you,' Alec said quietly. 'They watched you tear yourself apart for months looking for their child's killer. You sat with them, hour after hour, while they waited for news. You cried with them, Mac, and when they saw you at the hospital with Cara . . . Mac, I was there; I saw the state you were in. No one could have blamed you after that.'

Mac tried hard to steady his breathing and to slow his heart. It thumped against his ribs, deafened him. He couldn't remember – was grateful that he had somehow buried that memory so deep even he could not access it – but they had told him he had held on to the child, trying so hard to save a life that could not be saved: had held her in the ambulance, carried her into the hospital, laid her on the trolley and begged anyone who would listen to help her. He could not believe that all the months of searching had come to nothing, and then later, when he had been told that there were no new leads, that the case had been wound down pending later review, he had felt betrayed, not just because of Cara Evans and her parents, but also on his own behalf.

He wanted to go home now.

Alec opened the driver's door and got out. Mac followed, going ahead of his friend past the parked car and up to the front door. Becky Evans opened it. She stood stock still, staring at him.

'Mac,' she said. 'You've found him? Tell me you've found him.'

'We've been upgraded back to active,' Mac said softly.

Joe Evans appeared behind his wife, taking in the scene, a look of combined hope and dread fighting for precedence on his too-thin face. Joe Evans was never meant to be a skinny man. Mac knew what he was feeling. They'd never let go of the hope that Cara's killer would be brought to justice, but they had, nevertheless, reached some measure of, if not peace, then equilibrium, and now that was to be destroyed all over again.

Joe Evans, Mac knew, was wondering if he had the strength for it. As Mac watched, he stiffened his shoulders and lifted his chin, reminding Mac of Emily's Calum, the whole world resting on his back but determined to take his best shot at carrying it.

'You'd best come in,' Joe Evans said.

NINE

There was no way down to Frantham Old Town by car. The little fishing village had been the only Frantham before the Victorians had come along and constructed Frantham-on-Sea, with its promenades and boarding houses and now defunct railway. Frantham Old Town, by contrast, had never been intended for the tourist trade; it tumbled down the steep slope from coast road to seafront and little harbour via cobbled streets only just wide enough for a bicycle, and was occupied by a company of fiercely protective local families, many of whom had been there for generations.

Miriam, therefore, had two options. She could either park in the pull-in at the top of the hill and walk down the length of the little settlement to the boathouse, or she could drive a quarter of a mile further on, park at the newly built marina, close by the lifeboat station, and then walk back across to the boathouse, a matter of five minutes at a fast pace – and Miriam rarely walked at any other.

Miriam, unlike Mac, was not a creature of habit; it was a matter of nightly impulse as to which she should do. That and if she had shopping with her, in which case the marina was a better, flatter and more evenly paved option. Tonight, though, one of those cherished winter sunsets, witnessed as she had driven back to base from the scene of a serious road accident, was still hanging around when she had deposited her paperwork and box and left for home. Red still streaked a blackening sky, but close to the horizon a band of silver and peach remained, and she knew from experience it would still be there by the time she reached the pull-in on the coast road above her destination.

Miriam had never really been a weather-watcher before – in fact, she had always rather scoffed at the peculiarly British obsession – but, almost imperceptibly, she had come to realize that she had been caught by the cloud-watching bug and, in part at least, Mac was to blame. Frantham Old Town and the little boathouse apartment revealed the most delicious opportunities for the activity, and she had become as obsessed by the ever-changing view of sea and sky as Rina and Mac.

Having parked up, Miriam paused before wending her way down through the narrow streets. That silver streak still clung tenaciously to the horizon, though the sky above was solid black and the stars were starting to appear. Miriam was sure there was a sound meteorological reason for it all, but privately she viewed it as a bit of Frantham magic. She took little notice when a second car pulled up, just glanced over to see if the driver was anyone she knew, then dismissed it from her attention when she realized it was not. It crossed her mind that the driver might wonder what she was doing, standing there in the dark, staring down at the ocean, and she was mildly surprised when the driver did not move to get out. She glanced at him again, noting a middle-aged man, glasses perched on a rather broad nose. He too seemed to be staring out to sea. Another weather-watcher, Miriam thought, and when the man turned his head and looked her way, she summoned a polite smile. The man did not respond; he just continued to stare.

'OK,' Miriam muttered to herself. 'Just your friendly neighbourhood pervert then.' It wasn't all that unusual for courting couples to use the pull-in as a meeting place and, considering the view, Miriam could understand that. This man appeared to be alone, but, well, maybe he was meeting someone. Shrugging, Miriam set off down the hill towards the welcoming lights of Frantham Old Town.

Despite the fact that the streets were largely unlit, only the glow through curtained windows and the odd light above a front door breaking up the shadow, Miriam had never felt uneasy walking down alone. It was a friendly place, close-knit and welcoming, and though she and Mac were incomers, she had never felt that they were seen as intruders, a fact she put down to Mac's job and position in the community. Tonight, though, she felt oddly uneasy. Something in the way the man had looked at her was disturbing. He hadn't just glanced her way; he had looked and then kept on looking, and that bothered her.

Miriam always walked fast, but she realized that tonight she had almost broken into a run. Not a good idea on the steep cobblestones, even when, as now, they were fairly dry.

She blessed the fact that her work called for hours of standing and walking and sensible shoes. Heels were definitely not the footwear for Frantham Old Town. Above her, back at the road, a car door slammed, the sound carrying easily on the still evening air. For a second or two Miriam froze, listening for footsteps. From a nearby house issued the faint sounds of a television quiz show, the sound of children arguing from another across the street, and from behind her the unmistakable sound of someone following her down.

She hurried on, tempted to knock on one of the doors and ask for help, aware of how silly that might appear. Glad that her shoes had soft soles and made little sound on the cobbles, she threw away her caution and good sense and broke into a run, the steep hill quickening her pace way beyond the realms of comfort or safety.

Just ahead, round a bend, there was a pub, the King's Head, and the lights beckoned her. Chances were, even at this early hour, there'd be someone there she knew, who would walk her the rest of the way to the boathouse and not think her crazy. She could stop, have a drink, have a chat, wait for the man to go away, get this speculative friend to walk her home and maybe even invite them in for coffee. Well, maybe not that but . . . but what if there was no one there she knew? What if, what if . . .

God's sake, Miriam, get a grip.

Just opposite the pub was a tiny shop where Miriam had, in the summer, bought a bracelet for her sister. She had run into Mac, *almost* by accident, that day and they had spent the rest of it together, an *almost* unplanned act – utterly unplanned on Mac's side – that had led to everything else. At the side of the shop was a set-back doorway into a baker's shop. Breathing hard, Miriam abandoned thoughts of the pub and dodged back into the shadows of the recessed door. And waited, trying hard to control her breathing, waited for the man to go by.

Seconds passed. Minutes dragged, or seemed to. Maybe she was mistaken. Maybe there was no one there?

And then the footsteps, regular and deliberate and unnaturally loud in the stillness of the little town.

Miriam pressed as flat as she could, almost willing herself through the doorway and into the empty shop. She heard him pause. Maybe she could scream? She had no doubt that if she screamed someone would come. Screams in the night were unusual enough here and the population concerned enough, inquisitive enough, that she would not be ignored. She drew breath into her lungs, heard the man cough and then move again, footsteps coming closer and then passing by. Miriam watched as he moved past her hiding place, glancing from left to right as though looking for something. She was convinced that he had spotted her. He paused again, lifting his head and pushing the glasses back up the broad nose. Distractedly, she noticed that his hair had grown too long and brushed against the collar of his coat.

Then, relief. The man seemed to notice the pub, moved purposefully across the narrow street and went inside.

She almost laughed aloud.

Cautious, though, she left the sanctuary of the doorway and stayed in the shadows as she passed the door of the King's Head. Through the windows she could see the early drinkers chatting to the landlord. The stranger ordering something and the landlord lifting a glass to one of the optics.

Miriam was almost past, still in the shadows cast by the narrow shops and little houses, but busy telling herself that she had been a fool. The man had just come out here for a drink – that was all – and was probably meeting friends. She was letting her imagination run riot and to no purpose, none at all. And then he turned, drink in hand, and looked her way and Miriam was running again, even though reason told her he'd see nothing through the pub windows, looking out from bright light into dark. She ran and didn't stop until she was inside the boathouse and had locked the door, the conviction that she knew the man from somewhere – and that she really was the reason he had come here – now absolutely wedged tight in her mind.

TEN

Saturday

Mac had given up on the idea of going home; it just wasn't going to happen. Wildman had declared that there was to be a case review for all senior officers: a chance to go over old ground, discuss it as a group, be open to the possibility that the original enquiry may have missed something or that tiny details, overlooked then, may come into sharper focus in the light of new information.

Mac couldn't fault him on his logic and, though he knew they'd all worked their backsides off during the first investigation, was not even offended by the idea that something may have been missed. He knew just how easy it was to become myopic, particularly when emotions were running so high. That said, he was not exactly enthusiastic about spending his weekend in the close company of Wildman or even such pleasant colleagues as Alec. He felt himself being sucked down into the maelstrom intensity of the original enquiry and really would have welcomed time to breathe.

For the first time he began to wonder if he'd been right to come back; more worryingly, he'd begun to have niggling doubts that he even wanted to do this job any more. Even at the height of his involvement in the Cara Evans case, even at the deepest moments of despair that followed, he had never had that thought and he could not for the life of him understand why he should be having it now.

He took the opportunity to call home and Miriam's voice cheered him instantly. An instant more and he was aware that something was wrong.

'I hoped you'd call last night.'

'By the time I got back it was so late I thought you'd be asleep. We went to see Cara Evans's parents. It was a long visit.' He felt a momentary pang that he'd made time to phone Emily, but thought it best to keep that to himself. Miriam sounded tense, a little distant.

'That must have been hard,' she said. 'I just hate it when I have to meet with the bereaved. I never know what to say.'

'Are you all right?' Mac knew she wasn't. Just something in her voice, or something missing from it.

She hesitated. 'I'm sure it's nothing.'

'Miriam? Come on, you don't worry over nothing.'

'Don't I?' she managed to laugh but it sounded false. She began to tell him about the man who had followed her, or who she thought might have been following her, though she was sure now that it had been coincidence and nothing at all.

Mac listened, tense, and, as though her fear was contagious even in the retelling, his anxiety overwhelmed him.

'Miriam, listen to me. I want you to pack your stuff and leave, now, soon as you get off the phone. Jerry will be off today' – the boathouse owner was often around on Saturday – 'so get him to walk you back to your car and check the car when you get there.'

'Mac? I don't understand. And I'm not asking Jerry to walk me anywhere – he'll think I'm nuts. Anyway, it's broad daylight. Saturday.' She sounded braver now, relieved that she could be impatient with *him* instead of herself.

'Get in touch with DI Kendal – you remember him? His number should be in my book. Tell him you need to speak with a sketch artist and ask him to give me a ring.'

'Mac, you're scaring me.'

'Good. Miriam, I think there may well be something to be scared about.' He closed his eyes, swore softly under his breath. He should have called her last night, should have warned her then, but somehow he had assumed that Peel's attention would have shifted north when he did; apparently not. Miriam's description of the man struck a chord. Peel, with his too-large glasses and his slightly flattened nose. Like Mac, he'd been a rugby player in his youth and his face suffered the same indignities.

'There's some indication that Peel has been . . .' *Stalking?* Was that too emotive a word. 'Has had me under surveillance.' He took refuge in more formal language. 'Something he told a former associate makes us think he may have either been to Frantham or had someone down there on his behalf.'

'What? You must be kidding me? Mac, when did you find this out?'

'Yesterday afternoon. Miriam, I'm so sorry. I assumed, as I was no longer there . . .'

'But you still could have called, let me know. Mac, you know how lonely that road is at night, just how cut off I'd be.' She broke off and he hesitated, not sure what to say, realizing just how scared she'd been and that he was very firmly in the wrong.

Would 'sorry' do? 'I'm so sorry,' he said. 'Miri, I'm really . . .'

'Stupid at times? Yeah, you really are.'

He could hear her breathing, nervous and loud, as she held the phone close, and he could imagine her gripping it tight in both hands. 'I'm sorry,' he said again, meaning it absolutely, willing her to know just how much he was meaning it.

'Have you spoken to Rina?'

He would have lied now, if he'd had to, but fortunately he could be truthful. 'No,' he said. 'I've not spoken to anyone else yet. You think you can stay at your sister's?'

'You think he knows about my flat?'

'I think I don't know any more. Maybe . . .'

'Mac, I've got a job to do, so don't suggest I go anywhere. I'm not planning on running away.'

He seemed to be surrounded by people telling him that, Mac thought. Mostly they seemed to be women. 'I'd rather you left the boathouse though, stayed with someone. Don't be alone. Maybe Rina—'

'Mac, stop right now. I love Rina and Tim, and I'm really fond of the Peters sisters and the Montmorencys and all of them, but stay there? No, not in a month of Sundays, not to escape a whole boatload of Thomas Peels.' She was laughing now, but Mac didn't really think she felt amusement.

'Miriam. You will leave, won't you?'

The laughter ceased. 'Soon as I get off the phone,' she said. 'I love you, Mac. Come home soon, won't you?'

'I will,' he promised. 'And I love you too.'

Next on his 'to do' list was Rina. If he expected to surprise her with an early call, then he was to be disappointed. She listened to his concerns and then delivered hers.

Fitch and Abe Jackson had promised to look in on her today. Abe, a veteran of earlier Frantham crises, now had his own security firm in Exeter, mainly employing ex service people like himself.

Fitch, she told him, would be staying in the tiny spare room at Peverill Lodge. 'Eliza and Bethany are as overexcited as a couple of puppies,' she said.

'Well, so long as they don't wet themselves,' Mac joked. 'I mean, isn't that what excited puppies do?'

'I won't tell them you said that,' Rina said sternly.

'No, probably better not. Rina, are you really that worried? I mean, Fitch has to come all the way from Manchester.'

'And the Duggans have said they can spare him for as long as I need. Better be safe, I think.'

'Safe?'

'Well, with what you've just told me, I think I'm doubly pleased he's coming.'

'But you were worried even before that. About Karen.'

'Mac, I've learnt not to ignore my feelings, and I've a feeling about this. I don't know where Karen's been these past months, but what I can tell you is she left with little more than the clothes on her back and she's come back with a darn sight more. Let's just say she departed in Primark and returned in couture, and unless she's found herself a rich sugar daddy, I'm guessing she's earned it, and I don't think she's been working, if you see what I mean.'

'I'm being thick here, Rina.'

'Yes, you are,' she said bluntly. 'Think about it, Mac. Her father was a career criminal – a poor excuse for one, but nevertheless he moved in, shall we say, certain circles.'

'So does Fitch,' Mac pointed out.

'Which is what makes him so useful. The problem with Edward Parker was that he was a bear of a man but with very little brain. The mother, poor love, well, if anyone was born to be a doormat . . . but the children are extraordinary. George is a bright, sensible, wonderful child and will grow into a very special young man. Karen, however, she has single-mindedness, intelligence and her father's lack of respect for anything legal or respectable. She has the connections, Mac. And it's the timing that bothers me. It's almost as if she knew you'd be away.'

'I don't see how. You've spoken to Andy and Frank Baker?'

'I have, and Sergeant Baker is going to have a chat to that nice DI Kendal.'

'He's not that nice.'

'Jealousy doesn't suit you. But I believe in having insurance, and Fitch is insurance, Abe is intelligence, and Kendal is backup in case we need someone arrested.'

Mac laughed. 'You seem to have covered all bases. Rina, I'm not going to argue with you.'

'And Miriam?'

'Going to stay with her sister. Ben, Miriam's brother-in-law, he's built like the proverbial outdoor facilities and his brothers live almost next door, so I figure she'll be safer there, and now she knows there may be a problem . . . I told her to call Kendal too.'

'He's going to be a busy boy. Still, that's what he's there for. Seriously, Mac, you watch your back; we're all counting the days until you're home safe.'

ELEVEN

Fitch was a much-loved honorary member of the Rina Martin household. His introduction to life at Peverill Lodge had been somewhat dramatic; his boss's son had been killed and Fitch had come south with Jimmy Duggan to find those responsible for the murder. Not much happened in Frantham that did not eventually involve Rina, and she had been drawn into the investigations, both official – Mac – and not so official in the shape of Jimmy Duggan and Fitch.

His arrival had the ladies, Bethany and Eliza, in a major twitter. They'd been pacing back and forth from living room to hall most of the morning, occasionally retreating to practise the piano, leading Rina to assume that they had a special performance arranged for their guest. She hoped Fitch could cope with such adulation. The inviting scents filtering out from beneath the closed door of the kitchen told her that the men of the household were equally enthusiastic. Steven and Matthew had been closeted in there since just after breakfast, and Rina hoped fervently that Fitch had brought his usual appetite with him and not suddenly and unexpectedly taken to dieting.

The doorbell rang just on noon and doors all across the ground floor of Peverill Lodge burst open. By the time Rina opened the front door, a welcoming committee had gathered. Fitch stood on the step, grinning broadly, and Rina stood back to let the big man in. The door of Peverill Lodge was large and impressive as befitted such an elegant Victorian villa, but Fitch practically filled the same space.

Fitch dropped his holdall on to the tiled floor and swept Rina into his arms, kissing her soundly before opening his arms wide and sweeping both sisters into his massive embrace.

Rina straightened herself up and watched indulgently as the Peters sisters squealed and wriggled and pretended to protest, all the while snuggling closer. The Montmorencys stood close by the kitchen door, waiting for their turn at welcome; Rina wondered if they'd be content just to shake his hand.

'Bet Fitch is the only person who gets away with grabbing you like that,' a laughing voice said.

Rina turned, smiling. She might have guessed that Joy Duggan would be unable to keep away. 'I'd make an exception for you, sweetheart,' she said, welcoming Joy with a warm hug. They watched, laughing, as Fitch was escorted into the living room by his admirers.

'Is Tim here?' Joy asked anxiously. 'And, Rina, just how bad are things?'

Tim arrived just as lunch was about to begin and Joy pulled up a chair and seated herself beside him at the table. Rina smiled at them both. Joy Duggan, daughter of Fitch's now-dead employer, was more than a decade younger than Tim, but somehow Rina didn't think that was going to stand in her way. In many ways, she was the more mature of the two. She'd set her sights on him from the moment they had met and, though distance and college kept them physically apart, Rina knew they texted many times a day and spoke to one another nearly every evening, Tim managing a quick call between sets even when he was working.

Selfishly, she hoped that once they finally got together properly Joy would move south to Frantham rather than have Tim go north to be with her. She already missed her Tim now that he was more regularly employed and not quite as readily available for advice and support and just idle conversation, and Rina realized that she'd come to view the younger man as surrogate for the children she had never had. More than that, he was probably her closest friend.

Lunchtime talk was casual, catch-up time, the little news of life and learning and knitted scarves and magic and the plans for the Pallisades' Christmas extravaganza – the hotel was already booked solidly for the entire Christmas and New Year period. Serious discussion was never permitted to spoil a meal at Peverill Lodge.

Rina half listened, impatient for the meal to be over and to be able to tell Fitch just why he was here.

Abe Jackson arrived just as lunch was ending, but was brought with due ceremony to the table and supplied with cake in lieu. Joy went to the kitchen with Rina to help bring in the coffee trays.

'Mum sends her love,' she said. 'She wondered if maybe you and Tim might come and stay for a while after New Year. I know neither of you can get away before.'

'I'm not sure I can get away *then*,' Rina said. 'I don't like to leave them for long, you know.'

Joy laughed. 'Rina, they're not kids, not really. Mac and Miriam can look in on them all, and at least you know no one will starve. You deserve a break, and Mum would love someone to do the January sales with.'

'That sounds wonderfully normal,' Rina said wistfully. 'Yes, Joy, tell Bridie I'd love to. I can't recall the last time I had a proper break. It was probably back in my acting days, though I called it "resting" then and didn't like it one bit.' Not, she thought gratefully, that there had been many such gaps in her life; although fame, with *Lydia Marchant Investigates*, had come relatively late in her career, she had rarely been out of work.

'I can't recall the last time you saw Mum when there wasn't some emergency happening,' Joy added.

'That too. Joy, I love having you here, you know that, but things are getting more complicated by the day here and . . .'

'And I've probably been with you through worse,' Joy said. 'Hey, Rina, I had to come, you know that. Mum knows that. She says if you need reinforcements, you only have to say the word, but she knows I'd not miss the opportunity to see you all.'

'Especially Tim,' Rina said mischievously.

'Especially Tim. Mum knows we Duggan women won't be put off once we've got something into our heads and she reckons I could do a lot worse.'

'Have you informed Tim that his fate is sealed?'

Joy giggled and suddenly looked like the twenty-year-old she was, maturity slipping away. 'Oh, I think he knows,' she said. 'But I'm being sensible, getting on with my studies and all that. I promised Patrick I would and I'm not about to let him down.'

Patrick, Joy's dead brother. The maverick son not prepared to go into the family business with his father and older sibling. Patrick who wanted to make his own, legal, way in the world and who hoped his sister would do the same. Joy had grown up so much this past year, Rina thought; it was just a pity that so much grief should be the cause of that.

Back in the dining room, Rina poured coffee, noting a subtle change in mood seemed to have taken place in her brief absence. She intercepted what could only be described as a meaningful glance between Matthew Montmorency and Eliza Peters. She groaned inwardly.

Steven Montmorency took his cup from her and set it down purposefully. He steepled his plump fingers and leaned back in his chair. Bethany wriggled in her seat and exchanged an excited glance with her sister.

'Now,' Steven said. 'We've all eaten and we're all happy to be back together, but none of us imagines this is a social visit, do we, Matthew?'

Matthew Montmorency shook his head. Unlike his supposed twin, who was almost bald, Matthew had a mane of thick, grey hair that hung past his collar. He pushed a heavy lock back off his face. 'No, indeed, we don't,' he said. 'Do we, girls?'

The 'girls', neither of whom would see sixty again, chorused an answer. 'No, Matthew, we most certainly don't.'

Rina looked at Fitch, who shrugged. 'Well, you've got to admit, Rina, the last time we all got together was a tad dramatic, so it's a natural assumption. Who goes first?'

Rina took a deep breath. She looked at Tim, but he was busy playing with Joy's hand and seemed not to be giving the conversation a hundred per cent attention. Abe Jackson merely shrugged when she glanced his way.

'So,' Fitch prompted, 'what the devil are we dealing with this time, eh?'

Rina scanned the expectant faces around the table. 'A girl called Karen Parker,' she said quietly, 'who may or may not be about to cause us some problems.'

'Young George's sister,' Matthew nodded, satisfied. 'I told you that was her, Steven. I said, that's young George's sister and she's dyed her hair, didn't I?'

'Quite,' Steven said, 'but that's not the end of it, is it, Rina?'

'No,' Rina said quietly. 'When I asked Fitch to come and give me a hand, I thought what I had in mind was maybe some intelligence-gathering and someone to keep an eye on George should Karen try to coerce him, but I spoke to Mac this morning and it seems that his former life has well and truly come back to haunt him. To haunt us all, in fact. As you may know, Mac left to go back and work with his former colleagues. Now, I know you're all aware that when he came here he was recovering from a major . . . well, let's call it a collapse. He's so much better now, but I'm still concerned about the effects this whole thing will have on him.'

'Oh, poor Mac,' Bethany said. 'He is such a lovely man, and lovely people tend to be, well, fragile, I suppose.'

She looked to her sister for confirmation and Eliza nodded wisely.

'I would not suggest that Sebastian is fragile,' Matthew said. He and Steven were the only people, as far as Rina knew, who ever used Mac's given name. He tolerated it with a good grace. 'But any of us can suffer ill health as a result of stress – that's just the way of things, isn't it?'

'So,' Fitch said, 'suppose you start at the beginning and bring us all up to speed, Rina. You're suggesting we've got ourselves two problems – one big and one fairly small – so let's start with Mac and work our way out from there.'

Rina nodded. 'It began with the kidnap and murder of a little girl,' she said. 'Her name was Cara Evans, and Mac witnessed her death. He still can't get over the fact that there was nothing he could have done.'

For the next hour Rina told them all she knew about Mac and his previous life in Pinsent and the reopened investigation, and about the possibility that Thomas Peel had been watching Mac as he began his new life here in Frantham. She told them about Miriam's scare the night before and Mac's warning that Peel was intent on creating trouble for him, even as Mac attempted to track him down. She watched their faces carefully, anxious not to upset them all too much. Bethany and Eliza, though they may look like elderly, fragile flowers, were as tough as old boots. Steven was, oddly, much more vulnerable. This last year had been difficult, and Rina worried that this was one upset too far. Matthew's comment about anyone being vulnerable was, she knew, all about his beloved Steven, now arthritic of knee but well of mind for these past few secure, Peverill Lodge years.

'And so,' Rina said by way of conclusion, 'I'm worried about Karen because of what kind of life I suspect she has been leading since she left.' She had decided to leave out the implication of George's sister in the death of Mark Dowling;

that seemed a shock too far for the general company. 'George has settled here now. I don't want him pressured. The second problem is, I suppose, just as speculative. Thomas Peel may or may not be of concern.'

Now she had voiced all of this, Rina was aware of how flimsy it sounded and worried that she had overreacted. After all, Karen was the same age as Joy; she was just a girl. Why should Rina have been so upset, just because she turned up in decent clothes and possessed of an extra dose of confidence?

'I'm sorry,' she said. 'Fitch, Abe, I feel now that I've called on you for no reason.' She sighed deeply. 'I'm probably just being an old woman with too much imagination.'

A chorus of denial at the table. 'You're not old,' Joy declared.

'And I've rarely met anyone with more acute instincts,' Abe Jackson said quietly. The table fell silent. Abe had barely spoken since taking his place and being instructed to devour cake.

'You know something?' Fitch was suddenly more alert and Rina more painfully aware that he had originally come to her rescue, even though he doubted there had been anything to rescue her from.

Abe slipped some papers from his inside jacket pocket and handed them to Fitch. 'Rina, I used my contacts and did some checking. Your Karen has cut quite a swathe since she left here – little thefts and frauds all up and down the country. Nothing anyone's been able to pin on her, but . . .'

Fitch glanced up sharply from what he was reading and then caught on and followed Abe's lead. 'She's enterprising,' he said. 'I suppose when you've gone without for as long as she and George must have done, then other people's weakness and inattention must lead you into temptation.'

Rina studied them both, wondering what had not been said. Fitch, never a good liar, was avoiding her eye.

'Anyway,' Joy said, 'we're all here now and that's something to celebrate, don't you think? Matthew, Rina says George and Ursula are coming to tea. Is there anything I can do?'

Rina blessed her. The Montmorency twins at once began to clear the table, helped by the Peters sisters, and soon Joy was deep in discussion with them regarding the very important provision of 'High Tea'. Tim managed a quick kiss before being ushered off, and Rina led the way into her little sitting room at the front of the house – her private space in which she could escape the beloved madness of her household.

Fitch and Abe followed, Tim in their wake, looking back regretfully.

'Go,' Rina heard Joy whisper. 'We'll take a walk later, just the two of us, and I thought I might come and see you perform tonight.'

Rina chuckled to herself. Tim was well and truly out of his depth, she thought, and she approved completely.

The tiny front parlour seemed even smaller with Fitch and Abe and Tim all crammed in beside her, but they managed to seat themselves, Tim having brought an extra chair from the hall.

'Now,' she said, 'which of you is going to tell me what's going on?'

Fitch handed her the printed sheets that Abe had given to him, and Tim leaned in so he could read it with her.

Rina read and then read again. 'Are you sure about this? Of course you are.' She took a moment or two, wondering what else to say.

'Mac's absence is no coincidence, Rina; neither is Thomas Peel coming out from whatever hole he's been hiding in. And there's Karen, right at the heart of it.'

TWELVE

Mac was in need of a break. The briefing room had been filled to capacity with officers all morning and they had spilled out into one of the interview rooms. Mac had found refuge in Alec's office, only to find that Wildman had already staked a claim to the last available space and squeezed a desk into the corner by the door. The door crashed into the side of the desk every time it was opened, and getting to the chair required an effort of bodily convolution that a contortionist would have been proud of. That Wildman would be able to get in at all was a general source of amazement; bets had been taken on his ability to free himself from behind the desk once he was there. So far, Mac had seen no evidence of him even trying to do either. Wildman was a percher; desks, radiators, backs of chairs, all welcomed his rotund buttocks, but no chair ever seemed destined to be favoured with their pressure. Mac had begun to wonder if Wildman was even capable of bending at the knees.

Mac had spent the morning working his way through witness statements, reliving in memory the interviews and events he had supervised or attended or noted down. Faces, names, incidents, all seemed at once so long ago and so immediate, as though he recalled seeing them on a cinema screen. He found it very hard to feel he had a place in all of this, an odd sense of detachment, curtain-like and muffling, having fallen between him and what he did. He recognized it for what it was: his attempt to protect himself, to avoid the hurt of last time. Mac told himself that detachment was good, that he'd see more clearly and more precisely, maybe catch some small mention, some tiny revelation that had not been recognized before.

In practice, what was really going through his mind was that he didn't want to be there, in Pinsent, in close proximity to Wildman, the percher, who was poised, Mac felt, to catch him out, to take note of any weakness and seize upon it. He felt Wildman's eyes upon him again and looked up, met the man's gaze. Was the first to look away.

The file on the desk in front of him seemed to have been written in a foreign language. Words writhed and faded and came back into focus for a mere instant before fading out again. He had read that paragraph, what, three, four times? He just knew that Wildman had noted the hesitation, the lack of concentration, and as if to confirm that, he heard Wildman's sharp voice ask, 'Find something interesting there, Mac?'

Mac closed the file and stood up, brushed past his boss and went to find himself a coffee.

Down in the main briefing room, men and women examined financial records, phone calls, tracked movements of suspects who had seemed relevant eighteen months ago and who would now have had time to fade back into whatever murky world they inhabited. They had lost time, lost momentum. Now, all of that would have to be kick-started, urged into life, momentum regained – and how long would that take? Mac took a look at the hessian pinboards that lined the longest wall. On day one they had shown only the images of Cara Evans and Thomas Peel; now other images joined them, captioned and connected by arrows drawn on to scraps of paper, red cord that some enterprising soul had found and used to recreate more complex contacts, scribbled notes speculating about payments made or phone calls received. Two collators, both women – one a uniformed sergeant and the other a young, newly promoted DI – sat close to the board, one at a computer, one making handwritten notes on to the loose pages of a ring-binder. As new leads came in, new possibilities emerged, it was their job to cross-reference and to annotate. Others would join them, but it was important to keep this part of the team small, agile, constantly interacting. Computer databases were wonderful, but it was often the human being who recalled the little things, the tiny, broken fragments of information that had to be properly phrased before the computer could even begin to search.

He studied the faces pinned on to the board, thinking of all the glossy US television series he and Miriam liked to watch – and criticize – with their glass partitions on which the growing evidence could be displayed and their instant transfers of complex information, ready and available at the touch of a computer key, and he wondered, briefly, if it was really like that, anywhere. If the reality was always closer to what it was here: groups of people reading and comparing and talking, and making entries on to sheets of paper just as often as they did into vast computer systems, and where links were drawn out with pins and lengths of red string.

He needed air. He took his coffee and went out into the yard at the back of the police station. No view and not much in the way of fresh air as this space was now refuge for the few remaining committed smokers. They were clustered together, huddled with coffee mugs in one hand and cigarettes in the other, close to the perimeter fence. Officially, no one was permitted to smoke anywhere on the premises and they were still, technically, within the purview of the building regulations, but everyone turned a blind eye. It occurred to Mac, suddenly, that he knew very few people who smoked any more. Neither Andy nor Sergeant Baker did, though Baker had done in his younger days. None of Rina's household. He had become unused to seeing these huddled groups of dispossessed.

'Time for a break, is it?'

Mac groaned, looked up. A ramp led down into the yard from the rear door and Wildman now leaned on the railing, peering down. Mac figured the railing was too high to perch upon; he'd noticed that leaning was a secondary Wildman trait.

The DCI slouched down the ramp and commandeered a place beside Mac. 'So,' he said, 'how are you holding up?'

It was almost a relief that Wildman had actually asked the question. 'I'm doing all right, so far,' Mac lied.

'Can't be easy, though, coming back here, to where it happened, having everyone looking at you like you're the guilty one.'

'I can't say I'd noticed that they had,' Mac said steadily. Was that what everyone was thinking? He became aware, suddenly and intently, of a dozen imagined slights, of eyes that avoided his, of . . . 'I don't believe that's what everyone is concerned with,' he said more firmly. 'Our focus should be Thomas Peel: where's he's been, where he is now, why he's suddenly come out of hiding.'

'I'm sure Cara's parents agree with you,' Wildman said.

Mac turned to fully face the man. 'Actually, they do,' he said. 'Nothing can bring her back; the best they can hope for is some kind of justice, is . . .'

'Closure?' Wildman's voice was heavy with sarcasm.

'No,' Mac said. 'They and I both know there can be no closure. Some wounds scab over, even grow new skin, but they will always be there, raw and hollow beneath the surface, ready to bleed.'

He held Wildman's gaze, aware that this was not the response the DCI had been expecting. 'I suppose the truth is, both Cara's parents and I, we don't want closure, as you call it. I sometimes wonder if justice really has any meaning when someone has done something like that. Can you really settle for justice with a man like Thomas Peel?'

'So, what, then?' Wildman smiled, and Mac was horrified to realize that the DCI saw a certain kinship between them. 'You out for revenge, Mac? You'll get Peel in a dark corner somewhere, beat seven shades out of him, leave him dying with his throat laid wide open?' He laughed as Mac turned away. 'No, I don't suppose you would. I don't suppose you'd have the stomach for it.'

'You don't know me,' Mac said softly. 'You'll never know me, so don't pretend to try.'

THIRTEEN

Abe had left the Martin household by mid-afternoon and Fitch had made himself scarce, as had Joy and Tim. She had watched them all set off into what had turned out to be a clear afternoon, bright and breezy and cold, but blessed with that clarity of winter light that Rina had come to love and which seemed particular to this part of the south coast.

Fitch was driving into Dorchester, and Joy and Tim planned to be tourists for the afternoon. What Fitch had in mind he had not said, but Rina guessed he'd be meeting up with Abe. All had offered to stay and wait for Karen's arrival, but Rina had been very firm. No, this should be as normal an afternoon as possible. George would have enough to deal with, and she really didn't want Karen to feel that she was being ganged up on, even if that was the actual truth.

George and Ursula arrived just after four, one of the carers at Hill House giving them a lift on the way home. Peverill Lodge was a regular destination for the pair, and Rina was well known to everyone at the home. She would put them in a taxi later and George would call once they had arrived back, as per their normal arrangement. That was, Rina reflected, perhaps the only normal thing about this particular Saturday.

'You look very nice, Ursula,' Rina commented as she greeted the two teenagers.

'It's a new top,' Ursula said, though it did not escape Rina's attention that she was also wearing make-up, something she would not have bothered with on an ordinary visit. Unlike the other girls at Hill House, Ursula did not go in for 'paint and powder', as Matthew Montmorency called it. A little eyeshadow, maybe, but not much else. Today, she had taken extra care, looked older than fourteen; older than George.

George was quiet, nervous. He allowed the Peters sisters to usher him through to the living room, and Rina heard them telling him about the new piano piece they had learnt to play. They were teaching George to play on a casual basis; he wasn't very good, but he gave it a try as much to be nice to Bethany and Eliza as for any musical aspirations.

'Is he all right?' Rina whispered to Ursula who had hung back in the hall.

'No, not really. He told Cheryl that Karen would be calling in today while we were here; she wanted to know why she didn't come to Hill House and got all excited, said we should get a cake and all that.' Ursula rolled her eyes. Cheryl was their key worker at Hill House. Rina suspected that, despite Ursula's display, the two were really quite fond of her, and Cheryl was devoted to George. 'George told her Karen was shy and wouldn't like a fuss. Can you imagine?'

Rina had to remind herself that Ursula had never in fact met George's sister, so was really in no position to imagine anything. George, she guessed, must have told Ursula a great deal.

Ursula hesitated, then she said, 'I think he's scared, Rina. Not of Karen exactly, but he's kind of not had to think about anything since she left. Not about his dad or his mum or how they lived or anything.'

Rina nodded and clasped Ursula's hand. 'We'll look after him, love. All of us.'

The doorbell rang, the very real bell in the hall dinging loudly on its wrought-iron, spiral pulley.

'That will be Karen,' Rina said.

Ursula nodded and hurried through to join George, and when Rina ushered Karen into the large living room in which the welcoming committee had gathered, Ursula was standing firmly at his side, small, slightly built and only fourteen, but as protective as any grown woman. Rina winced as she intercepted the look that passed between Ursula and Karen as the older girl came in. Poor George, she thought briefly: if looks were weapons, he'd be torn limb from limb as each staked their claim.

Abe's security firm worked out of an unassuming little office on a small industrial estate on the outskirts of Exeter. His immediate neighbours were a company specializing in point-of-sale merchandise and a firm which, as far as Fitch could tell, sold novelty socks. When he met clients, it was either at their place of work or at a tiny little place in Dorchester that he rented as a sublet from a firm of solicitors, sharing their immaculate entrance, building and kudos, but not their costs. The fact that one of the partners in the firm of solicitors was an ex commanding officer in Abe's unit had secured him the use of what had been a storeroom and an agreeable rate; essentially, in exchange for a nicely furnished space, desk, filing cabinet, computer access and nameplate on the door, Abe did occasional surveillance work for the law firm.

Unknown to Rina, Fitch had previously visited both businesses, and Abe's expertise had several times proved useful to Bridie Duggan, Fitch's employer. The Duggan empire had been founded on very dodgy practices, but in later years Jimmy Duggan, now deceased, had moved into more legitimate areas, including two nightclubs. Since his death, Bridie had continued that move, her eldest son taking over part of the day-to-day running of their enterprises, but Bridie well knew that it took more than intent and one generation to completely make the transfer from illegitimate to legal and she liked to keep a close eye on previous colleagues and associates. She was an astute enough businesswoman to make use of inside information and to know when and where trouble might be brewing with Jimmy's former partners. Abe had been invaluable as a low-profile troubleshooter.

Fitch nodded to the woman on reception; they had met before when he had visited the office and, once seen, Fitch was rarely forgotten. She smiled nervously at him. 'Mr Jackson just arrived,' she said. 'You know where to go?'

Fitch thanked her and headed upstairs to Abe, knocking on the half-glazed door and then going straight in. Abe waved him into a chair and set a glass on the desk in front of Fitch, who raised it in salute and then sipped, savouring the taste of the single malt.

'Best just make it one,' Abe said. 'You've got to drive back.'

Fitch nodded. 'Joy and Tim have gone to look at some writer's house,' he said. 'She's all into that stuff now. Tim's influence, I suppose. Bridie thinks it's wonderful.'

'That would be Hardy's place, I would imagine,' Abe said wryly. 'He was pretty famous, you know, still makes good television.'

Fitch regarded Abe over the rim of his glass before setting it down. 'Taking the piss, are we?'

'Possibly. How is Bridie? I spoke to her last week and she was full of cold.'

'Better now. Got through a half-dozen boxes of tissues, nose like Rudolf. So, this kid of Parker's, what's she been up to then? I take it you kept most of it back?'

Abe produced a file from the desk drawer and pushed it across to Fitch. 'Some of this is speculation,' he said. 'I've got a couple of leads I want to run. Thought I'd wait to get the go-ahead. I don't want Rina knowing all this; she's got enough on her plate and anyway—'

'Rina's got morals. You and I gave them up a long time ago.'

'I still have a moral compass,' Abe protested.

'Yeah, but it certainly don't point north. Bridie says not to worry about pay; she'll foot the bill.'

'No bill,' Abe said. 'This one's on the house.'

'Getting sentimental, are we?'

Abe shook his head. 'Settling an account, that's all.'

Fitch snorted what may have been a laugh. 'Right,' he said. He drained his glass and looked regretfully at the bottle of Macallan. 'Get the kettle on, then. I'm a slow reader.'

For the next half hour Abe Jackson watched Fitch read. He made tea, strong enough to take the plate off a cheap spoon, and set a red mug beside the file. Fitch nodded but did not look up. He read like a child, following his finger as it tracked line by line. Some people, Abe knew, would take this as a sign of lacking intellect; Abe knew better. Fitch was meticulous, and something about keeping contact with the words of the page seemed to help that acute and accurate processing that passed for thinking in Fitch's head. Abe was a linear thinker, A to B with as few stops and sidelines as possible; get to the core, the heart. Fitch, for all his brawn, was possessed of a very agile brain and was anything but linear. Fitch made connections that Abe knew, from experience, he would either not see or would dismiss as being too far outside his original brief.

'So,' he said when Fitch finally looked up and closed the file. He took the red mug and gave him a refill. Two sugars, not stirred.

'There's been no ramp-up,' Fitch said. 'No one turns so naturally to violence, not without some kind of . . .'

'Oh, it's there,' Abe said. 'She put her dad in hospital,

remember. Justifiable, of course, but nevertheless she crossed a line. Then there was that Mark Dowling kid.'

Fitch frowned, touched the file as though doubting himself.

'No, it's not in there,' Abe told him. 'Not the Mark Dowling episode. My associate prepared that file. I got hold of the intel on Dowling from another source. Seems he was threatening Karen's little brother. It was in the papers earlier this year; I'll scan and email the clippings soon as I have everything. Rina's not given either of us a hell of a lot of notice. It seems Dowling is, or was, prime suspect in the murder of an old woman, lived down the street from Rina. Mac's first case not long after he arrived. Anyway, Dowling gets beaten to death, Karen disappears not long after. Mac was about to make the arrest, though he was somewhat lacking in solid evidence at that stage. I think he hoped she'd confess.'

Fitch shoved the file further on to the table. 'Some hope of that,' he said. 'So, Karen disappears and?'

'And she sent Mac a mobile phone. She'd photographed the murder scene.'

'She'd what?'

'Cold,' Abe agreed. 'Mac reported it to Eden, his boss back then. Eden was on the verge of retirement. Mac knew all he could do was prove that Karen had seen Dowling dead, photographed the scene. She'd gone anyway, so it all went into a file somewhere and nothing came of it. Then Mac had his hands full with your boss and his family. Karen Parker was the least of his worries.'

'And now . . . she's efficient, I'll give her that. Three clean kills. How does she make contact?'

'My sources tell me an ad is placed in the personal column of one of three national newspapers. She has a different day for each one. She replies, arrangements are made, money transferred, she does her thing, gets paid the balance. You read in the file about Percy Mears?'

Fitch nodded. 'Tried to renege on the balance once she'd completed the job.'

'So, she paid him a visit, extracted what was owed. Bank records show the last thing he did before he died was make the transfer. Talk is, she does the job, takes the money, is gone. As long as you don't mess with her, she's perfect.'

'And it's well known that she's Parker's kid? Parker was a

cheap thug. How did she convince anyone she was even capable?'

'Victim number one. Vido Feinmann. In the file.'

Fitch nodded, working it out. Vido was a man he knew well from Jimmy Duggan's not so legitimate days. 'Prostitution, drugs, extortion, usual mix,' he said, thinking aloud. 'Had a nasty habit of increasing the price. Wasn't there some incident with a young woman. Carlisle's daughter? GHB, date rape . . . He went to ground a bit sharpish after that.' He paused. 'So, young Karen Parker, knowing that Vido is not only *not* going to be missed; his absence, shall we say, is likely to be rewarded . . .'

'Did what Carlisle and his crew had been unable to do. Tracks him down, kills him, sends the pictures to Carlisle along with the bill.'

Fitch laughed. 'She's got balls; you've got to give her that.'

'Yeah, what I hear, Vido donated his. Anyway, she's then up and running. Kudos and start-up capital in one.'

'And two since. Apart from Percy Mears. Being a client, I suppose he doesn't count.'

'Apart from him, two more that we know about. It has to be said too that she's canny. Doesn't take out anyone who's likely to be missed or who's likely to start a vendetta. Vido overstepped the mark: no one was going to be seen to miss him or mourn him. Wesley Norman – number two in our report. He'd played one side against the other so often that no one would trust him to buy them a beer. Thought he was clever; didn't realize that you have to have someone out there willing to watch your back while you rip off the opposition. The names implicated in getting rid of him are, let's say, legion . . . way I figure it, someone passed the hat and everyone bunged a fiver in.'

'I never encountered Norman,' Fitch said. 'I knew about him, never heard a good word. So, where does Thomas Peel start to figure in this?'

'That, as they say, is the sixty-four dollar question. So far as I can ascertain, contact with Thomas Peel was part payment for victim number three, Edward Hutchens. She seems to have heard that Peel was being protected and who by. The Hutchens hit was, we think, put out by Igor Vaschinsky.'

'Vaschinsky? Russian Mafia? Well, his elder brother is, so . . .'

'Vaschinsky is, in part, a legitimate art dealer who uses his business as a front for a fine-art smuggling operation. Hutchens crossed him, threatened to go to the authorities and expose Vaschinsky, if, of course, he didn't pay up. One thing the Russians don't take kindly to is blackmail. It seems our Igor liked the idea of this young Turk being the one to take out his old friend; it amused him, so he made contact with Karen Parker, they agreed terms, and then Karen got wind of the fact that Hutchens and Peel had once been friends, that Hutchens was, possibly, still in contact. Anyway, it seems she persuaded Hutchens to tell her where Peel was hiding out before she killed him. She then hands over to Igor Vaschinsky and his people, who get hold of Peel for her and persuade him, shall we say, that it's in the best interests of everyone if he cooperates with her. Karen and Peel both have a gripe with Mac and so . . .'

'And so, Peel comes out of hiding and Mac goes back up north. Karen turns up here.' Fitch nodded thoughtfully. 'Which implies not only that she doesn't like Mac a whole lot, but also that he's the one person she's scared of.'

'Scared? No, I wouldn't go that far, and I'd also say she's wary of Rina, though Rina has so far been an ally. Mac, however . . . Mac wants Peel, and Mac knows enough about Karen to make life very hard.'

'I think it's more personal than that,' Fitch speculated. 'Rina told me once that Karen felt he let her down. Parker senior snatched his son, Karen called on Mac to help and she thinks he didn't act fast enough. That's how come Rina and Tim ended up on the cliff top that day, when Parker took his tumble. Anyway, we're trying to apply logic and reason here. Karen doesn't need a reason, the way I see it.'

He picked up his mug and peered despondently into the now empty depths. 'Truth is, when Rina called and asked for me to come down, I thought she'd just got a bee in her knickers over nothing. Teach me to think again, won't it?'

At Peverill Lodge, tea went much better than Rina expected. Karen heaped praise on the sandwiches and cakes and sausage rolls the Montmorencys had provided. She laughed at the jokes Bethany Peters told – despite the fact that it took the joint effort of both sisters to remember the punchline – and listened to the very hesitant duet George had been persuaded to perform with Eliza, clapping loudly at its end. Even Ursula relaxed her guard enough to tell Karen that George had been put up a stream at school and was now in second from top for most subjects. She sounded, Rina thought fondly, rather more like a proud mother than a de facto girlfriend.

'Well done, Georgie,' Karen said softly, and Rina could see the very real pride in her eyes. 'I knew you could do it. You just needed to be somewhere settled down.'

Rina looked anxiously at her young friend. Karen had just given him an opening; would he take it?

George did. He took hold of Ursula's hand – something Rina had not seen him do before so openly – and said, 'I like it here, Karen. I *am* settled. I'm getting on at school, I've got friends and I—'

'And I'm really happy about that,' Karen interrupted, 'and of course Ursula can come and visit any time she likes, but, George, you need more than that and I can offer that now. I've got us a little house and I've found you this great school and—'

'And I don't want to go.' There, he'd said it. George bit his lip and Karen stared. Rina was shocked to see bright tears fill Karen's eyes.

'Rina, can we, I mean, can George and I talk somewhere private, please?'

Rina hesitated. She looked at George, who took a deep breath and then nodded. 'You can use my room,' Rina said. Her little sitting room at the front of the house was usually off-limits to all but a select, invited few.

'Thanks,' Karen said. She got up and went out into the hall.

'George.' Ursula's eyes were wide with concern.

'It's OK,' he said. 'She's my sister and I love her. She'll understand.'

He let go of Ursula's hand and followed his sister. Rina showed them into her sitting room and quietly closed the door.

George accepted Karen's hug, returned it, recalling all those times when Karen's love had been the only thing between him and a world of pain. He sat down in one of the fireside chairs and Karen took the other, bringing it close so that the chair arms touched. 'I want you with me, little brother. I've made so many plans. You'll love the little house – look, I've got photos on my mobile.'

George looked at the pictures she had taken, noting absently that her phone looked as expensive and sophisticated as everything else Karen owned now. She was right: it was a lovely little house – small, Georgian-looking almost, with a pretty cottagey garden. There were pictures too of the inside and what would be his bedroom, and she had all these plans for what they could do together. 'There's a basement, George. We could turn it into a games room. You remember how we always used to joke about doing that. We'd have a TV and games machines and table football.'

George laughed, despite his misgivings. 'Like the one they had at . . .' He tried to think which of the many hostels and refuges they had been at. 'Well, that place, you know. We got told off for being out of bed.'

'Yeah, well, it was two in the morning and we were making enough noise to wake the entire house.'

'And I was only eight.'

'Yeah, well, that too.'

They both fell silent. It was just after their dad had come back, and George had seen first-hand just why his mum and his sister had dreaded his return. He'd been too young when his dad went to prison to recall what it had been like before.

'That was the first time we ran away from him,' he said.

'Second,' Karen told him. 'You were a baby; you won't remember.'

'Karen, why didn't she go away when he was in prison? Why didn't she just take us and go somewhere else? We'd have been all right. Just the three of us. Karen, do you miss her?'

Karen shook her head really sadly. 'You know, I think that's what hurts such a lot. I don't. She was . . . well, she wasn't like a mum; she was like someone else to take care of. George, I never knew what we'd be coming home to. If *he'd* be there, if she'd be . . . well. You know.'

'I can't believe she killed herself. We'd always been so careful. We always hid the pills, always made sure she couldn't . . .'

'I know,' Karen said quietly. 'That day, well, I guess I just didn't hide them. I gave Mum her meds and then I left and . . . I guess she must have found the rest.'

Something in the way she said it jarred on George's consciousness. They'd talked about it so often: what would happen if their mum did succeed in one of her suicide attempts.

She'd seemed so much better when they'd come to live in Frantham, even got a job. Then their dad had turned up again and everything had gone wrong.

'Did you . . . Karen, did you leave the pills where she could find them?'

For a minute he thought she was going to get mad with him or deny it, ask him how the hell he could even think such a thing. But she didn't. Tears poured down carefully made-up cheeks, and George found himself thinking that the old Karen rarely wore any make-up apart from a little lip-gloss. 'I didn't think she'd do it, George. But I was sick of taking care, of being the adult, of having to think about every little thing. I left the flat and then I remembered I'd meant to put the pills in my bag and I'd not done it. I thought about going back and then . . . then I just couldn't be bothered, if you want to know the truth. I just didn't want to know any more. All I could think about was what was happening to you – and Mum, well, I guess she'd just dropped way down my list.'

They fell silent, each immersed in their own thoughts. Then George asked, 'How are you paying for all this stuff?'

'What do you mean?'

'Oh, Karen, don't do that, you *know* what I mean. The house, the clothes, the car—'

'It's a hire car.'

'Yeah, but when did you learn to drive?'

'I took lessons before I left, remember?'

'Yeah, but, Karen, what are you doing? Do you have a job?'

She laughed. 'I work, if that's what you're asking. George, I've got this plan. There's this little gallery – the woman who owns it, she's retiring next year. We've talked and she's going to be selling up. I want to buy, take over from her. George, it'll be great, a proper home and a proper business.'

'Paid for how?'

She frowned. 'Does it matter?'

'Yes, it matters.'

She laughed. 'I don't see why. What matters is us; what's always mattered is us. Family. There's just you and me now, just like it always was, really. Difference is, George, I can look after you properly now. We can have a proper life with a proper home and a real future. By the time she's ready to sell next year, I'll have more than enough put away to buy the gallery, keep everything going while we get established. She'll be selling the business and the goodwill that goes with it, and it's right on the promenade, so there's all the passing trade in the summer.'

'Karen, stop, please stop,' George begged her. 'Just tell me something.'

'Anything.'

'Are you . . . are you like our dad?'

She stared at him. 'I'm nothing like our dad. Our dad was a mean-minded thug. He hurt us, he hurt our mum; he lived to hurt people. How can you say that, George?'

He took a deep breath. 'I know what you did,' he said quietly. 'About Mark Dowling. Karen, how is that so different from the way our dad was?'

She laughed then, actually laughed, and George, shocked and profoundly disturbed, did not know how to respond.

'Is that all?' Karen asked him. 'Look, George, Mark Dowling was an arse, a prick, a . . . Mark Dowling deserved what he got. I have no remorse to spare for the likes of Mark Dowling, or our dad, for that matter. I wish I'd managed to kill the bastard way back. Trouble is, I suppose, it takes a bit of practice to get things right – a bit like you and that piano.'

George felt his breath grow tight and thick in his lungs. 'And have you practised since?' he asked her. 'Karen, I don't want any of this. I want my big sister back, like it was before. I don't want all this, this stuff. I just want ordinary.'

She shook her head emphatically. 'No, you don't, Georgie, not really. That's just other people telling you what you should want, claiming to have the moral high ground. But tell me this, Georgie, where was their moral high ground when our dad was beating the shit out of our mum, out of me, threatening you? Who helped us then?'

'Rina helped us. Tim helped. Mac helped.'

'Mac?' She laughed again. 'Look, I'll grant that Rina and Tim stepped up when we needed them – Rina in ways I think she now regrets, but, anyway, I'll grant you that. But Mac? No way. Let me tell you something, George. I called him when I knew our dad had snatched you. I called him, but did he come? Did he hell! He was out there doing some bloody TV appearance. You were gone – our dad had taken you away

– and there he was, telling the world that they'd get whoever killed poor Markie baby, swearing he wouldn't let the killer get away with it. Friend? Yeah, I thought he was, but twice he let us down.'

'Twice?'

'Came to arrest me, didn't he?'

'You'd already gone.'

'Just as well, wasn't it? George, Mac is the *enemy*. He might say all the right words and he might play nice when it suits him, but don't think he gives a damn. Just don't you ever think that.'

George's mind was in turmoil. He knew that Mac had come to arrest Karen, hadn't really been surprised. He knew too that Mac had no choice, given what he'd figured out. That Mac had been absent at the precise moment his father had come for him was something George knew Mac regretted desperately – they had talked about it – but he also knew that no one can be in the right place at the right time all of the time. Should he say that to Karen? George decided it would be a waste of breath.

'I want to stay here,' he said as firmly as he could. 'I don't want to go with you. I don't want to be a part of whatever it is you're doing.'

'You wouldn't be. You think I want to involve you in . . . Oh George, I'm doing all of this for us. Like I told you, a year from now and we'll have a house, a business, a way forward for both of us. You'll finish school and maybe even do university. George, you've seen all those kids in care we met at hostels and homes and everywhere. Most of them would be lucky if they did anything with their lives. Thick, most of them. Had it all battered out of them. But not you and me. We're different. We survived, George, and now I'm going to make damn sure we do more than just survive. I'm doing whatever it takes now, to make sure of that.'

George stood up. 'No,' he said firmly and he saw it flash across his sister's face, even as it crossed his own mind, that it was the first time he had refused her anything. A brief, bright burst of anger, soon gone, she stood too, hugged him again, but George sensed that this time the embrace was somehow possessive and territorial, not a simple expression of affection.

'You'll come round,' she said confidently. 'It's all a bit much, isn't it, our kid? I'm pushing a bit too hard. Right, I'll be off for now, before Matthew offers me more cake – any more and I think I'll explode.' They returned to the rest of the company and Karen took her leave, laughing and joking again and telling the Peters sisters to make sure George kept up with the piano practice. George said nothing. He stood in the hallway until she had been waved off by the entire household.

Rina started towards him, but Ursula got there first.

'You OK?'

'No, not really.' He knew she wouldn't pester him with questions. One thing he and Ursula definitely had in common, they liked to tell things in their own time, if at all. Their relationship, George thought, was as much about all the things they could safely leave unsaid as it was about telling.

'We'd better get ready,' Ursula said. 'Our taxi will be here.'

Rina nodded. 'I'll get your coats,' she said. She looked anxiously at George and then at Ursula. Out of the tail of his eye, George saw Ursula shake her head. *No questions now; just leave well alone*. He was relieved to see that although Rina pursed her lips, clamping down on the very natural impulse to ask what Karen had said, she took Ursula's lead. She was, perhaps, the only adult he had ever met who knew when to leave things alone.

George took a deep breath, leaving it to Ursula to deal with the effusive farewells. He felt he ought to say something that was vaguely normal, but just couldn't quite remember how. 'How's Mac?' he managed as the taxi sounded its horn outside and Rina opened the front door.

'He tells me he's managing,' Rina said.

'I hope he'll be all right.'

Rina watched them as they opened the back doors of the car and scrambled inside. Vince, the usual driver from the local firm, waved at Rina and she waved back, standing on the doorstep until he drove away.

'I hope we all will, George,' Rina said.

FOURTEEN

It had been a frustrating afternoon, Mac thought. They had applied for the CCTV footage from the court on the day of Rains's sentencing, but been told that it no longer existed. Recordings were kept for a month and then overwritten, which meant there was no way of actually verifying Rains's story about Peel being in the public gallery that day. Mac was starting to think it had just been a wind-up, by Rains himself or suggested by Peel.

Nothing useful either on Ricky Marlow. A request had been made for a warrant for his financial records and had so far met with resistance from the local judiciary. Marlow had powerful friends and a reputation for tough but honest dealing; additionally, officers had gone back and talked to the bar staff who'd been on that day, and had also met with a customer they identified as being a regular on Wednesday lunchtimes. He thought he remembered Peel from the photograph they showed him, definitely recalled 'a bit of an altercation' and that Marlow had asked a rather drunk customer to leave. Recalled that the man said he hadn't finished his drink and that Marlow had offered a refund.

'I remembered,' he said, 'because I was ready to tell Mr Marlow that the staff hadn't served him above one drink, so he must have come in like that and the staff not noticed or whatever.' Mr Marlow was, apparently, very hot on his staff not serving the overly inebriated and the customer had not wanted Sally, a new employee of Marlow's and one the customer evidently admired, to find herself in trouble.

'Interestingly,' Alec told Mac, 'both staff on duty that lunchtime insisted that Peel had seemed stone cold sober when he'd come in and he'd only had the one drink.'

'Give the man an Oscar,' Mac muttered. 'So what's left?'

'John Bennet,' Alec said. 'We still need a word. He made a statement the day he reported seeing Peel. Time to see if he's remembered anything more.'

'Fat chance.' Mac was inclined to be pessimistic. It was that sort of day.

Alec laughed. 'Almost certainly right,' he agreed, 'but best go through the motions, eh?'

John Bennet lived on the outskirts of Pinsent on one of those bland 1970s estates that had sprung up just before the 1980s brought the building industry to its knees and shrank the size of new builds for ever. The houses on the Freelands estate were large and oblong and large-windowed, with grassy frontages and off-road parking, arranged in a curling mass of little cul-de-sacs that all seemed to be part of the same road.

John Bennet's house was in the third cul-de-sac they tried, found after they'd finally figured out that the numbers ran consecutively and not odd on one side and even on the other.

It was dark and cold, and Mac was ready to pack up for the day, out of patience with himself, with Wildman, with the minutiae of an investigation he somehow had little faith in. He could not explain his mood or his depression; only that it wrapped his mind too much in memory, in a time that had already been fixed and a quest that had failed, miserably. He could not seem to convince himself that this time would be different. Maybe, he thought, he had just forgotten how tedious some police work could be. True, he had been assigned a posting in the back of beyond, but, even when major events had finally been persuaded to pass Frantham-on-Sea by and go and play elsewhere, he had not been bored. He had, unwittingly, become something of a neighbourhood policeman, part of the community, at home with a job that called upon him to take half an hour to walk the few hundred yards along the promenade, just because everyone stopped to talk to him, and where, should he pause to look out to sea, he might become involved in a deep discussion regarding the next day's weather. He liked it; he was happy. Back in Pinsent, he was homesick and heartsick. 'Do you ever think about giving it up?' he asked Alec.

'Sorry?'

'Police work.' Mac stared vindictively at the semi-detached house they had now identified as John Bennet's. 'Seventies architecture,' he said. 'The decade of bland.'

'We discussing ambition or architecture?' Alec asked.

'Neither. Both. I don't know.'

Alec waited, but Mac was done with talk. He got out of the car and walked up the rough concrete path to the red front door set between two large windows. A rubber plant took up most of the entrance hall.

'Who the hell has rubber plants these days?'

'People who consider the aspidistra old-fashioned?' Alec suggested. He rang the bell, glanced anxiously at Mac. 'I can handle this. Want to wait in the car?'

'No, I'm fine. Just tired and . . .'

'Jaundiced,' Alec said.

The inner door opened and John Bennet came out into the hall. He recognized Alec, stood back. 'Go on through,' he said. 'Tea? Coffee? Millie, it's Inspector Friedman and – sorry, I don't think we've met.'

'Inspector McGregor,' Alec said, as though not trusting Mac to answer for himself. 'Sorry to disturb your Saturday evening.'

'Oh, not at all.'

The inside of the house was pretty much as Mac had expected. A long lounge-diner with patio doors at the end leading out into the garden. Millie was closing the heavy curtains as they came in. She turned, smiling. Two little girls sat at the dining table. 'The kids are just having their tea,' she said. 'Can I get you anything?'

Mac declined; Alec said he would like a coffee if it wasn't too much trouble. The room smelt of spaghetti hoops and tomato sauce, buttered toast. It was such an odd thing to do, Mac thought absently. Drown pasta in bright red sauce and plonk it on toast. George loved the stuff; Ursula, if she had to eat anything tinned and tomatoed, preferred beans. Funny, he thought, the random facts you picked up about people.

He took a seat on the plump blue sofa, aware of the wide-eyed children staring at them from the other end of the room.

'So,' John Bennet said, 'what can I do for you?'

'We're reviewing evidence,' Mac said, finding his voice. 'I know you've spoken previously to Alec here and other colleagues; I just wondered if you'd mind going over things again.'

Bennet looked slightly taken aback, then recovered himself. 'No, not at all, but I don't think there is anything I can add. I went out at lunchtime on Wednesday last. Well, actually it was the Wednesday before last now, wasn't it?' he laughed, suddenly slightly nervous, as though he felt he might be taking a test. 'I take sandwiches two or three times a week, but Wednesday

I usually go to the little shop on the corner. It's become a bit of a habit, I suppose. Friday too, most Fridays anyway.'

'Why Wednesday?' Mac wanted to know.

'Why? Oh I see, well, Millie has a little job – she works Wednesday mornings, Thursday afternoons and sometimes Fridays. The local chemist shop. Occasionally she'll cover other days too, but her hours are nine till two on Wednesday, two till six on Thursday and, as I say, sometimes on a Friday. Oh and evenings when it's their turn on the rota.'

'Rota?'

'For late opening. All the local chemists are on a rota. Emergencies, you know: people trying to buy paracetamol at eleven o'clock at night, I suppose.' He laughed nervously. Millie arrived with Alec's coffee. 'Ah, I was telling them about your job. About why I don't take a pack-up on Wednesdays.'

'Oh, I don't get time on Wednesdays, not getting the girls to school and me to work and all the breakfast things tidied away before I go. I can't bear the thought of coming back to it all at lunchtime.'

'Right,' Alec said. 'Well, I suppose that's . . . Right then.'

Mac tried not to smile. 'And this has been the arrangement for . . . how long?'

'Oh, just this past year,' Millie said. 'Just since I had this job.'

'And this Wednesday when you saw Peel?' Mac could see Alec begin to frown, knew he'd picked up the same detail as Mac.

'Oh,' John Bennet said, 'well, as I told you all before, I was coming out of the cob shop and I saw him hurrying down the road. I knew it was Thomas – in fact, I almost called out to him and then I remembered, you know, that he wasn't the Thomas I used to work with any more, not after . . . well, you know.'

'Not after he killed Cara Evans,' Mac said.

Millie glanced anxiously at her girls and then glared at him. 'Please, Inspector. The children.'

'So you followed him instead.'

'Yes, yes, I did.'

'You didn't think to phone the police straight away?'

'I . . . I didn't have my phone. I'd left my mobile in the office.'

Mac nodded. 'And you saw him go into the B & B where we now know he'd been staying.'

'Yes, as I told you before. That's what I did.' He frowned. 'Look, I'm not sure what all this is about and I'm not sure I like the way this conversation is going. You sound almost, well, accusing.'

'No, Mr Bennet, I'm not accusing. Just tell me one thing, though. When you worked with Thomas Peel, did you buy your lunch at the same shop on a Wednesday then?'

'Well, no, I told you, or rather Millie did. Just this past year, since she got her job.'

Alec drank his coffee and set the cup down on the tiled-top coffee table. Mac wondered if it had come with the house; it was certainly of the same vintage.

'Unlucky for him, then,' he said quietly. 'To come back to Pinsent and to happen to be in the street just as you happened to come by.'

Bennet frowned. 'I don't like your tone,' he said. 'I did the right thing. I saw him, I reported it.'

'You did,' Alec agreed. 'Thank you, Mr Bennet, Mrs Bennet. Have a pleasant evening.'

Sitting in the car, Mac said, 'So, either Peel was watching John Bennet and knew his movements or . . .'

'Or someone had the forethought to tell him.'

'If Peel wanted to be seen. I know that's the assumption but—'

'It's the right assumption,' Alec said. 'Peel shows himself. The investigation is reopened. I came up here.' He was thinking aloud now, not sure where the thought led.

'So, who told Peel where Bennet would be on a Wednesday lunchtime?'

Alec shrugged. 'Bennet?' he suggested.

'Why would he? Do we know how close they were before Peel went over to the dark side?'

'Peel did that long before we knew about him.'

'True. Did Bennet know? Did Bennet collude, or are we looking at an innocent man, and I'm just, as you say, jaundiced?'

Alec shrugged. 'I don't know,' he said. 'But I think we need to keep him in mind.'

FIFTEEN

Philip Rains was dead. The news came just as Alec had dropped Mac at the flat and was heading for home. He spun the car around and returned to find Mac already standing in the doorway waiting for him.

Alec drove while Mac tried to get extra details before they arrived at the prison.

'Stabbed to death,' Mac said. 'A shiv made from a hacksaw blade.'

'A hacksaw blade? How did that get past the searches? And what's wrong with the great tradition of the sharpened toothbrush handle?'

'Apparently his attacker took metalwork classes – they think he got the broken blade from the scrap bin. Whatever, it did the job.' Mac thought of Alec's comments about Rains the day before. About him being unable to join the main prison population because of his proclivities. It looked as though he hadn't been safe anywhere.

'What do we know about his killer?'

'His name . . .' Mac consulted the hastily scribbled note he'd made and tried to read his own writing. 'His name is Billy Tigh, convicted sex offender, though unlike Rains he prefers young women. Three counts of aggravated rape, just transferred this week, took exception to Rains from the moment he arrived.'

'No honour among perverts,' Alec said. He pulled up at the gatehouse. Three marked cars had already parked in the yard beyond, and the scientific support van pulled up just behind as Alec showed their ID. 'You should have had a cup of Bennet's coffee,' Alec said. 'It's going to be a long night.'

Fifty miles down the coast, a knock came at Emily Peel's door. Calum opened it, still on the chain.

'I'm here to see my daughter,' Thomas Peel said.

'You're what!' Momentarily too startled to react, Calum soon recovered and pushed the door closed, but the hesitation had been enough and Thomas Peel thrust something long and metallic into the space between door and frame. Shocked, Calum realized that the man was armed, that the metal thing was a shotgun, that he, Calum, was facing both barrels. Hastily, he backed away, pressed against the wall, staring at the weapon, appalled at how solid it looked.

'Open the door,' Peel said.

'I–I can't. It's on the chain.'

Peel took a step back. 'Contrary to what you might have seen in the films,' he said, 'wood won't save you from a shotgun blast, so I suggest you remember that. Shove the door to, take off the chain, open it properly and let me in.'

Calum stared. Behind him, Emily came from the kitchen and into the hall, Frankie at her heels.

'Oh my God.'

Thomas Peel heard the exclamation. 'I've come to see my girl,' he told Calum again. 'I'm not planning on hurting anyone. I just want to talk.'

No one, Calum thought, comes armed with a shotgun when they just want to talk. 'OK,' he said. 'I–I'll close the door and take the chain off.'

He's going to kill me. Calum's brain seemed to have switched from paralysis into overdrive. *He's going to kill us both no matter what we do.* He looked back at Emily and saw she knew that too.

'Run.' Calum mouthed the word.

She shook her head, eyes wide.

'Run,' he breathed. 'I'll be right behind you.' He swung the door closed, calculating the risk, how much time they'd have before Peel came through. Calum had no illusions. Peel might avoid the sound of the shotgun going off in the street if he thought Calum might be prepared to cooperate and let him inside, but . . . however you looked at it, Calum reckoned they had seconds to get away.

This was no time for caution. He slammed the door and threw himself down on to the tiled floor, scrabbling towards the kitchen as the world exploded and splinters of wood hurtled down the length of the hall and rained all around him. He crawled towards Emily and the kitchen door.

She turned, first heading back to him and then, as he regained his feet, back into the kitchen. She'd got the back door open by the time he reached her. Frankie snarled, not understanding, but prepared to defend them anyway. Calum grabbed his collar, dragging him outside. Lights had come on in neighbouring houses, people shouting from windows. This was a quiet street and the explosion of the gunshot had shattered the peace. Outside was a yard, brick-paved and slippery. A gate led to a ginnel, an alleyway between houses. Low walls separated the terraced row, one from another.

Calum dragged the gate open, slammed it shut behind them as he urged Emily through and pushed Frankie after her. What now? What if Thomas Peel ran down the ginnel? He'd see them and Calum knew they could not outrun a shotgun even if they could outpace the man.

'Over the wall,' he whispered and lifted Frankie unceremoniously into a neighbour's yard. Emily followed and then Calum. This, the next door house, was empty, the occupants out. Over the next wall and into the next yard. A security light came on and Calum swore. The back door swung open. Folk in this part of the world were not, Calum thought, easily intimidated.

A voice shouted, irritable at having his Saturday night so rudely interrupted. 'Who the bloody hell's there?'

'It's us.' Emily's voice sounded thin. Frankie whined.

'Emily? What the hell are you doing down there? What the bloody hell's going on?'

'He shot at us,' Calum said. It sounded like an absurd thing to say even as he said it.

'I told her it was. I said it was a shot, but no, she wouldn't have it, said it couldn't be, said this wasn't the flipping Bronx.'

Calum felt the laughter rising in his throat, fought it down, realizing it was just the adrenalin, the hysteria. 'Call the police, please,' he said.

'Already done, lad. Better get yourselves inside and I'll get a brew on. I told her, I said, I've heard enough shotguns in my time. Used to go clay pigeon shooting, didn't I, but she don't listen. Mark my words, women never listen.'

Cautiously, Calum and Emily approached the kitchen door. *This is a farce*, Calum thought. *This is just the most stupid thing. It isn't real.*

Light flooded out into the yard and Frankie bounded past them all and, tail wagging, yelping a greeting, he made himself at home. Calum glanced back over his shoulder, still uncertain. 'You said you called the police?'

'I did, lad, yes, I did.'

Hesitant, but profoundly relieved, Calum moved forward into the light, Emily beside him. He never knew just what it was that he heard, just that one second he had convinced himself that everything would be all right and the next he knew it would not. He heard a voice shout out, realized it was his own, grabbed Emily and bundled her down and on to the ground. A crash of sound and a flash in his peripheral vision. A woman's screams. And Calum knew that Thomas Peel had followed them.

SIXTEEN

Billy Tigh wasn't talking. He sat at one of the tables in the visiting room they had previously used to interview Rains, nursing a cup of coffee and staring at nothing. His behaviour was puzzling everyone, including the on-call psychiatrist who sat beside him. Prison guards stood by, but Billy Tigh was not restrained now; he had been handcuffed immediately after the stabbing and confined to a cell, but it was soon evident that he was a threat to no one else. Alec and Mac had been told that, after the stabbing, Tigh had dropped the shiv and then stood totally still, waiting for the excrement to hit the proverbial fan. It had – three officers jumping him and wrestling him to the ground – but he had offered no resistance then or later.

He hadn't spoken since, had barely even looked at anyone. It seemed that his anger was spent and he had no fight or even will left in him.

'Billy,' the psychiatrist spoke quietly, 'these officers are here to ask you some questions.'

Alec sat down, Mac drawing up a chair beside him. The table was small – they practically touched elbows. Billy Tigh did not look up.

'What did you have against Rains?' Alec asked. 'You'd only been here ten days – barely enough time to find out his name, never mind build enough resentment to kill a man. So?'

Tigh said nothing. He seemed to recall that he had a cup of coffee. He lifted it to his mouth, but did not drink, just peered into the cup as though not quite sure what it was. He was not a big man, stockily built with close-cropped hair and a square-jawed face, currently expressionless, dead-eyed.

'What did Rains do to piss you off, then?' Alec asked. He glanced at the psychiatrist, then looked at Mac. The doctor shrugged.

'Can we talk?' Mac said. He got up and wandered over to the coffee machine, wondering if it could be persuaded to produce something even vaguely drinkable. Alec and the psychiatrist joined him.

'Is this for real?' Alec said bluntly. 'Or just an act to get him off the hook?'

'I couldn't say. The guards reckon he just stood there, didn't do a thing to defend himself or excuse himself or explain. Rains had just come from the showers; he was crossing the recreation area. Tigh walked up to him, stabbed him, Rains hit the deck and Tigh just stood there. He's said nothing.'

'Great,' Alec muttered. 'Prior associations?'

'None on record. As far as we know, Tigh and Rains met ten days ago, but . . .'

'But—' Alec said. Mac's phone rang. He looked at the caller display and frowned. 'Alec, I'd better take this. It's Calum, Emily's boyfriend.' He stepped away from the others and listened. Minutes later they were leaving the prison and heading south.

'We're OK,' Emily told him. 'We're not hurt and Mr Macintyre, our neighbour, he's OK too. We were in his yard, trying to get away. Mr Macintyre opened the back door and we were just about to go inside and then . . . then my dad shot at us again. I thought Calum had been hit, and he thought I had, and splinters from the back door and the glass cut Mr Macintyre's face and hands, but we're all OK. The paramedics took him off to get some stitches in his face and his wife's gone with him. Frankie's still in the house. Mr Macintyre's son's there. Frankie's OK too.'

She sat in the police van, Calum at her side, blankets round their shoulders. They both looked pale and scared. The CSIs were on scene, and marked police cars were still parked along the narrow street. The officer in charge, an Inspector Collins, had wanted to take Emily and Calum away, but Emily had refused point-blank to go anywhere until Mac arrived, and she'd been so distressed he had decided not to press the matter. The fifty-mile drive had been covered at more than legal speeds, and Alec and Mac had arrived in less than thirty minutes after they had left the prison.

Alec leaned on the open door and Mac sat opposite the young couple. 'You should go to the hospital anyway,' Alec suggested. 'Get yourselves checked out.'

Emily shook her head emphatically. 'We're all right,' she said. She shook her head again, this time in disbelief. 'I don't get it,' she said. 'Why would he do this? It makes no sense. Why would he want us dead?'

'I don't know,' Mac told her honestly. While he had fully expected that Peel might attempt to contact his daughter, he had not for one moment anticipated that he would try to harm her. Peel was capable of murder – he'd proved that – but he'd made no threats against Emily, chosen to let her believe him dead for the past year and a half. It seemed perverse, wilful, unnecessary. Neither Emily nor Calum had or were capable of doing anything that might threaten Thomas Peel.

'Calum, this may seem like a stupid question, but do you think he—'

'Meant it?' Calum asked. 'Oh yes,' he laughed uneasily. 'Mac, this wasn't an exercise in frightening us witless, though he did that all right. He followed us, he fired, we hit the deck, and it was Frankie that saved Mr Macintyre.'

'Frankie?'

'Frankie barked, Mr Macintyre turned to look at him and the shot hit the door. Mac, if he'd been killed, we wouldn't have been able to forgive ourselves. I never thought Peel would follow us.'

'What happens now?' Emily said. She laughed, and Mac could hear how close she was to breaking down, even as she tried to make a joke out of their circumstances. 'We don't have a front door. Our landlord will go spare. You think we might lose our deposit?'

'You'll be taken somewhere safe,' Mac reassured her. 'You'll be looked after, I promise.'

She nodded, closed her eyes and pulled the blanket more tightly around her shoulders. The adrenalin rush had faded and left exhaustion in its wake.

'Emily, did you ever hear the name Billy Tigh?' The question from Alec was unexpected.

She opened her eyes again and looked curiously at Alec, frowned, then nodded slowly. 'I can't remember where, but yeah, I know the name.'

'Can you think about it? Let us know if anything occurs. And did you ever hear of a Philip Rains?'

She might have heard about him on the news, Mac thought. Tigh's was a less famous name; Rains had made the headlines.

Her first comment seemed to confirm that. 'I remember the

trial,' she said. 'It was just after . . . just after my father disappeared. After we thought he might have killed himself. I watched about the trial on the news because it seemed so weird, seeing Philip Rains on the telly, accused of those things.'

'You knew him before?' Mac was surprised. Nothing he had read in reviewing the case had led him to believe that there was previous contact, but, then, had anyone asked Emily these questions before? He recalled that Emily had lived apart from Thomas Peel for several years. Her mother had separated from him; Emily had been a child, like so many, with just a weekend father, and the assumption was that he had kept his two lives apart. Mac remembered too that Emily's mother had remarried and moved away, and that mother–daughter relations were not the best they could have been.

'So, how did you know him?' Mac asked again.

She thought about it, putting things in order. 'When Mum and Dad split up, I was twelve. We moved away and I saw him every other weekend at first, then once a month, and then just for a week or so, or maybe a few days, in the holidays. I must have been about fourteen? I went and stayed in the summer holiday. Philip Rains was there, had a room in Dad's house that was usually mine. I was meant to be at Dad's place for a couple of weeks, but, I don't know, Philip didn't like me and I didn't like him, and I was fourteen and stroppy and couldn't understand why my dad had someone else staying at the house when it was supposed to be my time.' She paused and looked at Mac, and he could almost feel the same thought occurring to both of them. 'Yeah,' she said, 'there was a time I actually got on OK with him, when we did things together like going to the park or the pictures or to the beach. It doesn't seem right, does it?'

Mac didn't know how to respond to that. 'So what happened?' he asked. 'That summer?'

'Nothing,' she shrugged. 'I got stroppier, so did Phil Rains, and I went home after a few days. Mum wasn't too pleased. She wanted some time to herself with my stepdad. Ironic, isn't it? In those days I actually wanted him in my life; a few years later and I'm trying to run as far and as fast as I can and he just wants me dead.'

SEVENTEEN

It had been five o'clock on Sunday morning when Mac finally tumbled into bed. Miriam had sent him a text and Rina a message on his voicemail, asking him to call as soon as he could. He figured 'soon' didn't mean right then. Despite what had happened and the frantic events of the night, he fell asleep almost as soon as his head hit the pillow. He woke, very reluctantly, a little after nine, mouth dry and head so thick he felt hung over. His phone was ringing.

'Wildman wants us at the office,' Alec said.

'What, now?'

'Well, I'm planning on a shower and food before I go anywhere, but yes. The Sunday lunch we promised may have to be delayed, by the look of things. You want a lift in?'

'No, I'll make my own way.' Mac turned over and dozed for another hour, waking again to the ringing of the phone. This time it was Miriam. She was settled at her sister's and would be there until Mac returned and everything was back to normal. He told her about the turn the investigation had taken and warned her to take care, but she sounded happier and more confident than the last time they had spoken, and Mac allowed himself to feel relieved that she was not alone.

He showered and took time to make tea and toast, knowing he was just provoking Wildman by his tardiness, but not caring very much. He was trying to get things clear in his own mind, to fathom what had caused Tigh to turn on Rains and Thomas Peel to vent such violent rage upon his daughter and her boyfriend. Emily had called her mother to warn her, just in case. It had been an awkward phone call, made still more difficult by the hour, and Mac had listened to the stilted, one-sided exchange. He had watched Calum's face, seeing anger and resentment there on Emily's behalf.

So, Emily had met Philip Rains. Who else did she know about? Mac and Alec had reeled off a series of names: previous associates, possible victims of blackmail, work colleagues who had been implicated by association, even if only briefly.

Of them all, she recognized only two: John Bennet because, as she'd told them before, he had worked closely with her father, and Richard Marlow because her father had been so proud of the work done at the Marlow residence. By the time they left, she was even more certain that she had heard Philip Rains mention Billy Tigh, but could not fix the context. It had, she said, been a long time ago and she'd expended a great deal of effort on not remembering things that had to do with her father.

Interesting, though, Mac thought. Previously they had thought of Rains as being just someone Peel knew about and was blackmailing, not someone he was close enough to that he let him stay in his house. Mac had asked the question again, feeling uncomfortable in doing so. 'Em, did your father or Philip Rains ever—'

She had shaken her head emphatically. 'No, like I told you. Dad never touched me; in fact, quite the opposite – there was never even any normal hugging and such. He just wasn't a demonstrative man, and Rains – no, I only really spent those few days anywhere near him, and all we did was try and wind one another up. Anyway, I was fourteen by then; from what they said at Rain's trial, I was much too old to be interesting to him, and anyway, they say he preferred boys.'

How old was Billy Tigh? Mac wondered. He checked through his records and found that Tigh was just twenty-one, though he looked a good five years more than that. Had Tigh been a victim? They knew now that Rains had been abusing children for at least a dozen years before Peel had shopped him. Would the maths work? Was there a connection? Or was Mac merely seeing connections where none existed? Billy Tigh had been in and out of trouble since he was ten years old, and no one – none of the social workers he'd had contact with – had ever raised the possibility of abuse. Not that this was a guarantee of anything, but Mac was familiar enough with the system to know that it would have been considered alongside all Tigh's other problems somewhere along the line.

Telling himself that he really must get on to calling Rina, Mac left for work, unable to put off the Wildman moment any longer and feeling vaguely guilty knowing that Alec would already be there. Something was nagging at the back of his brain, something about Philip Rains, but he couldn't quite pin down what it was. Something he had said that day they interviewed him . . .

Putting the thought aside for the moment – knowing that to let the thought process work, he sometimes had to let it well alone – Mac got into his car and drove to Pinsent police HQ, more aware than ever that he didn't belong . . . could no longer belong . . . wanted to go home.

Back in Frantham, Sunday passed quietly and without event. Mac hadn't called and Rina didn't want to keep trying; he'd get back to her when he could, she knew that. She spoke to Miriam who told her that Mac had his hands full and gave her a brief account of what was going on so far as she understood. Abe, who seemed to be able to use contacts Rina could only speculate about, filled in more of the background. It all sounded very dramatic and very unpleasant.

George phoned from Hill House mid-afternoon; not for any particular reason, he said, though Rina understood his need for reassurance. She and her eccentric household now provided baseline normality for George, something dependable in a world where not much was or ever had been. They talked for a while and she told him he had done the right thing in standing his ground with Karen.

'She had to learn that she can't run other people's lives for them, George. I'm sure her intentions for you are the very best, but that doesn't make them right.'

'No,' George agreed. 'I do love her, Rina, but . . .'

Rina decided the rest should be left unsaid, for the moment at least. She steered the conversation into the safe, if dull, harbour of homework and weekend TV, and was relieved that George seemed content to be thus steered. There were times when the normal and even the banal were to be craved.

Mac finally called her late that night, just as she was off to bed. He apologized, said it had been one of those days. He sounded, Rina thought, distracted.

'What was it you wanted to tell me?' Mac asked.

'Oh, I think it can wait. You're tired, I'm tired. Abe managed to piece together some of Karen's movements over this past year. It looks as if she's following in her father's footsteps, shall we say.'

Mac sighed. 'That's not good; not entirely surprising either. How's George holding up?'

'We're taking care of George, don't you worry.'

'Right, that's good. You're right, Rina, I am tired, fit to drop. I'll give you a call tomorrow and you can fill me in properly. Give my best to everyone.'

As she hung up, Rina Martin felt oddly alone, even though her home at Peverill Lodge was currently rammed full of people. Tim was working, Joy gone to watch again, and Rina was aware that a small but very perceptible gap was opening between *her* world and that newly created by Tim and Joy. She didn't grudge either of them that, knowing that happiness should be grasped tight and celebrated to the full. She'd had only five short years with *her* beloved. Even so, she mourned for Tim as though he had left and gone to some far distant place, and prayed to whichever gods handle such requests that he and Joy would still make some space for her in their lives.

Right now, Mac was so far away. Even having Fitch on call did not compensate for the fact that she now felt she was being left to cope alone.

To cope with what?

Rina could not say. Karen was a part of it, and keeping young George safe and happy – but what else? Abe had confirmed that Thomas Peel and Karen had been in contact, so what was going on there?

Rina pulled the blankets aside and sat down with a thump on the side of her bed. The camp bed was made up ready for Joy, though she'd not be surprised to find it had not been slept in tomorrow morning. It was reassuring, at least, to know that Abe had two of his men keeping watch over the Pallisades and Tim and Joy.

She took the photograph of her late husband, Fred, from the bedside cabinet and looked longingly into that familiar face, still young, always young, still so much loved, always loved.

'Oh Fred.' Rina stroked the glass. 'I still miss you as much, you know that, don't you? I wish you were here now. I just feel so troubled and I don't know why or what about. Just the sense that there is so much more to come and so much worse.'

EIGHTEEN

Monday

Miriam left at eight o'clock for the short drive from her sister's house to work. She was due to get in at eight thirty, and it was a twenty-minute run, even allowing for hitting a bit of heavy traffic for the last half-mile.

It had rained heavily in the night and she took her time on the back roads. Farm traffic moving from field to field and incontinent horses left mud and other debris on the narrow road, and on a couple of previous occasions even Miriam, experienced in country driving, had skidded alarmingly after heavy rain and nearly put the car into a ditch.

The sight of a vehicle skewed halfway across the road just after a particularly sharp bend did not, therefore, either surprise or particularly alarm her. There was no one in the driver's seat of the large saloon car and no way around it. Worried that the driver might have been hurt, knowing that there was a blind bend on the other side of the car and concerned for other traffic, she pulled on to the verge and got out, reaching into her jacket pocket for her mobile phone as she did so.

'Don't move, please; don't look around. Just put your hands behind your back.'

'What?'

Despite the warning, Miriam half-turned towards the speaker. Something sharp and metallic struck her hard against the temple. She staggered, momentarily stunned, and felt cold metal against her wrist as the cuff closed around it. Miriam fought, pulling away, too late realizing that her assailant had equipped himself with a pair of police-issue quick cuffs. She had seen officers use them often enough to know that the rigid bar across the centre, between the two cuffs, was also an object of control, the cuffs explicitly designed so that a police officer could subdue a violent individual, even with just one wrist contained. As you turned the cuff, pressure on the bar could be brought to bear against the wrist, the nerves, the tendons.

It hurt. It hurt a great deal. Her assailant twisted the cuff and she was on her knees on the muddy road, the pain in her wrist, as he bent it back, excruciating.

'Other hand,' he said. 'Give me your other hand.'

Miriam tried to resist, to keep her second hand out of reach, but, stunned by the blow, overcome by the pain now flaming all the way from wrist to shoulder, she could not. He had her other wrist, cuffed that, dragged her back on to her feet.

It was the man from the cliff top; Miriam was certain of that. It was Thomas Peel.

'Move,' he said, jabbing her in the back. Miriam moved.

She looked for escape, willed a car to come round the bend, but this was a quiet road with high hedges. Peel was taking a big risk, but not an unreasonable one. As she approached the car, she saw that the boot was unlatched, part open. Claustrophobia overwhelmed her as she realized what he had in mind. 'No, no, please, no.'

He reached around her and opened the boot. Miriam kicked out, making contact with his shin. Peel yelped and she began to run, slipping on the grass verge as she rounded the car. Peel was on her, though; he struck her again and she fell heavily, this time almost losing hold on consciousness completely. She felt him lifting her, then something pressing down on her nose and mouth. Then nothing.

Thomas Peel opened the rear door of the car, dropped the shotgun down into the footwell and pulled a plaid car rug down on top. He was getting into the driver's seat when a four-by-four rounded the bend. The driver braked hard, shouted at Peel and then, apparently thinking better of his anger, put his head out of the window and asked if everything was all right.

'Skidded on some mud,' Peel told him. 'I thought the tyre had gone, so I got out to check, but I must have just hit something.'

The man nodded. 'Happens all the time,' he said. 'Need a hand to shift the car?'

'Thank you, no. I should be fine.'

Peel got into his car and eased it back on line, then drove on, giving the other driver a wave in his mirror. For a mile the Range Rover followed him and then turned off down an even narrower road. Peel chuckled to himself. Timing had once more been fortunate; his luck had held for him today, much as it had for Emily and that wet idiot, Calum, on Saturday night. The memory of that still irked him, but there were other days and there would be other chances, and now he knew for certain that Emily was not his child, there was nothing to hold him back from getting rid. She was nothing to him now; neither was the woman he'd been married to and who had let him down.

Thomas Peel had a long and complex list of things to do, and Emily was still on it, no mistake about that; for the moment she'd just slid a little further down, but he'd get back to her and it would be soon.

The minibus was set to leave Hill House at seven forty-five to drop all the kids at their various schools, but its departure had been delayed by a small hatchback that had driven up the drive and parked across its path. Looking out from the landing window, George's heart sank as he recognized the car and the well-dressed blonde who stood beside it.

Almost sensing him, Karen looked up at him and waved, as though this was the most normal behaviour in the world.

'It's my sister,' he told Cheryl as he passed her in the hall.

Cheryl was not impressed. 'Well, she's got a funny way of carrying on, George. Tell her to move it to a parking space and that you've got to go to school.' She paused and looked more carefully at him, as it suddenly dawned that George was not exactly thrilled to see his sibling. 'Forget that, I'll go and talk to her.'

'No,' George said. 'I'll go, but I've got nothing to say.'

Cheryl let him go, but George could hear her quizzing Ursula as he opened the heavy front door and stood outside in the damp and cold of the November morning. The wind, as usual, was rushing in off the sea. It hit the cliff and rose sharply, creating strange eddies and gusts around Hill House and its gardens. Today it felt even more chill and damp than it usually did and even more richly scented with salt and seaweed. As he crossed the circle of drive in front of the house, with its little island of shrubbery, the scent of fallen leaves, rich with late autumn decay, added to the mix. George filled his lungs with the scent and the damp, chill air, 'You have to move,' he said. 'The minibus can't get out.'

'That was sort of the idea,' Karen said. 'I thought I'd give you a lift to school. I had this feeling you might just get on the bus and go sailing by if I didn't make you notice me. You seem determined not to, these days.'

'I notice you,' George said. 'I see you. I just think I'd rather ride with the others.'

'What, in that rickety thing with all the losers, rather than a nice comfy car with your big sister?' She laughed, as though he shared her joke.

'They aren't losers. Karen, please go, I've got to get to school. We can talk later.'

'I want to talk now.'

Behind him, George was aware that the other kids at Hill House were filing out and being loaded into the bus, the usual early morning squabbling interrupted by this far more interesting development. He felt terribly exposed, and discomfort flushed his freckled cheeks. Karen watched him, a half-smile on her lips that did nothing to soften the hurt and anger in her eyes. He didn't want to hurt her feelings, but, more than that, he didn't want to allow her to hurt him, and leaving would lead to pain; George was certain of that.

He glanced over his shoulder. Ursula was waiting for him, clutching her backpack and George's. Cheryl stood beside her, one hand on Ursula's shoulder, watching and clearly wondering if she should intervene.

'I have to go,' he said again. 'I've got physics first period, a double lesson. I've got homework to hand in.'

'Homework!' Karen stared in disbelief. 'George, I get the feeling you're not hearing me. I can't believe this. What have they done to you? It's as if you've been brainwashed.'

'No, no, I've not. I'm fine, Karen. I want you to be in my life.' Did he? Really? 'I love you, you're my big sister and we went through a lot, but I can't go with you. Karen, I've got to do what's right for me now and you've got to do what you think is right for you.'

He turned, began to walk back towards the minibus, hoping she'd just get in the car and go, worried that she wouldn't.

Cheryl moved towards him, suddenly really concerned as it dawned that this was not just some rather unconventional and unannounced sibling visit. 'George?'

'It's all right.'

'Get on the bus, OK. We'll take care of this now.'

George nodded, wondering if Cheryl and the rest of the staff would really be capable of handling Karen. He certainly wasn't, not any more. It was as though she suddenly understood that he meant what he'd been saying.

'You'd trade me for that lot of losers?' Karen shouted.

George faced her, tears streaming now and not caring who saw. 'No,' he yelled back, his voice breaking with the emotion of it. 'I want both. I don't want to have to make choices, but you're the one making me choose – and I choose not to be blackmailed. Dad did that, Mum did it too. It was always "do as I say or I'll hit you" or "do as I say because I might top myself if you make me unhappy", and now you're doing it too. I can't live like that, Karen. I didn't know how much I hated it until I didn't have to do it any more. Don't tell me to choose.'

He got on to the bus and Ursula followed him. An unaccustomed silence had fallen and all eyes seemed trained upon them as the other kids stared. The engine choked into life and the bus pulled off. Karen made no move to shift her car, so the driver eased round her, hoping the wheels would not sink into the sodden lawn. George breathed a sigh of profound relief as they regained the drive and rounded the bend that took them out of sight of Hill House.

'What do you think she'll do?' Ursula whispered. Around them, conversation had begun to buzz. George knew he'd be the subject of most of it, but he didn't care any more.

'I don't know,' he said. 'I've never seen her like this.' He wiped his eyes on the back of his hands, grateful when Ursula produced a pack of tissues and handed him one.

'You must have been really close,' she said tentatively.

'She was all I had; I was all she had. Dad was just violent and Mum was in bits most of the time. Karen kept it all together, kept us away from him, kept us moving. When we settled here, we thought we'd lost him, then he came back and Mum took pills and . . . then there was just me and Karen for real, and then there was just me.'

Ursula took his hand and held it tight. 'My dad's in hospital,' she said. 'He's been there since I was little. Mum couldn't cope. She left me with my gran and then my auntie, and then she just went off somewhere.'

George was shocked. They'd both avoided talking about the past, just touching on the less painful elements, but not wanting to dwell on those parts so hard to face.

'You don't know where she is?' he asked.

'She left with some man she met at work. Said he made her feel wanted and important. Gran was too old and then she died, and my auntie works abroad a lot, all over the place. Anyway, there was no one else, you know? Stuff happened and I ended up at Hill House. I hated it, until you came.'

George squeezed her hand and welcomed the firm pressure in return. They fell silent then, each buried in their own memories, aware that around them the morning gossip and quibbling had regained its normal volume. They said nothing more until they got to school.

NINETEEN

Mac had been trying to contact Miriam all morning, but her mobile phone kept ringing and then going over to voicemail. Eventually getting someone to answer the office phone, he was told that she had not come in that day nor had she called in sick.

Worried, Mac phoned her sister, only to be told that she had left as usual, her sister thought, just before eight. Could she have broken down en route? Surely, if so, she'd have called someone.

'She has breakdown cover,' Mac said. 'She had her mobile with her?'

'Oh, I'm sure. It's like an extra limb; she takes it everywhere.'

True, Mac thought; like him, she was used to being summoned at odd hours and the habit of keeping the mobile close carried over even to those times when she was not on call.

'I could drive her route,' Miriam's sister offered. 'Just in case.' She sounded really worried now, more so when Mac instantly said no to her suggestion, then regretted the sharpness in his tone. 'You think something happened to her, don't you?'

'I don't know,' Mac said truthfully. 'I'll get someone to go out and look for her. Can you tell me which way she'd be most likely to go?'

Minutes later Andy Nevins was mobilized and Sergeant Baker was alerting their colleagues in Exeter, just in case this should turn out to be more than Miriam merely being late for work.

'She's probably gone straight to a job,' Mac told Miriam's sister when he called her back to let her know what was going on. 'She maybe had a call-out on her way in.'

'Maybe,' the sister agreed cautiously, clinging to that little bit of hope, but as Mac put the phone down, it was with the awareness that neither of them thought for a second that could be true.

* * *

Andy found Miriam's car halfway between her sister's house and her workplace. He called Mac.

'It's parked on the roadside, as if she's pulled over deliberately on to the verge. There are tyre marks crossing the road in front of her car – looks like someone turned round, clipped the verge front and back when they manoeuvred. Mac, I've spoken to DI Kendal. He said I should secure the scene best as I can and wait for him to get here.'

Scene? Oh God. 'Signs of a struggle?' Mac's heart was pounding, but he tried hard to keep his tone normal. He heard Andy hesitate.

'Scuff marks on the road that look like shoes have scraped on the gravel, and . . . and, Mac, there's blood, just a few drops, looks like cast off and then drips as if she . . . as if she stood for a moment and the blood dripped on to the gravel at the side of the road. Mac, I may be wrong, I'm no expert.'

Mac took a deep, sustaining breath. Andy was, in fact, very good at reading a scene. He was fascinated by the technical side of policing, and Miriam had talked him through a number of crime scenes, arranged for him to have a place on one of the new training courses her department was setting up to improve the skills of new police recruits. If someone knew how to secure a scene and what to secure, then the chances of preserving vital evidence were massively improved.

'Let me know as soon as Kendal arrives,' he said. 'And thanks, Andy.'

'Trouble?' Alec had picked up on the tail end of the conversation.

'Miriam didn't make it into work,' Mac said. 'They've just found her car. There's blood, Alec, signs of a struggle.'

'Thomas Peel,' Alec said.

TWENTY

Miriam woke with a head that thumped and pounded so loudly she thought the sound came from somewhere else, until the pain told her that the sound was inside her.

Her hands were no longer bound and she lay on a narrow bed in the corner of a room with a gently arching ceiling. Painfully, she tried to focus on the brickwork above her. A basement, then. An old one, substantially built but – she inhaled, concentrating on the smell of the room and trying to shut out the worst of the pain – not damp and not particularly cold.

She struggled to sit, but her head threatened to fall off and she was forced to lie still for a little longer. Beneath her fingers she could feel the texture of rough blankets and, beyond that, metal. The mattress on which she lay was a little smaller than the frame of the bed and it was the metal structure that almost burnt her fingertips with its sudden coldness.

She tried again to sit and this time succeeded, though it was several minutes until the contents of her skull ceased slopping about and she could manage to open her eyes.

'I have a concussion,' she said aloud, oddly startled by the sound of her own voice. She could, when she focused, hear no other sound, just her own breathing and the chink and squeak of metal against metal as she shifted on the bed. She wondered how long she'd been out.

Beside the bed stood a small folding table and on that was a plastic jug, half-filled with water, and a paper cup. Beside that a chocolate bar. Somehow she was unsurprised to find that it was a chocolate cream, her favourite. 'Of course it is,' Miriam muttered angrily. 'Does his research, doesn't he?'

She touched walls that were painted white over flaking brickwork, though her first impression had been right and there was no feel of damp. The room was cool and she guessed at night it would be cold, but there must be at least some heating to keep it dry. Squinting, her eyes still not fully able to focus, she could see pipes running around the room just above the level of a rather battered wooden skirting-board and a tiny, cast-iron radiator near the corner of the wall opposite the bed. At the other end of that same wall was a door. That at least looked new and heavy and solid. A single light bulb, suspended from a braided cable of a type she was sure was now illegal, shed about forty watts of light on to a concrete floor. The only other furnishing was a zinc-plated bucket in the corner furthest from the door. Next to that another folding table on which was set a single pink toilet roll.

'Great,' Miriam muttered. 'Thanks a lot.'

She closed her eyes again, thinking that at least he could have left her some aspirin beside the water jug. She was determined not to be afraid. Her wrists hurt and her head felt like it had an army of Morris-dancing bears performing inside it, but she felt oddly calm. Probably just the effect of the concussion, she thought.

The fact was, he could have killed her. Mac would have no way of knowing if she were alive or dead, and would have to believe Peel, but here she was, still alive, so Peel must have something else in mind and that meant . . . well, she wasn't quite sure what it meant, but she was determined to feel optimistic about it. It was either that or break down and give in to complete despair. *That* she was certainly not going to do.

Miriam shivered; she was still dressed in her outdoor clothes, but even so felt chill and shaky. She recognized that part of this was shock, part physical trauma. Shifting her weight slowly, she managed to get off the bed and stand on her own two feet – that they felt like someone else's feet was little comfort when the pins and needles began. She pulled the coarse green blanket from the bed and, with a bit of difficulty, draped it around her shoulders, grateful that it had been meant for a double bed and so reached right down to her feet. Coarse it may be, but it was warm.

She tried to move, feet still not obliging at first. She poured some water and drank, sipping slowly, trying to ignore the nausea which confirmed her thoughts about concussion. As she set the cup down, she glanced at the wall behind the bed. And froze. Pictures of children adorned the brickwork, innocent-looking images of children playing, kids with their families, in school yards and on climbing frames. Children, arranged in a rough circle on the bricks beside the bed. And in the centre of the circle, one child – smiling face, light brown, almost blonde hair, clutching a doll: Cara Evans.

TWENTY-ONE

Mac was trying to focus on the lunchtime news and not succeeding very well. He'd spoken to Kendal and to Andy Nevins several times already and was wondering if he could call again, reminding himself that the last conversation with Andy had taken place only twenty minutes before and if anything new had happened they would have let him know. Or would they? How often, Mac thought, had he delayed speaking to family because he'd known he might have to contradict himself some time later? Then again, how often had family contacted him, not because they really expected new developments but just for the assurance they had not been forgotten?

And how often had he wished they'd lay off and just let him do his job?

Alec had briefed Wildman regarding events down in Frantham, and Mac had been glad of the intervention. Wildman stood, watching him. One eye on Mac, one on the television. Peel's little exhibition of Saturday night had taken a while to permeate, largely because reporters had been first kept at bay and then given no additional information until the Monday morning. First reports had concluded that this was a violent domestic; drama but little promise of long-term content. By Monday morning, someone had got hold of the fact that Emily Peel was the daughter of Thomas Peel. *The* Thomas Peel, child killer. That reports of his suicide had been unfounded; that, for reasons as yet uncertain, he had come looking for his daughter and her boyfriend; and that he had been intent upon murder.

It seemed to Mac that just about everyone in the street had been interviewed at least once. Reports from officers stationed at the end of Jesmond Street revealed three local news crews, two national papers and four television vans – 'one satellite, two proper', according to one comment – and that Emily and Calum's neighbour, together with Frankie the dog who was still in residence with him, had attained celebrity status.

Mac listened as Mr Macintyre told, once again, how he had heard the shot, looked out of his front window and seen a man with a shotgun enter his neighbour's house. That he'd come downstairs and told his wife to call the police, and that then the security light in his yard had sparked on.

'They were hiding out behind the wall,' he said. 'Young Calum had carried the dog and poor little Em – she was in bits, so she was. I said to them, you come along in, I'll make you a brew. Then all of a sudden, there he was. I tell you, if Frankie hadn't barked when he did, I'd have been a gonner and the young 'uns too. Then we heard the sirens, just after the shot, and he scarpered, that Peel.' He nodded emphatically and Frankie barked, just to show how he'd done it that night.

Had Mac been in a better mood, he might have joined the laughter. As it was, Macintyre's good humour just set his teeth on edge.

'Weren't you scared to open your door?' The interviewer was very young, very pretty, and the old man was clearly enjoying his moment of glory. 'No, my love, we don't scare easy round here. Not that we expect trouble, mind; this is a respectable street, and Calum and young Emily are a lovely pair, even if they haven't found the time to get married yet.'

Mac walked away, stared instead out of the window and down into the car park. He took his phone from his jacket pocket and studied the screen, checking just in case it had rung or a message had been left, and he, somehow, had not heard.

'If you're not going to be any good to me here, you'd best fuck off home,' Wildman said.

Mac started, so absorbed in his own thoughts he'd not heard his boss. 'I may well do that,' he said. 'Miriam is missing. Right now that's all I can think about. Peel has her.'

'And the last time you and he crossed swords, you lost, far as I remember.'

'I don't need reminding.'

'I think you do. I think you need to be reminded of it over and over again until you realize you can't solve anything on your tod. You need the rest of us. Policc work is about team work, not playing the bloody hero. That way people get killed.'

'I never played the hero, as you put it. I followed a lead. I didn't have time to wait. We'd waited before and Peel had slipped through our fingers in the time it took backup to get there. I didn't ask for what happened. I didn't want to be the one there, facing him. I didn't make it happen. Peel did; he called the shots right from the very start and he's doing it now.'

'Good,' Wildman said.

'What?'

'I said *good*. Time you brushed that frigging chip from your shoulder and realized you aren't alone in your suffering.'

'What?'

'You think any of us got away with it? Any of us here that didn't go home and rack our brains wondering if we could have done more, done anything to save that little lass? It was chance. Chance Peel decided you were the one he wanted to fuck around with. You were the one he could watch suffer and enjoy the most, but get this straight, Mac: it could have been any one of us on the beach with him that night, and ninety per cent would have done exactly what you did. Run to the kid and let him go. Peel was playing his luck that night, betting on the odds.'

'And you'd have done it different, would you?'

'Damn right I would, but, you know what, Mac, I don't see myself as being a better person for knowing that. I don't hold myself up against the likes of you and pass judgement; that's your game, not mine. I just know *me*, just like Peel knows himself, just like Peel knew you. Like he knows you now. You're not the most able opponent, Mac, not the best copper, not the meanest, not the strongest – just the one that provides him with the best game. Remember that, then, when it all goes tits up again, which – mark my words – it will; you might get to play him a blinder. You don't want another death on your hands, and no one that knows you wants to deal with your bloody conscience either, so do us all a favour.'

Mac stared, lost for words. Angry retorts rose to his lips and died there. The room had fallen silent, only the television breaking the tension and that was now delivering the weather report. Absently, Mac absorbed the fact that fog would be blanketing most of the country from late afternoon.

'You've no right . . .' he said at last, but there was no heat in his protest, just a profound weariness.

'No right to do what, Mac? To make you less of a martyr? Martyrs don't make good cops. Remember that.'

He turned on his heel and left the room. Mac watched him go, wondering if and how to make his own exit.

Alec appeared at his side, a mug in his hand. 'Tea,' he said. 'Drink. You OK?' he added.

Automatically, Mac took the mug from him. Conversation resumed, drowning out the weather forecast.

'Is that the general view?' he asked.

'General? No. Common? I imagine so.'

Mac took that in, accompanied the knowledge with a slug of tea. Found he felt oddly cleansed by Wildman's anger, by his own response – or lack of it. He nodded.

'Look, everyone sympathizes, everyone knows, fears, it might be them next time. We all hope we'd make the right call, but none of us knows how it would pan out when we're actually in that position.'

'And how did you feel, afterwards? When they brought her back from the beach, when—'

'Mac, along with every man Jack of us – women included in that – I was glad I'd been somewhere else.'

TWENTY-TWO

Somehow Mac made it through lunchtime and into the afternoon. Kendal phoned, but there was nothing to report, only that blood at the scene was the same group as Miriam's, but that traces had been minimal.

'We can probably assume she's not badly hurt,' he said. 'Or at least not losing blood.'

Was that compensation? Mac had to hope so. He thought again about just dropping everything and heading for home, but something told him that Peel would not remain so far south, not for long; he would stick with familiar terrain. And the thought that he might be halfway down the motorway should Peel make contact, and he would then have to back-track and lose precious time, was the one thought that kept Mac from leaving.

Peel needed to know where to contact Mac, and Mac needed to be able to be contacted.

Mid-afternoon brought a shred of news. A driver of a Range Rover, heading for home and encountering the police cordon, had described an event he had witnessed that morning.

'The timing's right,' Andy Nevins told him. 'And the description of the man. And he's remembered part of the reg number. It's something.'

'It is something,' Mac agreed. But what? Was the number plate genuine? Was he even driving the same car? The Range Rover driver had seen no woman passenger and had said that the car was a saloon – a BMW, he thought, or something similar. 'Big,' he'd said. 'Nearly wedged itself across the road.'

Mac knew that meant there was only one place Miriam could have been and that was in the boot of the car. He could not help but wonder what Peel had done to her; she may not be bleeding, but she wasn't fighting either, or Range Rover man would have heard.

He closed his eyes for a moment, summoning the energy and the courage to phone Miriam's sister. Andy was acting as liaison – the family knew him and Mac understood how much a familiar voice could help under these sorts of circumstances – but it would not be enough just to hear news from Andy, and Mac knew he had to call them too, talk them through their fears, just as he was trying to do on his own account. He was about to find their number in his contact list when the phone rang again and Mac looked at the display. Miriam's phone.

For an instant he thought that it might be her. That this whole incident was a mistake and a normal, unpainful explanation would emerge. They'd all be relieved, all go home. *He'd* go home, tell Wildman he was right and he really couldn't hack it any more, to count him out.

He pressed the button to accept the call. The voice was not Miriam's. 'Hello, Inspector,' Thomas Peel said. 'I think I have something you may want back.'

It was half an hour before anyone noticed that Mac had gone. At first everyone assumed he was just somewhere else in the building; then, as another fifteen minutes passed, it was obvious that he was not.

The desk sergeant recalled him leaving. He said that Inspector McGregor had been talking on his phone and had seemed in a hurry.

Alec tried Mac's mobile number: no response, just straight to voicemail.

'Peel made contact,' Wildman said bitterly. 'He went.'

'What would you have done?' Alec queried. 'Or have you never cared enough about anyone for that to be an issue?'

TWENTY-THREE

The weather forecast had been right about the fog. It rolled in from a cold ocean and sat heavily upon the land. Mac had grown up not twenty miles from Pinsent and he remembered well the thick fogs that descended so suddenly on a previously clear day. Walking on the beach in winter, he had learnt early to keep one eye on the sea and watch for the mist that came in so often with the turning tide. Once it came down, even those familiar with the area could become disorientated, and Mac had learnt that listening out for the sound of the sea was no sure guide to finding your way off the beach. The north-east coastal fogs seemed possessed of an almost mystical power of deception. Mac remembered well the story of six children and their teacher from a local riding school who'd been lost one winter because the fog had come down and they had turned their horses out to sea, instead of heading back for the beach above the strand line. Three had been drowned, horses and riders. One was never found.

The fog descended in thick blankets when he was only a few miles out of Pinsent, and Mac was forced to slow right down. He could, at times, barely see the front of the car, and oncoming vehicles slipped out of the gloom like diffuse ghosts, internally lit and seeming insubstantial.

Peel had given instructions: where to go, how to get there, when to be there. To come alone. Mac knew this was foolishness, but what else could he do? A full-scale police operation would only scare Thomas Peel away, and Mac could just imagine that Peel would either take Miriam with him or leave her like Cara Evans. Mac could not bear to consider either scenario.

Briefly, he wondered if he'd actually have a job to go back to after this, but it was a fleeting, unimportant thought.

Rowleigh Bay was thirty miles from Pinsent and ten from the beach where he'd seen Cara Evans die. It should have been an easy drive, but the fog on the twisting coast road was daunting, taking every ounce of his concentration. Once, twice, he saw Alec's name flash up on the caller display. Once, Wiseman's. He let the voicemail take them. Wiseman left no message. The route was not a complicated one, but at each turn he had to stop the car in order to see the sign-posts. Twice he had to get out and peer through drifting cloud at the battered, rusted signs. Rowleigh Bay was a beautiful place in summer, though even then it was remote enough to avoid the glut of the tourist trade. This time of year, it was left to the seals and the birds, and the few brave walkers who came down from the cliff path to cross the rocky beach and maybe walk the mile back to Rowleigh village and the Cross Keys pub, though those that did were either local or frequent visitors: they had to be to know that Rowleigh village even existed, that Rowleigh Bay was even there.

A mile to go. Mac glanced at his phone, telling himself that he could call for backup now, that this was the sensible thing to do. That he was an even bigger fool than he'd taken himself for when he'd left Pinsent almost an hour before. He was, though, unsurprised to see that he had no reception here. That his phone was useless. Did Thomas Peel know that? Likely so.

Mac drove through the little village of Rowleigh, noting the absence of cars in the pub car park – still too early for opening – the lack of people in the street – too cold, too damp, too dark now – and parked his car at the break in the cliff, the dip that gave access from the village and the road on to the beach and into the bay. Once, he'd been told, there'd been a lifeboat station here. Once a jetty that took pleasure-seekers round the headland to watch the seals. Nothing here now but cold and damp and despair. No other cars parked either. Did that mean that Peel had parked elsewhere, had been delayed by the fog or . . . was not going to show after all?

Something very close to despair gripped Mac at the pit of his belly and cramped hard. What if Wildman was right and he had made the wrong call again? Could he live with that?

No.

He looked at the dashboard clock. With the engine off and the lights doused, it was hard to see anything. He could just make out that it was five fifteen. He rummaged in the glove compartment and found a torch, detached his mobile phone from its cradle, hoping irrationally that it might find a signal down on the beach, then left the comparative comfort of his car and began the long, painful walk down on to yet another lonely beach.

Miriam was back in the boot of Thomas Peel's car. She was cold and stiff and scared. He'd cuffed her hands again, behind her back, so that each time the car rounded a bend or took a corner she was rolled sideways with no means of controlling her momentum. Her shoulder was stiff and bruised from lying on it with her arms wrenched back, and her hands were now almost numb. What wasn't numb was bruised and sore.

He had fastened tape across her mouth, wrapped a blindfold around her eyes. Frantic rubbing of her head against the boot carpet had shifted the blindfold, and though there was nothing to see in a space that was too dark for vision anyway, she felt slightly better for having at least fought back in that small way.

Peel had barely spoken to her. He had given instruction but that was all, and any attempt she had made to engage him in conversation had simply been ignored.

When he had tipped her unceremoniously back into the car boot and slammed the lid down, her first thought had been to be thankful she was still conscious. The lingering smell of chloroform in the boot made her feel nauseous and helped to explain the massive, hangover-like headache that seemed a separate symptom to those simply caused by being hit about the head with the butt of a shotgun. Soon, though, she found herself wishing that she had been drugged. The sick feeling remained, the nausea worsening by the minute, the scent of chloroform exacerbated by the shaking and buffeting she experienced with each swerve and bump of the car. She was convinced he was doing everything he could to make her feel worse.

Her biggest fear was that she'd be sick, vomit with the tape across her mouth, choke to death. She'd seen people who'd died that way, choking to death on their own stomach acids. The thought of it horrified her now.

Miriam forced herself to breathe slowly. Having freed the blindfold by rubbing against the boot carpet, she now tried it with the tape. Gave up. The only result of that exercise was carpet burns. She then willed herself to listen out for anything that might give her a clue to the route they were taking, but apart from crossing a set of railway tracks, little seemed to vary. She then made herself count. Sixty. Sixty again. Counting seconds – one elephant, two elephants – just like she had as a child when she and her sister had tried to guess what a minute felt like. Kate, her sister, was always better at that game than she was.

She kept losing count.

After forever, the car slowed and continued to move slowly for what seemed like another term of forever. Miriam had hoped, briefly, that they would be stopping somewhere, that she could then make a lot of noise by kicking at the boot lid and that she might be heard. Would anyone hear?

And then, another worry. She knew that some boots were airtight; what if she ran out of air? Angry with herself for not thinking of that earlier – though what she could have done differently if she had, she didn't know – she focused on conserving air, trying to breathe, slow and shallow, not easy when every minute or so a bump in the road jolted her and thumped the air from her lungs.

That was different, she realized. The road had not been so rough before.

Minutes later they had stopped and she heard the car door open and then shut. She braced herself, determined she would deliver at least one good kick before he got her out.

The boot opened and Miriam lashed out, but Peel was ready for her. She kicked and he slammed the boot lid down on to her leg. Miriam howled in pain behind the tape, her throat clamping shut as the sound became trapped there and, for a terrifyingly long moment, she could not breathe. Then he dragged her from the car, forcing her out into a world that was chill and damp and dark, even when he fully removed the blindfold from her eyes.

'Walk,' Peel said and pointed the shotgun he was holding straight at her face. 'That way.'

Miriam turned and walked. The heavy fog closed about them, cutting them off from the world.

Mac stood on the beach and waited. He could hear the sea lapping a few feet away and, when the fog drifted, make out the high outcrop of the headland and the lower exit of the track he'd followed to get here. The fog swallowed every other sound and caused the sea to sound thicker than it was, more like oil than water, dragging against wet sand.

He strained his eyes, trying to see through the cloud that had settled all around him and soaked his clothes. His mind was barely aware of the chill, and it was only when his body reacted by violent shivering, taking his mind by surprise, that he was conscious of being cold.

He had expected Peel to follow the same path he had done and watched for movement from that direction, angry with himself for not getting hold of a map and studying the lie of the land. He was, therefore, taken by surprise when Peel – Miriam just ahead of him – appeared through the drifting fog, walking along the length of the beach.

There must be another way down.

Miriam halted at Peel's command, and Mac moved forward almost without thinking.

'Stay where you are, Inspector.' The gun was now in Peel's left hand and pointed at Mac. He wondered if Peel could fire left-handed, but the thought was short-lived, replaced by a more pressing and familiar fear. Peel had moved closer to Miriam and now he held a knife in his right hand. His arm around her body, the knife at her throat.

'I think we've been here before, Inspector,' Thomas Peel said.

Mac froze. He did not have to ask himself if Thomas Peel was capable of carrying out his threat; he already knew the answer to that. Miriam's eyes were wide with fear. Tape covered her mouth and her arms were pinioned behind her back. Peel's face was expressionless as he studied Mac. Experimented with him, pushed him to the limits of what he could endure.

Mac breathed deeply, the chill air filling his lungs. He kept his gaze fixed on Miriam, willing her to know how much he loved her, that he wasn't going to let her down. 'Why are you doing this?' he asked quietly, surprised at how normal and controlled his own voice sounded.

'Why? Because I can. Because it gives me pleasure.'

'What kind of pleasure? Is it just the power you think you have over people?'

'No,' Peel said. 'It's the power I *actually have*.'

Mac eased closer. He had no idea what he was going to do, but for now just engaging Thomas Peel was a beginning. *Miracles can happen*, he thought. *Miracles do*.

'Did you tell Billy Tigh to kill Philip Rains?' he asked and was shocked to see a flicker of surprise cross Peel's face.

'Rains is dead? Pity; he was once a friend of mine.'

'Until you gave him to us. Is that what you do with your friends – keep them while they're useful and then sell them out to the highest bidder?'

Peel cocked his head to one side and looked thoughtfully at Miriam. 'I think your policeman is trying to annoy me,' he said. 'We should tell him that's not such a good idea.' He brought the knife up, pressing it more tightly against Miriam's neck. Mac could see blood seep from behind Peel's hand.

'No,' he said quickly. 'I'm not trying to make you angry. I'm just trying to understand.'

Peel laughed. 'Now you're sounding like a shrink. Forget it, Inspector. I'm way off the scale of your understanding. Way, way above you.'

I'm losing him, Mac thought. *I'm losing him again*.

He tried another angle; mention of Rains and Billy Tigh had at least elicited a response, however slight. 'So, if you didn't have Rains killed, who did?'

'You're asking me? A man like Rains made enemies. I could make you a list, I suppose. Could be any one of a dozen people. More, maybe.'

'And was Billy Tigh his enemy? Was Tigh a victim?'

Peel laughed. 'How the hell should I know? I didn't keep a list of Rains's conquests. Like I said, a lot of people would want him dead.'

'Karen Parker among them?'

Peel laughed again and tightened his grip on the knife.

He's scared of her, Mac thought.

'Our little Karen might have Rains killed just because she'd like to piss me off. She doesn't have to have a better reason.'

'And does it? Piss you off, I mean. Someone killing your friend.'

'No,' Peel told him. 'I'd outgrown Rains long ago. He was fun for a while. No one lasts, though. I use them up and throw the husks away; you know that, Inspector.'

Peel smiled, and Mac knew for certain he was failing. Peel was bored and time was running out.

He risked another look at Miriam: no fear in her eyes now, just resignation. She wanted this to end, could not see how they could win, had all but given up.

Mac saw – or thought he saw – a movement behind Peel, but when he focused it was gone. Just drifting fog and enclosing, greying dark. He looked again: a whisper of movement, there and then gone. For a mere instant he allowed the fantasy that Alec or Wildman had tracked him down and they had come to the rescue. He cursed himself for not accepting Wildman's insistence that what mattered was the team.

'You finished, then, Inspector?' Peel said.

'No, I've not . . .' Mac began, but he got no further. A blade flashed, a body fell heavily on to sand and Mac was screaming and running. And all the terrible memory of that other night was falling in on him again.

TWENTY-FOUR

By midnight the fog had lifted and the sky was clearing. Dragon lamps illuminated the beach and the cordoned area where the body lay. Mac still did not understand what had happened.

Someone from the pub had brought hot soup, and Mac held a mug between his hands, sipping cautiously. Beside him, in the back seat of a police car, Miriam, swathed in blankets but still shivering, held her own portion and tried hard to show interest in drinking it.

Paramedics had treated the cuts on her head and throat and the bruising on her wrists. One side of her face was rubbed raw where she'd struggled with the blindfold and the gag, and around her mouth the skin peeled and oozed blood where the tape had ripped it sore. She looked a mess and she was the most beautiful thing Mac had ever seen.

'What happened?' she whispered. She had asked this same question at least a dozen times. Each time his answer had been the same.

'I don't know. There was someone else there.'

He had watched the shadow move behind Thomas Peel. Seen the hand, the knife; seen Peel fall on to the sand, Miriam taken down by the weight of the man as he collapsed. He had thought the worst, been convinced that Miriam was dead, and only when he'd hauled her out from beneath Peel's body, held her close, run careful hands across her body, looking for blood, was he convinced that she had survived.

The keys to the quick cuffs had been in Peel's pocket and he had released her, then rubbed her hands and arms, wincing as she moaned relief and pain as the blood returned, though even now her hands felt chilled and numb.

They had left Peel's body on the beach, hoping the tide would not come in before the police and CSIs arrived, and returned to the village to find a phone. The Cross Keys pub was now the centre of operations in a murder case.

Wildman had arrived and statements had been made, and Mac knew that his story had not been believed.

He didn't care.

Miriam was safe and Peel was dead, and he could think no further than that, not now, not tonight.

There was, however, one thing that had permeated his cocoon of pure relief. He had seen the knife that had killed Thomas Peel and recognized it. One from a set he had in a block in his kitchen at the boathouse. One of those or one just the same, and he knew that Miriam had seen it too.

'It's going to be bad, isn't it?' she said, as though tracking his thoughts.

'Yes.'

'They'll think it was you.'

'Yes, yes, they will.' He had said in Wildman's presence that he wanted revenge. That would be remembered.

'But you didn't do it. There was someone there.'

'Yes, there was.'

'But they'll still think it's you.'

Mac slid an arm around her shoulders. Miriam shivered and laid her head against him. 'What do we do?'

'We tell the truth,' he said. 'That's all we can do.'

'They'll still think it was you.' She closed her eyes and Mac took the mug from her hand as she slid into sleep. He drank his soup and watched the figures moving on the beach, and knew that this time, even more than when Cara Evans had died, everything would change. He was not the man he had been then, not even the man he had been when he returned to Pinsent. There had been a shift in his thinking, in his being. That sense that he no longer wanted to be doing this – putting those he loved or, indeed, himself in harm's way – had crystallized, though he had more than a suspicion that the decision was now well and truly out of his hands.

TWENTY-FIVE

By one o'clock they had been returned to Pinsent police headquarters and Mac taken off to one of the interview rooms. Wildman looked angry and Alec grave.

'I need to phone my sister,' Miriam said. Kate knew by now that she was safe, but Miriam badly wanted to hear her voice and give her own reassurance.

'I'll find you a phone.'

'It's OK, I've got Mac's. Alec, what will happen now?'

'What *should* be happening is me taking you to the hospital,' Alec said.

'I'm all right. The paramedics checked me out.'

'Even so. If not that, then at least to a hotel.'

'I want to stay here.'

Alec nodded. 'Look, wait in the briefing room; there's a comfortable chair in there and you can make your call in relative peace at least.'

'Thanks,' Miriam said. 'Alec, can you tell me where the loo is first?'

He pointed out the briefing room and then told her where to find the toilets. A quick glance at the briefing area as she passed by confirmed her anxiety that there would still be people about in there. Clutching Mac's mobile in her pocket, she went to the toilets, taking refuge in a cubicle, hoping no one would come in to overhear. Would anyone actually be up at Rina's this time of night?

To her profound relief, Tim picked up on the third ring. He had just returned from work 'Mac?' he demanded. 'What's the news? Is Miriam all right?'

'Oh, Tim. Thank God. I'm fine.'

'Miriam?'

'Please, Tim,' she interrupted him. 'I have to be quick and this is really important. Does Rina still have a spare key to the boathouse?'

'Yes, I'm sure she does.'

'Listen, please don't ask questions; there isn't time. In the kitchen, there's a knife block. One knife will be missing. Please, Tim, take the block and lose it somewhere. Please.'

'Miriam? You're not making sense.'

'Tim, I have to go. Please do it. Bless you.' She hung up, praying he would do as she asked and wondering what Mac would say if he found out. The police would search the boathouse; bound to. Mac was a suspect in a murder. Hopefully, the search would be done by the local police and, hopefully, nothing would happen for a few hours yet.

She heard the outer door open and flushed the toilet, came out of the cubicle. A female officer in uniform stood just inside the door. 'I came to see if you were OK,' she said. 'DI Friedman said you might like something to eat or drink, and then he wants you to make a formal statement, if you feel up to it tonight?'

Miriam made a show of washing her hands and grimaced when she saw her reflection in the mirror. Bruised and scraped and cut, and obviously exhausted, her face showed every second of the time since Peel had abducted her. 'A cup of tea would be really welcome,' she said. 'And yes, I feel fine to do that. I just want to call my sister first and tell her I really am all right.'

A few minutes later, tea in hand and ensconced in the old red leather chair – Miriam, hearing the tradition, figured she really did qualify on the grounds of having a truly terrible day – she phoned her sister on Mac's mobile phone and hoped no one ever had cause to look at the phone records for that night.

'Rina, wake up.' Tim and Joy had debated what to do. Joy was in favour of getting straight to the boathouse and doing Miriam's bidding; Tim, typically as a long-term member of the Martin household, had asked himself the inevitable question – *What would Rina do?* – and though the conclusion he reached was to concur with Joy, there was the small problem of not having the key.

'Tim? What's wrong?' Rina sat up, immediately alert.

'We need the key to the boathouse. You still have the spare?'

'Yes, dear. But why?'

'Because Miriam wants us to get rid of some evidence,' Joy said.

'What?' Rina looked from one to the other, clearly wondering just what they'd had to drink. 'Tell me.'

'You don't know it's evidence,' Tim objected.

'What else could it be?'

'Tell me,' Rina said again. She listened as Tim recounted the content of the mysterious phone call, taking in the fact that Miriam was, presumably, safe and that Mac was, it seemed, in some kind of trouble.

'Joy, the key is in the jewellery box on the dressing table. Yes, that's it. Now get going, the pair of you, and for goodness' sake, be careful. Don't be seen.'

Tim gaped at her, then snapped his mouth shut. 'You're not coming?'

'Tim,' Rina said patiently, 'it's the middle of the night. Sixty-three-year-old ladies do not go gallivanting in the middle of the night. Young people who work late in hotels and perform magic tricks go gallivanting in the middle of the night.'

'With their girlfriends,' Joy added.

'Most definitely with their girlfriends. Now go.'

They left and Rina stared at the now-closed bedroom door and wondered what was going on. She wanted desperately to call Mac, but, in common with gallivanting, ladies of a certain age tended not to make phone calls, even to their friends at – she glanced at the clock on the bedside table – two fifteen in the morning.

But they did make tea and eat biscuits when they couldn't sleep.

Donning her pink fleece dressing-gown, she went downstairs and put the kettle on, found chocolate biscuits and sat down to think and wait for Joy and Tim to return.

Wildman had permitted Alec to be the second officer present for the interview. At two fifteen, the only sound in the interview room was a soft whirring of the tape machine as he waited on Mac's response.

'I did nothing,' Mac said quietly. 'I admit to being stupid, admit to going it alone when I should have asked for help. Admit to maybe nearly getting Miriam killed, I don't know, I really don't, but I did not kill Thomas Peel. There was someone else on the beach. I saw them, in the fog.'

'So, describe this mystery man.' Wildman was clearly unimpressed.

'I saw a shadow,' Mac said. 'I saw movement and someone behind Peel. Then I saw the knife, or thought I did.' He sighed. 'It was dark, it was thick fog. I thought I saw the blade, but most likely I just interpreted in retrospect.'

'*Interpreted in retrospect*,' Wildman mimicked. 'What the hell's that supposed to mean?'

'It means, I saw a movement, I saw Peel fall, I thought . . . He dragged Miriam down with him as he fell and I thought . . . I thought she'd been . . . I thought she was dead.'

A beat or two of silence. Alec asked, 'You can make no judgement about the third person, then? Height, weight? Anything at all?'

Mac's gaze flickered towards his friend's face and then back to focus on Wildman. 'No,' he said. 'Not tall; Peel wasn't tall and they were behind Peel and I didn't see them. Not heavy. They ran. I heard them run. I *thought* I heard them run.'

Had he actually heard anything, seen anything he could swear to? He was certain that the third person on the beach had been Karen Parker, but he didn't even want to try that idea on in front of Wildman. Karen didn't feature in Wildman's world, and for the moment Mac felt he'd rather keep it that way. After all, on the face of it, there *was* no connection. He wondered if that was the actual fact. No connection. If, in his head, Rina's anxiety about Karen had become confused with his own obsession with Peel, and everything was warped and changed by that perception.

He only knew that he was tired, that he wanted to get this over with. That as soon as it was over he'd be heading home and he didn't care if he never left again.

'You killed him,' Wildman said.

'I never touched him. There was someone else.'

'And you think your girlfriend will back you up? Perjure herself?'

Mac rubbed his eyes wearily. 'She'll tell you the same thing,' he said. 'I was standing ten feet or so away, trying to talk Peel out of killing her. I was failing, really doing an appalling job of playing the hero. Peel was going to kill Miriam the way he killed Cara Evans – I could feel it, I could see it in his face. He was enjoying every minute. But I didn't kill him; there was someone else.'

'Convenient.' Wildman was sarcastic. 'The cavalry arriving just in time.'

Mac nodded. 'It was,' he said. 'It truly was.'

Frantham Old Town was silent and chilly. They had walked around the headland, the first time either Tim or Joy had followed the wooden walkway above the waves at night, and Tim decided on the spot that it would be the next to last, allowing for the fact they'd have to return the same way.

The sound of the sea churning beneath them was disturbing, the wet surface slimy and insecure. The whole experience vertiginous. They did not speak. Tim was very aware of just how far and how clearly sound travelled late at night, and their footsteps already sounded far too loud. He was relieved to step off the wooden causeway and on to concrete, then on to cobbles. The boathouse was only a couple of minutes away. He clasped Joy's hand and led her through the quiet streets and down to the old slipway, at the head of which the boathouse, once used for lifeboat launches, was situated.

'This is it?' Joy asked.

'Yes.' He slipped the key into the lock and opened the side door, glancing round to check that no one watched.

'There's no one to see,' Joy whispered. 'They're all asleep.'

Not daring to switch on the lights, they felt their way up the stairs and into the little flat. Eyes used to the dark now, Joy looked around, taking in the open-plan living room cum kitchen diner. 'Aw, it's cute,' she said. 'And tiny. My bedroom's bigger than this.'

'Your bedroom's bigger than most people's houses.'

Joy giggled.

'OK, let's find this knife block and go. Right, that must be it. Miriam was right: one missing.'

Joy had brought a shopping bag from Rina's kitchen and they slipped the knives, still in the block, into the bag. 'Right, I need a cloth,' Joy said. 'That will do.' She picked up a tea towel and took something from the shopping bag. 'I took these from the kitchen too,' she said. 'They're ones Matthew and

Steven don't use much, so it'll be all right. Matthew likes the carbon steel ones and these are stainless.'

'What? You've brought knives?'

'Sure I have. It'd look a bit suspect, a kitchen without sharp knives – someone's bound to notice.'

He watched, slightly awed, as she polished the blades and wiped the handles on the tea towel and then slipped them into the cutlery drawer. 'You look far too good at that,' he said.

'My dad taught us kids to be careful,' Joy said. 'Even the straight ones among us. Force of habit, I guess. Right, let's get out of here.'

Tim nodded, sudden panic gripping him. They were doing something important, he felt; also something he was pretty sure was illegal, and while that did not of itself worry him unduly, he felt oddly bad about involving Joy.

Down the stairs and out of the door, closing it quietly, though the sneck seemed terribly loud as it shot home. Back on to the cobbles, the concrete, the causeway, round the headland.

'What should we do with these?'

'Drop them into the sea?'

'I don't know how deep it is here,' Tim worried.

'Right, so we spread them about.' Joy took the bag from him and took the knives, one by one, pulling down the sleeve of her sweater and wiping them before launching them in a high and long arc way out into the ocean. Tim was impressed.

'Where did you learn to throw like that?' he asked as the block followed the blades. 'Something else your dad taught you?'

'No, a mix of netball training and playing cricket with a couple of brothers,' she said. 'Only way they'd let me play was if I learnt to bowl right. What if the block floats?'

'Hopefully it won't. The tide should be on the way out. Anyway, anyone who sees it will think it came off a boat; all sorts does.'

'Hope so. Right, we've done all we can; let's get back. Even *you* don't work this late and we don't want anyone asking questions.'

Fitch was in the kitchen with Rina when they arrived home; light sleeper that he was, he'd heard them leave and Rina come down. He was relieved to hear that it had all gone well, worried about the implications; he was in agreement with Tim that they had probably just now been guilty of concealing evidence and, most likely, perverting the course of justice.

'It can't be justice if they're blaming Mac for something,' Joy said. 'My dad reckoned Mac was a truly honest man, and there weren't many people he said that about.'

'Well, in his line of work, there weren't many that qualified,' Fitch observed.

'True,' Joy concurred.

'So, what now, Rina?'

'Now, Tim, we go to bed and then see what's on the morning news. By then it will be perfectly normal for me to give Mac a call; maybe we can find out what's going on.'

'I feel too awake to sleep,' Tim complained.

'I don't,' Joy told him. 'Way past my bedtime.' She yawned and stretched and then bid them all goodnight and headed upstairs. Rina too trekked off to bed. She was unsurprised, when she reached her room, to find that the camp bed was unoccupied and Joy nowhere to be seen.

TWENTY-SIX

Despite so little sleep, Rina was up early and watching the breakfast news. Fitch joined her. Tim and Joy were still unavailable for comment and, though she was sure Fitch knew where Joy had spent the night, Rina decided not to mention it. Joy was an adult, after all, and Fitch was not her keeper.

The breakfast news was a disappointment. A small mention of the shooting that had taken place two nights before, and more speculation as to why Thomas Peel should be trying to kill his daughter and her boyfriend. Something more about a body found on a beach at a place called Rowleigh Bay, but that was all.

Rina tried Mac's phone, but it was off. She and Fitch breakfasted on speculations and found it an unsatisfying diet.

At eight, to Rina's profound relief, Miriam called. She sounded distressed and confused and very tired. She wanted to come home and was about to call her sister and see if someone could come and get her.

'What's happening, Miriam? We heard you'd been reported missing, then nothing else.'

'Oh, Rina, it's all so . . . They think Mac killed Peel. He told them what happened, that there was someone else on the beach, that he didn't stab Peel, but no one believed him. Rina, I want to come home. I want Mac to come home with me.'

'Is that likely?' Rina asked anxiously.

'I think so. I don't know. They're going to search the boathouse, something about a knife.'

Ah, Rina thought, so that was it.

'I don't know much, but I think they'll release him later on police bail and we can come back. He'll be suspended, of course, pending full investigation, but I don't know any more than that. His car won't be released for a while, though. It's still considered part of the crime scene, and they're still trying to figure out where Peel kept me and . . . oh Rina, it's all so bloody awful.'

'We'll come and get you,' Rina said stoutly. 'Fitch is still here and he has a vehicle. We can be there by . . .' She looked at Fitch.

'Somewhere around midday if we leave now.'

'Somewhere around midday. Now, don't you worry, we'll soon be there and everything will be fine.' She could feel Miriam wanting to ask about the knife block, but could think of no way of letting her know that Tim and Joy had done their stuff without incriminating them. In the end she said simply, 'Tell Mac we all send our love, especially Tim and Joy. They've been really worried about the stress he must be under.'

'Thank you, Rina,' Miriam said. 'I'm truly grateful.'

'We have a vehicle here,' Rina said firmly. 'We may as well make use of it.'

'Right,' Rina said firmly. 'I'll get my shoes and write a note for Steven. He and Matthew will have to get breakfast this morning. You get on to Abe Jackson and tell him what we're doing. I want to know where Karen Parker has got to. Poor George was very upset by her behaviour yesterday; I want to know what else she's up to. And later we'll call Joy and Tim, and they can meet George out of school and find out if Karen told him anything useful.'

Fitch nodded. 'Right you are,' he said. 'Rina, do you think Mac may have . . .'

'Killed Peel? No, I don't. Oh, I've no doubt, given the right circumstances, he may well have been tempted, maybe even capable, but if Miriam says he didn't do it, then I believe her. If she says there was a third person on that beach, then I believe that too.'

'Looks like we may be the only ones,' Fitch said gravely.

'Then we'll have to help him convince everyone else, won't we?' Rina said.

Karen stood in the basement where Thomas Peel had briefly held Miriam Hastings prisoner, and felt both satisfaction and disappointment. This house was hers now, part of a deal that had nothing to do with killing Peel. That act had been a bonus, both for her and her current employer. Peel was an irritation to many – a blackmailer, a cheat, someone who had been protected only because he had information that could make trouble for certain business rivals his protectors had, and which had, for a while, made him useful. But, as Peel of all people should have known, usefulness can be outlived, and when Karen had asked for him as part-payment for other work she had undertaken, no questions had been asked. She'd then seen the safe house he'd been using and decided she'd like that as well. It was as close to perfect as she could imagine.

The trouble was that her pleasure at the acquisition was diminished by George's refusal to join her. She'd had such hopes. It would be like it used to be, only better. All of the pleasure and none of the pain.

Karen knew that her relationship with her younger brother was much closer than most sibling relationships, and that was because they'd both had to grow up so fast and take so much responsibility. Childhood had simply not been an option for Karen; she had done what she could to make it possible for George to have a semblance of one. And now she felt betrayed, abandoned and very angry, not with George but with just about everyone else. It pleased her immensely that Mac would take the blame for Thomas Peel's death. Maybe George would think him less of a hero. George seemed to think that taking life diminished Karen; why would Mac be viewed in such a different light?

Karen did not try and justify what she did. She wasn't some righteous vigilante, ridding the world of those who afflicted the innocent. Those she had rid the world of were no better or worse than those who paid for her to do so. They were, in Karen's view, mostly vermin, mainly unimaginative, generally driven by pure self-interest, but Karen understood their type and their motivations and was perfectly at ease with the implications. She earned her money using her skills. End of story. And if someone should raise the question of her only being twenty years of age, she would point them in the direction of the frontline troops currently serving in Her Majesty's forces. There were snipers her age, doing what they had a talent for and being paid a darn sight less for it than she was. That, as far as she could see, was the only difference between her and them. Oh, and the fact that she wasn't restricted by the need to kill at a distance, a fact to which the dead body of Thomas Peel, among others, could now testify.

George would come round, she thought. Just give him time. Just let him realize that everyone in the world except for Karen would let him down.

She took the pictures of the children from the basement wall, stacking them and then, leaving the basement, taking them upstairs. In the dining room, overlooking the small but pretty garden, was a wood burner, lit and ready and throwing out welcome heat. She opened the door, dropped the photographs on to the glow of wood and coal, and watched them curl and burn.

Pity, she thought, that all memories, all trace, all difficulties could not be disposed of in that same way: burnt to ash, transformed into heat and light and comfort, gone in a small blast of purple flame.

TWENTY-SEVEN

Pinsent was not ready for the arrival of Rina Martin. She had spoken to Miriam twice more on their journey and, by the time she walked into reception at Pinsent police HQ, had worked herself up into a most vengeful mood. Miriam was waiting for them there, clearly upset. Her face, now the bruising and scabbing had had time to develop, looked even worse than it had the night before.

Rina hugged her, then held her back at arm's length and surveyed the damage. 'What on earth are you wearing?' she demanded.

Miriam was nonplussed. 'Trace evidence,' she said. 'They took my clothes. Someone found me some trackie bottoms, and I borrowed a jumper from Alec. I'd got blood on my coat.'

Alec's jumper was dark blue and hung almost to Miriam's knees. The red tracksuit bottoms must have belonged to someone very tall with a love of loud colours, Rina thought. On Miriam's feet, half-hidden by rolled-up trouser legs, were bright pink socks and a pair of the blue waterproof covers she would normally have worn at a crime scene.

'You need some cream for that face. Come here; let me see what I have in my bag.' Suiting action to words, Rina rummaged and brought forth a pot of calendula cream. 'Here, let me.'

Looking like a child dressed up in her parents' clothes, Miriam stood obediently as Rina applied cream and affection in equal quantities, tutting all the while and muttering her displeasure.

Fitch saw the desk sergeant glance uneasily their way. He'd seen that look before when Rina was in moods like this. He decided to divert her.

'What's going on?' he asked as gently as he could. 'Is Mac all right?'

'You must be Fitch,' Miriam said. 'Thanks for coming. I didn't know what I was going to do.'

She hadn't cried yet, but she did now, breaking down completely and allowing Rina to draw her into a comforting, motherly hug and then to dry her eyes and tell her to blow her nose on a proffered tissue.

'Don't we have somewhere private we can go?' she demanded. 'And I want to see Inspector McGregor.'

'I'm sorry, you can't do that right now.' The desk sergeant eyed Rina and then Fitch with considerable suspicion. Fitch was used to that, but he could see it riled Rina. Not a good thing to rile Rina.

'And why can't I see him?'

'Inspector McGregor is not available,' she was told. 'He's with DCI Wildman. I don't know any more than that.'

Fitch intervened again. 'There's a café across the road,' he said. 'Rina, I could do with a coffee, a bite to eat, and I'll bet Miriam could do with a break from this place.'

'But I can't leave Mac,' Miriam said.

Fitch took a business card from his pocket and laid it on the counter. The desk sergeant picked it up. To Rina's surprise, it was very expensive-looking: cream card, embossed, neat black lettering. 'My mobile number is on there,' he said. 'If Mac becomes available, we'd be grateful of a bell, all right?'

The sound of Fitch trying his best to be polite and businesslike, and still sounding like some 1950s gangster, caused Rina to smile and the desk sergeant to drop the card back on to the counter as though it might nip his fingers.

'I'll see what I can do,' he said. 'But you may be waiting a while.'

Across the road, Fitch settled the ladies in a corner and went to the counter with an order for tea and whatever looked edible. Miriam had been given a sandwich at some unearthly hour of the night, but she had been too upset to eat; she had not eaten since breakfast the day before. 'Oh, and a chocolate cream,' she told Rina.

'A what?'

Miriam half-smiled. 'Peel took me to a basement. I woke up and there was a water jug and a chocolate bar. My favourite kind. Rina, he knew what chocolate I liked.'

Rina patted her hand. 'He knew a lot about both of you,' she said. 'But it's over now, sweetheart. He's gone.'

'And Mac is going to get the blame.'

'No, he's not.'

'Tim?'

'Did as you asked. No more questions about that. It didn't happen. Now, tell me what's been going on, as much detail as you can; we need all the ammunition we can get.'

Miriam had been unable to speak with Mac. She had been questioned, asked to make another statement, pressured by Wildman to say that Mac had been lying.

'There was someone else there,' Miriam insisted. 'I kept telling them. Peel was attacked from behind. I could see Mac all the time, but they're insisting that I'm lying just to protect him.'

'What do they say must have happened?' Rina queried. 'Miriam, just try to be calm and tell me. I've got thinking to do.'

Miriam nodded.

Fitch returned with a tray of tea and news that lunch was on its way. 'Bacon and sausage baps,' he said. 'I got a mix 'cos I didn't know what you'd prefer.' A thought struck him. 'You're not a veggie, are you?'

'No,' she laughed through tears that threatened to start again. 'I am hungry, though,' she said, wondering at that.

'Good, because we need you thinking straight,' Rina said. 'Now drink your tea and tell me everything you can remember. Then we'll go back over the road and sit there until they let us talk to Mac.'

They returned to the reception area to find Alec Friedman talking to a young couple who held hands tightly and looked as pale and battered as Miriam.

Alec and Rina had not met, but the desk sergeant had told him about the old lady and the bouncer, shown him Fitch's card, and Alec had guessed who she must be.

He left the young couple, came over with his hand outstretched. 'Mrs Martin? I'm Alec, a friend of Mac's.'

Rina shook hands. 'This is Fitch,' she said.

'Mr Fitch,' Alec turned to greet him.

'No, just Fitch.'

'Right. OK.' Alec let it pass. 'Can I introduce you to Emily and Calum? Emily is, or was . . .'

'Thomas Peel's child,' Rina said quietly. 'Mac told me a lot about you, my dear. This must be a terrible time.'

'They're saying Mac killed my father,' Emily said. 'Mrs Martin, I almost wish he had, but Mac wouldn't. It's not in him.'

'Of course it isn't,' Miriam said. 'I keep telling them there was someone else, but no one is bloody listening.'

'I'm listening,' Rina said.

'I know, but . . . you know what I mean.'

Alec sighed. 'Look,' he said. 'I can show you to somewhere you can all talk.' It was irregular, he knew, but then so was a group of five would-be defending counsels having a case conference in the reception area. 'I'll have a word with DCI Wildman, see if he can come down and have a chat. Please, come on through.'

He opened a door off the main reception area and ushered them all inside. It was a room kept for waiting relatives or for anyone needing a quick, private word. It was small and cramped, but just now it was the best he could do.

Rina nodded her thanks. 'I'd like to speak with whoever is in charge,' she said.

'I'll tell Inspector Wildman,' Alec said and retreated to the safety of the briefing room.

Rina made the introductions and surveyed the little group thoughtfully. 'Now,' she said, 'we'd better talk, find out what each of us knows and see how best to get Mac out of this mess.'

Three fifteen, and Tim and Joy waited outside the school George and Ursula attended, watching kids fight for places on the school buses and parents double-park on zigzag lines before grabbing their offspring and bundling them into waiting cars.

'What if they get on a bus?' Joy said.

'They don't; they go down into town and meet the minibus there. It has to pick up the younger ones first.'

'OK.' She grinned at him. 'Don't they all look young? I was never as young as that.'

'She says from her ancient position of just turned twenty. If you think they all look young, imagine how I feel.'

'Cradle-snatcher,' she teased.

'Don't,' Tim said seriously. 'Really, don't.'

Joy, disturbed by the sudden serious note, looked up at him in concern. 'Sorry,' she said. 'I didn't mean anything.'

'No, I know. I just worry what people think.'

'The people who matter are happy about it. Mum thinks the world of you.'

'Bridie thinks the world of Rina. She figures I come as part of the package.'

Joy laughed. 'You really think that? Tim, you may have noticed that my mother is as ready as Rina when it comes to speaking her mind. If she disapproved, you'd know about it. She loves Rina; she approves of you. She thinks you're sophisticated.'

Tim almost howled with laughter. 'Just as well she's only seen Marvello,' he said, thinking about his now-deceased other persona as children's entertainer, the Great Stupendo. 'Really, Joy, I made the most appalling clown. There's George,' he added, spotting the sandy hair, Ursula's blonde ponytail visible just behind. 'Hey, George. Ursula. Over here.'

George turned, a look of concern on his face. He came running over. 'What's wrong?' he demanded. 'Is Rina all right? Is Mac?'

'Hello, Joy,' Ursula said. 'Have they caught Thomas Peel yet? It said on the news he'd been shooting at people.'

It must seem almost exciting when you're fourteen, Tim thought, suddenly feeling very old and worldly wise, and then reminding himself that, compared to George and Ursula, he had very little to feel worldly about. They'd been through more in their short lives than he ever had. He noted that both avoided mention of Karen and wished he could do the same.

'Peel's dead,' he announced, childishly gratified when they both stopped and stared at him.

'Trouble is,' Joy added, 'the police seem convinced that Mac did it.'

Twenty minutes of walking and waiting for the minibus, twenty minutes to exchange so much news. Tim wanted to tell George about the knife block, knowing he and Ursula would love the adventure of it, but he resisted; better that fewer people knew any of it. Twenty minutes of getting George to recall everything Karen had said, anything that may give a clue to where she had been and how to track her down. Tim felt guilt, as though inviting George to betray his sister, but found that George had moved beyond that and that the recounting of

'Karen' conversations was the easy part. He had now talked it all through with Ursula so many times that it felt almost like it was someone else's story.

By the time the minibus arrived, George had explained about the house and the gallery and the old lady selling up, and the fact that it was on the promenade somewhere and there would be a lot of passing trade. He had described the house and its tiny front garden, its formal, imposing door and sash windows and every single thing he could think of.

'Did she want a gallery before?' Joy asked curiously. 'I mean, was she into art?'

George thought about it. 'She liked pictures,' he said. 'She used to draw cartoons for me to cheer me up, but she said there was no money in drawing; she had to get a proper education and a real job.' He frowned, as though remembering something awkward or remote. 'The house,' he said. 'It reminded me . . . you know when little kids draw a house and it's always got a door in the middle and four windows and a chimney on top?'

'Yeah,' Joy said. 'Like when they draw the sun with rays so it looks like a spider.'

'Well, I always drew houses like that, and Karen said one day we'd find a house like that and live in it. The house she showed me, like I said, sort of Georgian but not quite.' He shrugged. 'There are a lot of houses like that. Probably a lot of galleries too. It could be anywhere, couldn't it?'

Privately, Tim thought so too, but he tried to sound encouraging. 'We'll find it,' he said. 'We've got Abe and Fitch and Rina.'

He saw George nod and try to smile, but Ursula voiced what he really felt.

'Up against whose army?' she said.

TWENTY-EIGHT

At three fifteen in Pinsent, conversation had run out and Calum and Emily decided they had better leave. They'd been at a safe house while Emily's father still posed a threat; now they wanted to get back to something like normal and were wondering how and what and where. To go back to their little rented house seemed untenable; for one thing it was still a crime scene, cordoned off and under guard. For another, there was no longer a front door and the hall was peppered with shotgun pellets, splintered wood and plaster from when Thomas Peel had twice discharged the weapon. Calum now understood that it had only been because Peel had had to reload that he and Emily and Frankie had had those precious seconds in which to get away. Had Peel been armed with anything better than a shotgun, he was convinced their families would now be arranging funerals.

Meantime, they thought they'd go and stay with Calum's parents for a few days and consider their options. The idea of being somewhere under police protection was an uncomfortable one: a reminder of the past that both were eager to put behind them. Too eager, Rina thought. Fail to face up to what had happened now and it would surface with even greater intensity at a later, maybe less convenient moment, but she could appreciate their point of view.

Her other worry was that all of this might not be over. What if Karen had taken an interest in the young couple? What if Peel had associates who might want revenge?

Maybe she just worried too much. She wanted to talk this over with Tim, but a long discussion over the phone was not the same as a face-to-face conflab.

After Emily and Calum took their leave, Rina sat, thoughtful, while Fitch paced a room too small for meaningful pacing. Miriam sat at the little table in the corner of the room, head resting on her arms, trying hard not to doze. Sleep was what she really craved, but it seemed inappropriate and unfeeling, knowing Mac was still . . . wherever he was.

Give her action any time, Rina thought. Forced inactivity was something she just did not do well.

At half past three the door opened. Alec came in and motioned them to come out into the reception area. Rina bristled, thinking they were about to be thrown out or fobbed off with excuses, but Miriam was looking past her and jumped to her feet. 'Mac!'

She ran past Rina and grabbed at him, holding fast to the lapels of his jacket, pressing her face against his chest. He held her tightly, blinking as though he'd been in half-light for too long.

'Are you all right?' Rina asked.

'Suspended pending enquiries,' he said. He was pale and exhausted, dark circles under puffy eyes, and Rina would have sworn he looked thinner than the last time she had seen him. Smaller too, somehow diminished; even his skin looked grey and dull, as though he'd faded over the past few days.

'Take us home, Fitch,' Rina said. 'I think I've seen enough of this place.'

TWENTY-NINE

After Fitch had driven them back to Frantham, Mac and Miriam walked back along the wooden causeway to the boathouse, Mac half afraid of what he might find there and Miriam too tired to care. She had still worn the blue plastic crime-scene slippers, and Joy insisted on lending her a pair of shoes. Miriam had waited in the Range Rover while she fetched them, unable to face the exuberant welcome home she would have to accept from the Peters sisters and the Montmorencys; not wanting to hurt their feelings by rebuffing them.

They had spoken to DI Kendal on their way home, asked if it was OK to return. Dave Kendal was sympathetic and had been a little put out at being asked to conduct the search of his friend's house. He told Mac that he had supervised things himself, kept it all low-key, and that Mac's home was now available to him once more. The neighbours would probably not have noticed anything untoward. Mac thought that was an unduly optimistic hope, born of Dave Kendal's unfamiliarity with Frantham Old Town.

'What were you looking for?' Mac had asked.

'Your laptop, for one thing. Andy brought me that, says you hardly ever take it home anyway. And kitchen knives,' Kendal said. 'Wildman wanted us to look for a specific type, but all we found were the two old ones you keep in the drawer. I've had to take them, so I hope you don't want to chop anything tonight.'

Mac thanked him, noting that Miriam was avoiding his gaze and Rina suddenly showing great interest in the view from the side window, despite the fact it was now too dark to see a whole lot.

He said nothing until they reached Frantham Old Town and the familiar shape loomed out of the shadows at the top of the old slipway.

Mac let them in, switching on lights, looking round to see what Kendal's people had disturbed. It was such a minimal space, Mac thought, they'd have been in and out in less than half an hour, surely. It still felt intrusive and unpleasant, though, knowing that someone had rifled through his things and examined his personal possessions, maybe discussed his taste in music or his lack of a big-screen television or . . . Impatiently, he shoved such random thoughts aside, watched as Miriam paced the perimeter of the living room, as though establishing her territory, and then went through to the bedroom and stripped the sheets from the bed.

'What are you doing?'

'Changing the sheets, doing the washing. I don't know.'

He reached for the sheets, threw them into the bathroom hamper, then took both her hands and kissed them, rubbing his thumbs across the sore and broken skin of her wrists, the bruises now fading from black to purple, on their way to green.

She pulled away. 'I need a shower, I need to get clean. I need to be in my own clothes.'

'I need to know why my knife block is missing.'

She froze, half-turned towards the shower room.

'Miriam?'

'I don't know where it is,' she told him truthfully.

'You asked Rina to remove evidence?'

'Not Rina, no. Mac, leave it, please. I did what I had to do, that's all, and those who love you helped out.'

'And if anyone finds that out?'

'Why should they? Mac, I did what I had to do, same as you did. Maybe we both got it wrong, but we did our best. I'm alive, you're back here.'

'I nearly got you killed, and I may be back here but I'm still suspended, still under investigation.'

'No,' she said sharply. '*Thomas Peel* nearly got me killed. You did what you thought you had to do. You came for me, Mac; that's all I need to know. And I had the knife block disappeared; that's all *you* need to know.'

It wasn't. He slumped down on the bed, wondering exactly what she'd done. Who had come here, if not Rina? Tim, then; he'd have to have used Rina's key. Joy too? Could any of this be traced? Suddenly it was all too much. In the morning he might try and make sense of it, but now all he wanted was, like Miriam, to get clean, to eat, to sleep with her beside him, to forget about the world and all of its problems.

He could hear the shower running and he went through to the kitchen to put the kettle on and see if there was anything in the fridge that he could use to produce a decent supper. Preferably, something that required no sharp knife to prepare.

He looked at that place on the counter where his knife block had stood and remembered the beach and Thomas Peel dead. He had brought the flashlight from the car, gone through Peel's pockets to find the key to the handcuffs he had used on Miriam, and then he had seen the black, polymer handle protruding from the dead man's side, and he had known. His knife, from his block, in his kitchen.

Karen, he thought now. She had been here, she had taken it, she had used it.

He heard Miriam turn off the shower and the cubicle door open and then close. He crept back down the stairs, half-ashamed of the fear that now gripped him, knowing that fear is an infectious thing and not wanting Miriam to be infected. For the first time since he had moved into the boathouse, he shot the bolt on the outer door and used the deadbolt to lock it fast.

Fitch had driven from Rina's straight for a meeting with Abe Jackson. They met in a little pub Abe had found that served good food and at which Abe had now become a regular. Fitch tucked into beef and ale pie and some very good mashed potato, while Abe brought him up to speed on what he had discovered so far.

Billy Tigh, the young man who had killed Philip Rains in prison, had not been one of Rains's victims, but there was evidence that his brother had been.

'The parents separated. Billy went with his dad, and his brother, Terry, with his mum. Same mother, different fathers, which might explain it, I suppose. Anyway, the mother took up with a man called Brian Curtis, who, it turns out, was a friend of Philip Rains.'

'Curtis?' Fitch frowned, a forkful of pie halfway to his mouth. 'Why does that ring a bell?'

'Because Sara Curtis was a prison visitor. She went to see Rains on several occasions. Brian is her brother. Peel implicated him, but there was no evidence and it was passed off as vindictiveness on Peel's part. Sara had, of course, gone through all the necessary checks when she became a prison visitor; it was just assumed that Peel was trying to make trouble for a pillar of the local community.'

Fitch rolled his eyes. 'And do we know different?'

'About Sara Curtis? Not yet. About her brother, yes. Terry killed himself a year ago. He left a long and very rambling letter in which he implicated Brian Curtis, said that while Curtis was seeing their mother, Brian regularly abused him – and we know there was a strong connection between Brian Curtis and Philip Rains.'

'And Peel knew about this, presumably. Maybe told Billy Tigh that Rains was guilty too. No, wait. Mac said he told Peel that Rains was dead, and Peel seemed surprised, very surprised that Billy Tigh was involved. If Peel didn't tell Billy about Rains . . .'

'Maybe Karen did.'

'Why would Karen take an interest in Terry or Billy Tigh?'

'Because her dad also knew Rains, did time with him when Parker was in for armed robbery. Rains had been a driver on a couple of bank jobs, and like attracted like, presumably. No one knew about his other proclivities then, but . . .'

'But it all links together one way or another. Karen looks set to get her own back on anyone she thinks might deserve it. I mean, apart from any financial advantage she may be getting out of all of this, she seems set on getting rid of anyone who came within a whisker of harming her brother.'

'Or of failing to protect, in Mac's case,' Abe pointed out. 'She blames him for letting their dad take George away. Karen's logic isn't what you might call objective.'

Fitch shovelled mashed potato, thinking hard. 'So,' he said, 'Sara Curtis may have carried a message from her brother or from Peel to Rains, kept him in the loop. Miriam said there were pictures of kids on the wall in the basement. Do we know where Peel's been hiding out?'

'Not yet. He seems to have moved about a lot. No one actually wanted his company for long. I know he was being protected, and I have some idea of who and why, but until I firm it up I'd rather not add to that speculation.'

'And the gallery Karen told young George about?'

'Interesting. Particularly as there is already an art dealer in the mix. Our Igor Vaschinsky. We know he has a legitimate business and we also know his brother deals in stolen artworks.'

'And launders some of his money through his brother's legitimate galleries.' Fitch nodded. 'So . . .'

'So we get a list of his holdings and business interests; see if there's a gallery coming up for sale in the New Year.'

Rina had retreated with Tim and Joy to the peace and quiet of her front room. The family had been ecstatic at their return and effusive in their welcome. It had been a while before Rina could escape without them feeling slighted.

'So,' she said, 'the priority is to find Karen Parker. Abe and Fitch are doing their part; what can we do?'

'Fitch can use my dad's old associates,' Joy said. 'Mum still has plenty of clout in that direction; plenty of people owe her favours.'

'And Abe has contacts in some really odd places,' Tim added.

'So that leaves us.' Rina was aware that they looked expectantly at her.

'Karen worries me,' she said. 'Where is she, what is she planning, what will she do when she learns that Mac is back here? She planned to hurt him, inflict the maximum pain; I'm certain of that. She enlisted Thomas Peel, and when she did, I think she knew he'd want to replay that night on the beach when little Cara Evans died. I think she expected him to kill Miriam; that maybe she got there too soon. I don't know.'

'What if it wasn't her on the beach?' Tim said. 'I mean, a lot of people wanted Peel dead. Maybe someone else was following him or . . . something.'

'Or *something*?'

Tim shrugged awkwardly. 'It's just a thought, Rina, but what if Mac *did* kill him? Miriam wouldn't rat him out, would she? And I mean, no one could blame him if he did.'

'Well, I think the law might,' Joy said.

'I suppose so, but hopefully we've taken care of that side of things. I mean, no one that matters.' He looked hopefully at Rina.

She shook her head. 'Tim, I believe Mac; Miriam too. There was a third person on that beach and I'd bet my life that person was Karen Parker. She's killed once that I know about.

I suspect Abe and Fitch are *not* telling me that she's upped her score since then. Karen is a very angry, very able and very destructive young woman, more than capable of manipulating a situation to her own ends – and, I suspect, a lot cleverer than Peel gave her credit for. He thought he was manipulating her for his own ends, and I don't suppose anyone could have been more shocked than he was to find out he was wrong. But we should take note: those who underestimate or cross Karen Parker tend to end up dead or in very deep trouble. We've already done the second of those things. I think we should be very careful indeed not to do the first as well.'

Up in Hill House, Ursula had crept into George's room and they sat together on his bed, staring out of his window across the ink-black sea.

'What do you think is going to happen?'

George shrugged. 'Karen will find out that Mac is home and then she'll be mad. She'll come back here, or wherever he is. She doesn't let up once she's made up her mind to do something.'

'So, what do we do?'

'There's only one thing she wants more than Mac and that's me.'

'George, you can't.'

'I'm not going to go with her. I told her, I told everyone: I want to stay here, with our friends, with you.' He glanced anxiously at her. The light was out and her face was pale in the starlight. He knew that both he and Ursula were a bit slow about doing things. Some things. There were plenty of kids in his class who had . . . well, who claimed to have . . . though George didn't believe most of them. He swallowed nervously, leaned forward and kissed Ursula rather clumsily on the mouth.

She stared at him, and he thought for one awful moment that he had offended her. Then she kissed him back and he was relieved to find that she was about as bad at it as he was.

'I'd better go,' she said. 'We'll be in deep trouble if Cheryl catches us.'

Deep trouble, George thought as she closed the door very softly behind her. It seemed ironic that they should worry about such an ordinary thing as being caught in one another's rooms so late at night, what with all the big stuff there was to worry about. Stuff like having a psycho sister and knowing, despite everything, that he still loved her very much and wanted her to be all right. Knowing too that he was probably going to have to be the one to stop her before she put ‘being all right’ way beyond the reach of any of them.

THIRTY

Wednesday morning and the breakfast news was full of it. The child killer, Thomas Peel, had been found dead on a remote beach the morning before, and the media, annoyed at being so behind the times, were going into overdrive in their efforts to catch up.

Mac had described to Rina just how remote Rowleigh Bay was, and, watching the helicopter circle now, she realized just how right he was.

She watched intently, taking in the tiny village with houses huddled between church and pub, narrow road leading in and even narrower track leading out, both now crowded with vans and people and the paraphernalia of the modern media. The helicopter was turning now, the commentary explaining that Rowleigh Bay was popular with walkers in the summer, that the cliff path dropped down on to the beach and many took refuge in the village pub either for lunch or to spend the night before continuing on. It looked as though it would be a pretty place in summer, Rina thought, but it was her experience that just about anywhere along the north-east coast looked bleak from October through till March.

'And it was to seek refuge in the Cross Keys pub that a man and a woman came the evening before last,' the reporter intoned. 'The landlord described them as being wet and cold and very frightened. They asked to use the phone because their mobile, as many of *us* have found today, couldn't get a signal here. And then they left again. Not long after that, the police and ambulance arrived, although it seems likely now that the ambulance was too late to be of any help; Thomas Peel was already dead.'

Helicopter transmission handed over to their man on the ground and Rina listened on. 'Details are sketchy. The landlord of the Cross Keys said he'd noticed a car passing his pub about an hour before with one person inside. I think viewers have got to understand, this is such a small village that any vehicle passing through at this time of year is going to draw attention. I'm told there's a little pull-in up on the headland, just before the cliff path descends on to Rowleigh beach, and that police have been up there since yesterday morning. The locals tell me that, although it would have been dangerous and difficult in the dark and with thick fog swirling, visibility minimal, it may be possible that either the couple or Thomas Peel came down that way. The car the landlord saw pass his pub was taken away by the police yesterday afternoon. It is believed to be an estate, dark blue, maybe a Volvo.'

'Boy, are they scrabbling round for something to say,' Tim commented.

'You're up early.'

'Couldn't sleep. Too much going on in my head.'

'And Joy?'

Tim actually blushed. Rina tried not to laugh.

'Sleeping. It's all been a tad exciting.' He turned his attention back to the screen.

'Police have said that no one is being held in connection with Thomas Peel's death and that a formal statement will be issued later this morning. There are rumours that the woman had previously been a hostage taken by Peel, but these have not been verified. It was thought, briefly, that she might even have been Peel's daughter, Emily. We do know that, a few days ago, Thomas Peel went to the house that his daughter shared with her boyfriend, Calum Heaney, armed with a shotgun, and that he attempted to kill both his daughter and her boyfriend and succeeded in wounding a neighbour who went to their assistance.'

The report then turned back to speculation about the shooting and 'our woman on the spot' standing outside Emily's damaged house.

'Don't know much, do they?' Tim helped himself to tea from Rina's pot.

'No, they don't, and I get the feeling that they're annoyed the breaking news, as they're calling it, didn't break until twenty-four hours after the event.'

'Slow up north?' Tim suggested.

'From what Mac told me, you have to know the place exists in order to find it. The Cross Keys pub became the command centre up there, so I imagine everything was wrapped up pretty tight, and maybe the locals were slow to welcome that kind of media invasion. If it happens here, you can be sure the inhabitants of Frantham Old Town won't be rolling out the red carpet. The new town might put up with it for a while, if it brings some extra winter income but . . .'

'You think that likely to happen?'

She shrugged. 'We'll have to see what comes out in the media statement. One thing's for sure, though: Karen will now know that Mac isn't being held as a suspect.'

Tim nodded. 'That isn't good,' he said. 'Not good at all.'

George and Ursula had managed to sneak a few minutes of news, standing in the TV room with plates of toast and hoping, in the morning chaos of Hill House, that their presence would not be missed. They weren't supposed to watch the television first thing in the morning. All the kids had their bags to get ready, breakfast to eat and small chores to do, and the prevailing and understandable sentiment among their carers was that early-morning television interfered with that process.

They watched with the sound turned down and subtitles on, one ear straining to hear what was going on in the kitchen and hall as Cheryl dealt with lost PE kits and homework that hadn't been done and a mountain of breakfast that, thankfully, it was not their turn to help prepare.

It did not take long for Ursula to reach the same conclusion as Tim and Rina.

'Karen's going to be mad as hell,' she said. 'Do you think she'll come after Mac?'

George shrugged. 'Probably,' he said.

Down the hall they could hear Cheryl calling them and Ursula killed the TV.

'Did you get your history done?' Ursula asked as they raced for the front door, grabbing backpacks as they went.

'Yeah, but I think I've screwed it up.'

'Sure you've not, but, anyway, you've got Mrs Peace for history, don't you? She'll give you an extension if you ask. She likes you.'

George nodded and climbed aboard the minibus, wondering again at a world that seemed to place history homework almost on a par in their lives with the fact of a friend nearly getting killed and his own sister roaming around the countryside knifing people in the back.

He was finding it hard to focus on the school stuff, finding comfort in the normality of it at the same time.

Ursula cast him an anxious glance and he managed a smile. 'You've been through worse,' she said quietly

George nodded. He probably had, but that time Karen had been on his side and he'd been grateful for it. This time he was not so sure he wanted that.

Abe Jackson and Fitch were at Abe's main office on the industrial estate. The solicitor's office was great as the public face of his business, but here, in this more anonymous setting, he had the computers and the faxes and the phones and the personnel.

Fitch had been on the phone for the past hour, talking to previous associates of his late boss, and was building a picture of a Karen Parker that even George would have had trouble recognizing. Her father had been little more than hired muscle; even Jimmy Duggan had once employed him for that purpose, though, finding that he lacked finesse, it had not been a job opportunity that had lasted long enough to become a career. All agreed that Karen was far more intelligent, reliable and ruthless.

'No nerves,' Fitch was told. 'A real ice maiden and with the looks to go with it.'

Fitch also gleaned the impression that Karen was not in this for the long haul. She would make her money and then get out. 'She's a flash in the pan,' Fitch learnt. 'Give her a year and she'll burn out.'

'Give her a year and I reckon she'll be off, find herself a rich old man.'

And they were all right, Fitch reckoned. Karen did not plan a lifetime as a hired assassin; she was in it for the short term, for the instant cash it afforded and which she would have the sense to invest in something more solid and steady and life-changing than the mere destruction of a handful of individuals whom few would mourn and whose deaths many would rejoice over. Five years down the line, Karen would be something else, all trace of this episode in her life gone.

He found himself thinking that he'd almost like to know her then, when the anger had been consumed by action and she had her life on track; trouble was she was threatening now those Fitch was determined to protect.

'What have you got?' he asked Abe once he'd got off the phone and told him what he had learnt.

'Well, the Reverend Tom Longdon seems clean, as far as we can tell.'

'You sound disappointed,' Fitch grinned.

'Maybe. Maybe I just don't like vicars. There's some bits and pieces about Ricky Marlow. You remember, Peel went to his pub and Marlow threw him out? Well, Marlow definitely knew Rains as well. He gave him a reference for a driving job. A proper driving job, not as in fast car, clean getaway. Rains worked it for six months, then decided honesty was hard work.'

'How did you turn that one up?'

'Got one of my associates to go back over Rains's work record. He called round a couple of his previous employers, said Rains had applied for work and given their names for references.'

'And no one twigged that he was asking about a dead man?'

Abe laughed. 'It seems not. I think people don't like to think they've been associated; they'd rather lie to themselves. Having said that, Rains worked all over the country, and some may genuinely not have made the connection. Needless to say, my man wouldn't be employing him on the strength of previous recommendations. Nothing more, though, on John Bennet. Apart from having the misfortune to work with Peel and know Ricky Marlow because he helped with the survey on his extension, there's nothing to suggest that John Bennet is any more interesting that he purports to be.'

'Can't win them all,' Fitch observed.

'And the investigation? Has Wildman made any more progress?'

'My contacts tell me that DCI Wildman now accepts that Peel brought Miriam down from the cliff top. His car was still there and a second set of tyre tracks. They've taken impressions, but—'

'But he's now accepted there was a third person on the beach?'

'Has he hell. No, still convinced that Mac did it.'

'What's Mac done to piss him off?' Fitch queried.

Abe leaned back in the black leather chair. 'Oh, the animosity goes back to long before Cara Evans was killed. It seems there was evidence, planted as it happens, that Wildman was on the take. Mac was the man who found that evidence and then headed the investigation. Eventually it was all handed off to Internal Affairs and Wildman was finally cleared, but it took six months and he's never got over it. Then, the night Cara Evans was killed, Wildman was in the office next to Mac when Peel phoned him, summoned him to the beach and told him to come alone. Wildman was convinced that if Mac had briefed him, asked for his help, they might have saved the kid and got Peel.'

'Is that likely?'

'I doubt we'll ever know, but the pair of them have to live with the possibility.'

'And then Mac does the selfsame thing when Peel takes Miriam, and it damn near ends the same way.' Fitch nodded. 'I can see how that might gall a man like Wildman. It would bloody gall me. In fact, when this is over and I've got time to say my piece, our friend Sebastian McGregor is going to find out just what kind of a bloody fool I think he was.'

Abe smiled. 'I think you may have to join the queue,' he said.

THIRTY-ONE

Despite everything, Mac and Miriam had slept and slept late, waking to find the sunlight pouring into the flat above the boathouse and the view from the porthole window of a clear sky and calm sea, most uncharacteristic of November.

Breakfast was bread, taken from the freezer and hacked into rough slices with a penknife Miriam found in the boathouse below. The still-frozen slices were defrosted under the hot grill and made fairly decent toast.

'We have to go shopping,' she said. 'We need groceries and a bread knife at the very least.'

Mac nodded. 'Can we call into work?' he said. Corrected himself. 'Call in to see Andy and Frank Baker. They'll be worried. I feel bad about not having spoken to them.'

Miriam nodded. 'Sure,' she said. 'I'll call Kate while you shower, tell her I'm car-less and will get over to her soon as I can.' She felt oddly reluctant to go and see her sister: it meant travelling the road where Peel had blocked her route and kidnapped her. She wasn't ready for that yet.

Half an hour later and they were on the wooden walkway that led from Frantham Old Town to Frantham new. Bright sunlight sparkled off the slightly choppy water, and the sky was such a clear blue it might well have been high summer, but for the freezing chill that blew in off the ocean.

Miriam had clothes of her own at the boathouse, but she'd had to borrow a fleece from Mac, her coat still most likely residing in an evidence bag somewhere. She added it to her list of things needed, though today she'd settle for getting a couple of warm sweaters and a fleece that did not actually drown her.

'Oh and I need a hat,' she said. 'Something bright and totally outrageous.'

'Ask Eliza and Bethany. I'm sure they will oblige.'

'I'll do that, but not today. I don't think I could deal with all the sympathy and love-bombing.'

'Love-bombing?'

'You know, like they do in cults to make you feel needy, or maybe it's to fill the neediness; I'm not sure about that one. Anyway, that's why people stay: they're love-bombed into submission.'

That was a new one on Mac, but he didn't argue. Right now, Rina and Tim were part of the bad times over the past few days. Later, maybe even later today, he would want and need to speak with them and be reassured he was still a part of their family – to be love-bombed, as Miriam put it. Just now, though, he needed distance and brightness and fresh air, and to do the ordinary things like buying bread and finding Miriam an outrageous hat.

They passed the police station on their way to the promenade, but put off their visit until they'd seen to shopping and spent more time enjoying the unexpected sunshine. Several people spoke to them, one or two asking Mac if he'd been away. How long, he wondered, before the media storm once again broke over Frantham and everyone knew just where he'd been and why?

One of the shopkeepers asked Miriam about her face. 'That looks sore. Gravel rash, is it?'

Miriam nodded, delighted to have an explanation handed to her. 'Came off my bike,' she said.

'You should have worn your helmet.'

She found her hat, purple with a blue and red bobble and ear flaps. Mac didn't think even Eliza Peters could have produced anything more garish. Then, shopping in very heavy bags, they turned back towards the police station and reality.

Andy Nevins glanced towards the door as they came in and his face lit up. He came round from behind the counter, shouting to Sergeant Baker in the rear office, and Mac got the distinct impression that he only just avoided a hug. Miriam did not get off so lightly.

'Mac, boss, you're OK. No one would tell us nothing. DI Kendal's been trying to get some information, but they're saying nothing up there.'

Baker came bustling out and, to Mac's surprise, Dave Kendal followed him.

'You've saved me a trip,' he said. 'How are you, Mac? Miriam?'

'Suspended.'

'Alive.'

'Come on through, we were just about to watch the news. Wildman is supposed to be releasing a statement.'

Mac felt his shoulders sag. Couldn't he just go home and forget about everything? They crowded into the little office that was officially Mac's; might be his again when all of this was done. For now, though, he felt like a visitor and was glad when Miriam took the chair behind the desk. Kendall had set up a laptop to receive web television, plugging it into Mac's Internet connection. The news was about to begin.

DCI Wildman announced that he had a prepared statement to read out.

He was, Mac noted, still dressed in that same, loud dogtooth jacket, though the bald patch seemed to have grown. He put such random meanderings aside and tried to focus on what he had to say.

'On Monday morning at approximately eight a.m., Thomas Peel is known to have abducted a young woman on her way to work. He is then known to have held her for a period of several hours at a location as yet undisclosed. Later that same day, he took this young woman to Rowleigh Bay, threatened her life. As I'm sure everyone here can appreciate, we had every reason to believe he would carry out his threats.

'Thanks to a covert police operation, the young woman was released, largely unharmed, and is now back with her family. As a result of that operation, Thomas Peel died. The investigation of that death will, as is procedure, be carried out by the Police Complaints Authority and we will afford them every assistance. We are, however, satisfied that nothing could have been done to prevent the death of Thomas Peel and are just relieved at the positive outcome for the young woman he threatened.'

Wildman closed the folder on the statement and nodded to the waiting press. 'That's all I have to say just now. I'm sure you realize that the investigation is still in its early stages and further statements will follow.'

The room erupted. Mac saw journalists he recognized (and a lot he didn't) get to their feet as one and fire questions at the DCI as he prepared to leave the little stage. He picked out some of the questions from the hubbub, registering that someone asked if the young woman was Peel's daughter. Another, why there had been no earlier statement. Several wanted to know the background to the shooting two days before Peel's death. And one froze Mac to the spot. Miriam heard it too and gasped.

A journalist fought his way to the front of the pack, his progress noted by the cameraman recording the chaotic scene. Wildman paused and looked his way, and the rest of the journalists, realizing that one of their number had scored, fell quiet.

Wildman walked on, but the journalist repeated his question, the satisfaction in his voice evident as he realized his information was correct, even though Wildman refused to give confirmation.

'I wanted to know, Chief Inspector, was the woman on the beach a CSI called Miriam Hastings? And the man who came back to the pub to raise the alarm – that would be DI McGregor, would it not?'

Wildman had disappeared through the swing-doors at the end of the sports hall the police had borrowed for the event. But the journalist hadn't finished. He had another question which threw doubt on everything Wildman had said.

'Funny sort of operation, wasn't it? So covert that none of your radios worked, no mobile phones that could get a signal anywhere. Funny the way your man had to walk back from the beach and use the pub phone to call for help.' He looked around, clearly enjoying his moment, and the camera that had been about to pan away, to cut to the next item, stayed fixed upon him. 'Funny kind of covert operation that seems to have consisted of just one man. I mean, I know the cuts have been bad but . . .'

Laughter, cut short by Kendal muting the sound.

'It was bound to come out,' he said. 'Wildman put on a good show, but it was bound to come out. What you did, that you were alone.'

'But they have our names.' Miriam was furious. 'Who gave our names?'

'Any number of people could have leaked that information,' Mac said gravely. 'Miriam, I'm sorry, maybe you should go and stay—'

'With my sister? Oh yeah, great idea. Look how that turned out last time.' She sighed. 'We need more shopping.'

'What?'

'Enough to last at least a week. I'm not going anywhere until this has been sorted out and gone away. We buy a shopping trolley, get more groceries, stock the freezer.'

'Hide away in the boathouse?'

'Unless you have a better idea.'

Mac nodded. 'Maybe I do.'

One short call to Bridie Duggan and it was settled: that's where they would go. Mac had sheltered people at her home before; now he was the one who needed help and he could think of no better place. Fitch was summoned, and Joy, reluctantly, agreed to head for home with him, but with the proviso that she was coming back as soon as the fuss died down. An hour later and they were on the road, Mac having grabbed a few essentials from the boathouse, knowing that Bridie would provide anything else they might need.

It felt odd, though, claiming sanctuary from the other side, but just now there were few people he felt he could trust with Miriam's life; certainly not his colleagues who seemed intent on blaming him. Certainly not himself: his judgement so far had been not just wide of the mark but practically off the map.

I'm not running away, he told himself, remembering that earlier time, when Alec had intervened to keep him sane. *I'm just retreating.*

In the little house that Peel had once called sanctuary, Karen watched the television news and heard Wildman make his statement. She was furious that Mac had been allowed to get away with Peel's killing. What were the police? Utter incompetents? But Karen was not outmanoeuvred yet; she'd get what she wanted somehow. The phone call she'd made earlier that morning seemed to have paid off anyway. The look on Wildman's face when he had heard the names of Miriam Hastings and DI McGregor had been priceless. The journalist would be able to tell them nothing, just a woman's voice, put through from the central switchboard, claiming to be his sister. She had merely suggested he ask Wildman that question, left the rest to him.

Karen left the living room and wandered through the house. She'd begun to redecorate, painting walls and stripping paper. She'd have to get someone in to measure up for carpets, though she'd probably leave the bare boards in the kitchen and dining room and would definitely not touch the perfect tiles in the hall. The honey glow of softly polished wood was very nice, even if it wasn't in keeping with the period of the house. Whoever had stripped them back had really gone too far, removing the years of patina that would have built up; years of waxing and dusting and the tread of feet. Same went for the doors, but there was nothing she could do about that. She paused in the room that she had allocated for George. The bed was already in place, a big brass bedstead she had seen in an antique shop and which she knew he would love. Furniture was something he should choose himself, and the blue carpet was fine for the moment – it matched the heavy velvet curtains, which, again, she felt George would appreciate. Better than anything he had at that Hill House place.

He just needed persuading, and Karen was sure that would not be so hard. She'd made the mistake of allowing herself to be carried away. Put too much pressure on, when the poor kid was, most likely, just getting over their mum's death and Karen having to go away. It was her job to persuade him that she'd not be going away again, not his just to believe her.

Satisfied that all would be well in George-and-Karen world, she went back downstairs, put on the wellington boots she'd left by the kitchen door and went out to weed the rose bed.

Of all strange things, Karen had discovered gardening. George would piss himself laughing at that. His sister – first in the family to have green fingers.

THIRTY-TWO

Abe had been doing some informing of his own, passing on what he'd discovered about the Billy Tigh connection to DI Kendal, who had duly passed it on to Alec with the suggestion that they talk to the brother of prison visitor, Sara Curtis. See who may have talked to Billy Tigh about Curtis and Rains and the abuse of his brother.

He also had a possible lead on the gallery. Igor Vaschinsky had an aunt who ran a small gallery. It was an independent operation, though Igor had invested in it, and the aunt was also an illustrator. She had set up the gallery as an outlet for her own work and also for a group of local artists. It had a very good reputation; she had a knack for recognizing talent and also a real skill when it came to marketing. Now in her sixties, she was talking about retirement and looking for a buyer.

Abe thought it all sounded about right.

The Southern Gallery at West Bay Harbour had a website, and Abe downloaded some pictures of the outside to show George on the off-chance Karen might have told him something useful.

In addition, this now narrowed his search for Karen's house. She'd want, presumably, to be close to the gallery, so all he had to do now was find a house that matched George's slightly sketchy description to one within, say, a twenty-mile radius of Bridport, and that would be that. Easy.

Abe leant back in his chair and thought about it. Fitch had called, telling him about the sudden change of plans, but Abe was glad to hear that Mac and Miriam and Joy would now be out of harm's way. Three less people to look out for. He needed now to talk to the gallery owner, see if Karen had left any leads. No way on earth did he look like someone who might be interested in art.

Rina, Abe thought. Rina could do the intellectual, arty bit, and he could just hang around and look lost.

He picked up the phone. 'Rina, it's Abe. I've got a little

project for you. Get your glad rags on and try to look affluent. We're going on an art hunt.'

Back in Pinsent, Alec was involved in a major argument with DCI Wildman.

'You think I leaked that information?' Alec was furious.

'Some bugger did and it sure as hell wasn't me.'

'And what reason would I have?'

'He's your bloody friend. You've undermined me every step of the way, Alec. Like you didn't know McGregor had gone. Like you back him up on the lie he and that bint concocted. He bloody did it, Alec, and you're intent on making us a laughing stock. "Didn't know the cuts were that bad",' he mimicked.

'Listen to me,' Alec said slowly. 'I leaked nothing. I did not know Mac had gone or where. I have no more wish than you do for us to look like fools, but if you go to a press call with a story so full of holes a child could drive a truck through it, never mind a room full of journalists – whose sole mission in life is to sniff out the lies, turn them round and use them against you – then what the frigging hell do you expect? The landlord at the Cross Keys knows that story is full of shit – so do his staff, so does half the village, not to mention any and everyone who's been working the case since. Covert police operation? So covert none of us had managed to turn up? Where had we been hiding out, then? You've seen the size of that village; a chihuahua couldn't pass through without the locals seeing it. And, for the record, I don't believe that Miriam Hastings lied to protect Mac, though, fucking hell, Wildman, who could bloody blame her if she had?'

'Mac killed Peel. End of story.'

'And the forensic evidence to back that up? It isn't there. You have nothing, nada. The only blood on Mac's clothes was a smear on his sleeve consistent with him having searched Peel's pockets for the handcuff keys.'

'On his *sleeve*. Consistent with him stabbing Peel in the side. He'd have been protected from the spatter by the man's body so—'

'On his *right* sleeve. His *right sleeve*. The angle of thrust is consistent with Miriam and Mac's story. The killer came in from behind Peel, stabbed him in the left side and, from the angle of entry, with their left hand. They'd have had to stand at the side of him and thrust in and up to do it with the right, and I seriously think Peel might have moved out of the way if he'd seen anyone standing next to him and then come at him with a knife. And, if Mac stabbed him with his right hand – in the side, as you suggest – then no, Peel's body would not have protected him from the spray. There'd have been blood all across the front of his coat, all over the sleeve, not just a smear on the frigging cuff.'

Wildman was not about to give up. 'So, it was unexpected. Mac made a run at him, took a chance. He took every other bloody risk he could. You're not telling me he wouldn't have done anything imaginable not to have a repeat of what happened to Cara Evans. He didn't want to get another one killed. So he took a chance. I don't know, maybe Peel got distracted and McGregor was able to take him. Split second, that's all it would have taken. Peel looks away, Mac gets him.' Wildman took a deep breath, tried for conciliation. 'Look, any way you look at it, there was provocation; I'll give you that.'

'Generous of you.'

'A sympathetic jury, good lawyer . . . But he bloody did it. I know he bloody did it.'

'No,' Alec said quietly, 'you wish *you* had. That's what this is about, isn't it? Twice, Mac left you out of the loop. You think if you'd been there that night, then Cara Evans would still be here. You believe you'd have taken Peel down. You can't accept the fact that *you* might have failed, just like Mac failed. And then he goes and does the same thing all over again. More than you can take, isn't it? Knowing that Mac didn't trust you, didn't trust any of us, with Miriam's life.'

'This isn't about me.'

'Isn't it? I was there, remember. I saw the look on your face when Mac was brought into the hospital with that little girl. I saw the look on your face that night and you couldn't forgive him. The rest of us – well, we all thanked God it hadn't been us put to the test like that; all you could think was that you wished it had been you. Wished you'd been there because, in your own fucked-up little head, you could see yourself playing the hero, taking out the killer and rescuing the kid. Well, it wasn't like that, was it? Not so neat and clean as all that? Truth is, Wildman, I don't think anyone could have stopped Thomas Peel from killing Cara Evans, because he got off on it; he relished it, enjoyed every minute. If he could have arranged for someone to film it for him, then I don't doubt he would have done it. He liked the buzz and he liked to be reminded how good it felt, and that's why he set Mac up with Miriam: he wanted to capture the moment all over again.'

He looked away from Wildman, something echoing, something deep in his memory.

Wildman noted the change. 'What?' he said.

'It was a clear night. The night Cara Evans died. Bright, clear, you could see for miles.'

'So?'

Alec shook his head. 'I don't know. Just . . . Rains, he took pictures. Peel knew Rains was employed to take pictures.

'So what?' Wildman scoffed. 'Where are you going?'

'Back to talk to Billy Tigh. Oh, and you should organize an interview with Sara Curtis, the prison visitor who went to see Rains. *Her* brother abused Tigh's.'

'How the hell do you know that?'

'Information received,' Alec said and left before Wildman could say more.

The coast road was clear this time of year and the drive pleasant, Rina thought. Bare trees and hedges thinned of their summer growth meant that it was possible to look across the fields and see the sea for a good deal of the journey, only the section of road near Abbotsbury being sufficiently inland and the road between high enough walls for the open view to be blocked.

She and Abe talked, running through what they knew so far, and Abe finally told Rina just how deep Karen had buried herself in what had been her father's world. Knowing that because she had warned Karen and given her time to run, others had died, depressed Rina thoroughly.

Abe was more sanguine. 'If not Karen, then someone else,' he said. 'The life they led would have ended in violence one way or another.'

'I don't find that comforting,' Rina said tartly. 'Abe, my world has not been one that featured a great deal of violence until fairly recently and, frankly, I am heartily sick of it. I'm not cut out for this kind of thing at all. No, don't you dare laugh; I mean it.'

Abe's attempt to control his humour ended in a choking fit, and Rina seriously worried they might crash as the car veered across the road and dangerously close to a dry stone wall. 'Rina,' he said at last. 'Given the choice, I'd have you watch my back any time.'

'You're laughing at me again.'

'No,' Abe said seriously. 'No, I'm not. I mean every word.'

Bridport confused them for a while, West Bay Harbour being on the other side of the river from where they'd expected it to be. 'Should have used the satnav,' Abe said. 'I'm sure this was just called the quayside last time I came.'

The gallery was small, tucked back in the middle of a row of little shops and cafés, looking rather upmarket for its location, but also friendly and welcoming with its array of pretty Christmas decorations featured in the window, all made by local artists. Rina paused to admire the glass stars and little wooden ornaments, quilted baubles and plump ceramic choirboys. Through the window she caught the glimpse of an avant-garde Christmas tree, a twiggy affair hung with what looked like gold medallions and stained glass. She was less keen on that.

An exhibition by a local printmaker faced them as they entered. Woodblock prints created in the Japanese manner, intricate and multicoloured. Rina moved closer to examine a street scene. Streetlights giving way to stars in a rich blue sky, hurrying crowds intricately described.

'Beautiful, isn't it?'

Rina turned to the woman who had spoken. Adrienne Kossof, the gallery owner, sat behind a wooden desk on which was set a cash register, card reader and a stack of pastel-shaded tissue paper and another of tiny, oriental boxes. She was about Rina's age, but very slender and willowy and with grey hair in an elfin cut that suited her delicate features. She wore jeans and a heavy sweater and still managed to look chic and neat. Rina had given up on jeans years and years ago; she had never been that keen.

'Very beautiful,' Rina said, glancing back at the print. 'It just seems so sad that the block is completely destroyed in the making, doesn't it?'

The woman raised an eyebrow and smiled warmly. 'It does, rather. Of course, in Japan, in the heyday of printmaking, the artist would hand the work over and a whole troop of makers would create each colour block from the original. Richard, the artist here, he does the whole process himself. This exhibition – twelve prints – that's two years' work.'

'Well worth it,' Rina said and really meant it. She looked at the price of the street scene and inwardly flinched, but that didn't stop her from wanting it. There was a vibrancy about the scene that really appealed. Anyway, she rarely treated herself and, also anyway, it seemed like a good way of breaking the ice. Look affluent, Abe had said.

'I'd like that, please,' Rina said. The woman looked first shocked and then pleased.

'Wonderful! I'll mark it sold. Richard is due to take down this weekend. Will it be all right to send it on then? Unless you'd like to collect it, or, of course, if you want to take it now?'

'No, the weekend is fine,' Rina said. 'It seems a shame to disturb the exhibition, and we're only just along the coast.'

'Oh, it's mostly locals this time of year,' the woman nodded. 'Really, I wanted to feature Richard in the summer, but it just didn't happen. But he's picked up a bit of pre-Christmas trade. We go entirely over to the Christmas display from next week.' She smiled confidingly. 'To be honest, some of the Christmas stuff is just well-made tat, but it sells and this time of year that really matters.' She glanced from Rina to Abe, noticing him for the first time. Her look was curious, as though she tried to work out what their relationship might be. Abe might be young enough to be Rina's son – had she started a family very early – but they looked nothing alike and he was clearly younger than Rina was, so . . .

'The window display is very pretty, though,' Rina nodded sympathetically. 'I heard you might be selling the gallery?' she added.

Raised eyebrows from Adrienne Kossof. 'How do you know that?' she asked. 'I've told very few people yet. I don't want to give the wrong impression, you understand. I'm retiring through choice, not because the business isn't doing well.'

'Oh, no,' Rina said. 'That's what I heard. No, a young friend of mine is interested in taking over. She wants me to think about being a sleeping partner in the business.' Rina smiled as she handed over her credit card. 'You see, Karen is very young; having a, shall we say, older financial partner gives her a lot more credibility.'

'Oh yes, I see.' Adrienne took the card and inserted it into the reader. She frowned. 'I thought her name was Carolyn.'

Rina didn't miss a beat. 'Carolyn Johnson is her given name,' she said. 'She was named after her mother.' She leaned in, confidentially. 'They never really got along. We've always called her Karen. That would have been her father's choice. I said I'd call in and look around on my way to see her today. See what I thought. I must say, I'm very impressed.'

'Thank you. Pin, please,' she turned the card reader towards Rina. 'Well, we have talked about it, of course; she said her solicitor would be in touch this week.'

'She'll be using Rawlinsons, I expect,' Rina said. 'They arranged the purchase of her house recently.'

'No, Deerhams, I think. Take your card, please. Now I'll need your address for delivery, and the artist usually sends the occasional catalogue to his customers, if that's all right?'

They left ten minutes later and Rina was frowning. 'I think I gave more away about me than we found out that was useful. Still, couldn't be helped. At least we know what name she prefers to go by and the name of her solicitors. Now all we need is an address.'

Abe nodded. 'I don't think the Kossof woman swallowed any of it,' he said.

'Of course not. She's a businesswoman and she's the aunt by marriage of Igor Vashinsky. I imagine she's used to con artists.'

Abe could tell she was annoyed with herself. 'Rina,' he said, 'you did a good job. You've given us another lead and bought yourself a pretty picture.'

Rina scowled at him. 'You didn't like my picture?'

'Not a lot, no. I'm more of a Constable man, or Turner before he got all abstracty. Oh and I don't mind a nice Pre-Raphaelite. At least you can tell what it is.'

Rina shook her head. 'Take me home, Abe Jackson,' she said. 'Then go and investigate something: contact Deerhams and find out where Karen's house might be.'

'Yes, ma'am,' Abe said. 'Whatever you say. We are only here to serve.'

Alec had to wait before they'd let him in to see Billy Tigh. He'd been placed on the medical wing and, though he'd eaten well, slept soundly and watched television avidly – all normal behaviour for Billy Tigh – he'd said nothing more about the killing of Philip Rains. He'd been formally charged, received legal advice, been seen on a daily basis by the visiting psychiatrist, but shown no sign of remorse, concern or even acknowledgement of what he'd done. He'd certainly offered no explanation.

Alec had to get clearance from the psychiatrist before he was allowed to see Billy Tigh. They took him to the medical wing, settled him in a side room and brought Tigh in, a guard remaining by the door, both protector and chaperone.

Alec knew he was breaking with protocol by coming alone; maybe being around Mac, such breaches were catching. He hadn't let on to Wildman, but he too was angry with his friend. Mac had never been a team player, not really, but he'd at least given the impression of being so until now, and the doubt festered; what if he *had* told Wildman what was happening, alerted him to Peel's call? Would Cara Evans still be alive?

Alec, in his heart of hearts, believed that Wildman was more likely to have driven roughshod through Mac's attempt at negotiation and the result would have been the same. Alec could appreciate just why Mac had not taken Wildman into his confidence back then; he was having a harder time dealing with the fact that Mac had, this time, excluded Alec too.

Billy Tigh looked bored, as though he anticipated Alec's questions; the same ones had been asked time after time. Alec studied the young man. Light grey eyes stared back, non-committal and wary.

'Tell me about Terry,' Alec said.

Tigh blinked, the wariness more emphatic.

'I know about Brian Curtis,' Alec said. 'What he did to your brother. Did he hurt you too, Billy?'

A slow, hesitant shake of the head.

Alec caught his breath, and the look on the guard's face told him this was totally unexpected. *Don't rush*, Alec counselled himself. *Take it easy.*

'We know there were pictures of Terry and Brian Curtis.' He knew no such thing, but it was a reasonable bet.

A blink this time, wariness exchanged for something else. Something feral and angry.

'Billy, can you tell me, do you know who took those pictures? Was it Philip Rains?'

He nodded then: a small, slight movement of the head. 'He told me Rains did it. Took them pictures.' Billy's voice was hoarse, harsh.

'Terry told you that?'

The feral look died. Boredom again. Alec knew he had missed the clue, overshot the mark.

'Peel,' he said, mentally crossing his fingers. 'Thomas Peel told you?'

Again, the sharp nod. 'He told me. Rains took them pictures for him. Rains took all *his* pictures too, all them kids; he had a book, he said. Not like a real book, a book on the computer where people like that bastard Brian Curtis could order pictures off. Like it was a catalogue, he said. He laughed at me. A catalogue like me mum used to order stuff, clothes and stuff, like for Christmas. He took them pictures and Peel put them in his book. Our Terry, like he was a toy or a pair of jeans. He said he had loads of pictures.'

'When did he tell you this, Billy? When did you talk to Thomas Peel?'

Billy shrugged. It didn't matter to him when. Just that he had. His gaze drifted from Alec to some point on the bare, green walls.

'Billy,' Alec said, 'was it before or after Terry killed himself?'

Attention snapped back, and Alec quailed beneath a look so intense and hate-filled that he glanced instinctively at the guard by the door and saw that he too had noted that change and was now tense, expecting trouble. Was this the look that Philip Rains had seen, just before he died? It occurred to Alec that the mode of death had been the same. Rains and Peel: a strange echoing, as though whoever had killed Peel had known where and how to strike, had seen . . .

He shoved the thought aside. It was irrelevant for the moment and also inaccurate when he thought about it. True, each man had died of a single stab wound, but Billy Tigh had walked up to Rains and driven the improvised blade home while looking straight into his victim's face. Peel's assailant had attacked him from behind.

'Before,' Billy Tigh said, his voice small and strangled. 'I was angry, told Terry. Terry didn't tell no one about what Brian done. Then Peel told me about the pictures, showed them to me, and I went to Terry, said I know and why hadn't he told me. He cried. I never seen my brother cry, not since we were kids. Then he topped himself. What else could I do when I found out Rains was 'ere? I waited, found a blade, did him.'

End of story. Not quite.

'Billy?' His attention was sliding away; Alec could feel it. 'Billy, how do you know Thomas Peel?'

Billy Tigh laughed. At least that's what Alec thought it was; the sound was painful, reluctant. 'He was screwing Sara,' he said. 'Sara knew me mum.'

Sara? 'Sara Curtis? Brian's sister?'

'Yeah, her. Sara.' The blankness returned then as Billy Tigh shut down once more and Alec knew he'd had everything he was going to get. Far more than he had hoped for. The links were revealing themselves now, and Alec was sure they had, as yet, only glimpsed the web.

He watched as Billy Tigh got to his feet and the guard led him away.

Leaving the prison, he phoned Wildman and gave him the news. Sara Curtis, he learnt was on her way to the police station to 'help with enquiries'. Wildman listened without comment to what Alec told him, but Alec could feel the intensity of thought as Wildman took it in.

'Best get yourself back here,' Wildman said at last. 'Best she hear it from the horse's mouth that she's accused of screwing a child-killer as well as having a brother.'

Alec hadn't realized that possession of a sibling was now a criminal offence, but he decided to leave off baiting Wildman for now. His thoughts returned to Billy Tigh: that look, that anger, that grief. He pulled over, searched through his phone for the number of the psychiatrist and called him at home.

'I think he'll end up like his brother,' Alec said as he explained what had happened. 'Just thought you should know.'

'What gives you that impression?'

Alec thought. 'That's exactly what it is,' he agreed. 'Just an impression.' How do you explain the look? That sense that they are just going through the motions of living. That they have already given up. Alec had once seen that look in Mac's eyes and it was not one he could forget.

'I'll have them keep an eye,' the psychiatrist said, but Alec could tell he resented an outsider presuming to tell him his job and he had to leave it at that. He drove back to Pinsent, oddly disturbed by his meeting with Billy Tigh.

Mac called Rina that evening to let her know that all was well. Bridie Duggan was her usual hospitable self, and Miriam was feeling better in the shelter of her large house, within its walled garden and with its state-of-the-art security system, which Fitch had let Miriam play with.

'It's all quiet here,' Rina said. 'I talked to Andy and he said there'd been some calls from the media, so I expect all that will change, but they'll get short shrift in Frantham Old Town.'

'True. Fitch will probably head back tomorrow. He'll give you a ring and so will I. Miriam sends her love.'

Rina set the phone back on its cradle, feeling better now she knew that Mac and Miriam were out of the way, though she could not help but feel troubled at how tired he sounded: so like the Mac she had first met, world weary and lost.

She hoped that everything would be more settled by Christmas. She'd give a great deal to have a normal, celebratory festive season, and then the promised trip to Manchester for early in the New Year – a few days' shopping and socializing with Bridie and Joy – would be lovely.

Tim mooched in, looking despondent. He was relieved that Joy had gone but was missing her terribly.

'Oh my poor lovelorn boy,' Rina teased. 'You've got it bad, haven't you?'

'Terminally,' he agreed, brightening a little. 'Rina, do you think it matters, me being older?'

'No,' she said. 'Joy knows her own mind. But, Tim, take it slow, enjoy it, don't rush headlong. You've been thrown together by circumstances that were far from ideal; take time to get to know one another now, to do the ordinary things.'

'I will, Rina. Or, at least, I will if Joy does.' He bent to kiss her on the cheek. 'Don't worry, Rina darling. I'm going to enjoy every single minute, just like you did with Frank, and I know if he was still here, that's what you'd still be doing, even now. I've had a good teacher.'

He left her then to get ready for work, and Rina dabbed the tears that pricked the corners of her eyes.

THIRTY-THREE

Fitch had originally decided to drive back on the Thursday morning, but circumstances intervened in the shape of Igor Vaschinsky.

'He wants to talk to you,' Bridie told Mac. 'No offence, but I'm not having that man in my house. I do have my standards. You can meet him at the club; you'll be safe enough there.'

'Safe enough?'

She shrugged. 'Better that than sorry. You sleep well?'

'We did, thank you.'

'She's a lovely girl, Miriam is. You going to make her an honest woman?'

'I hope so,' he said, surprised to realize the truth of that. He'd never really thought in terms of marriage.

'I think our Joy hopes for something similar,' she said.

'Tim. Yes. They do seem to have become very close.' Mac was cautious.

'He's a good man,' Bridie announced. 'I'd like it better if they were a bit closer in age, but when I think of some of the idiots she's dated in the past, I just count my blessings, frankly. Mac, why is it that teenage girls always seem to go for the himbos and the bastards?'

'Himbos?'

'Male bimbos,' Miriam said, coming into the dining room. 'Who's that, then?'

'We were just talking about teenage girls. The boys they choose.'

'Oh, don't,' Miriam shuddered. 'Lord, when I look back, it's scary.'

'Help yourself to breakfast, love. All on the sideboard. Mind you, I don't think I was any better. I met Jimmy when I was Joy's age, though, and that was it for me. Him too. I never had reason to worry.'

Fitch took his place at the table, Joy following behind with a plate piled high.

'Hungry?' Mac asked.

'Starving. I'm normally just toast or muesli, but this morning I could eat a horse.'

'Don't give Bridie ideas,' Fitch warned. 'So,' he continued, pouring himself some coffee. 'What do you suppose Vaschinsky wants?'

'Has to be something to do with Karen and Peel,' Mac speculated.

Fitch nodded slowly. 'Abe turned up a few connections,' he said. 'He thinks Vaschinsky's people delivered Peel to Karen. That she knew where he was but couldn't get to him; Vaschinsky, shall we say, facilitated.'

'And Peel cooperated.' Mac frowned.

'Not so odd,' Fitch said. 'I think it's safe to assume that pressure was brought to bear on Peel, but that he'd also have the inclination. He liked that sort of challenge and, besides, Karen gave him access to you. Miriam, you remembered anything else about the house?'

'Not over breakfast, Fitch,' Bridie said. 'Let the girl eat.'

'Oh, I don't mind and I can think and eat at the same time.' She speared a mushroom, regarded it thoughtfully as though it might provide the answer to something. 'No damp in the cellar,' she said. 'It wasn't warm, but it wasn't freezing cold. I think I was in just one part: when I heard Peel come down the stairs, he walked across another room. I could hear his footsteps. The door opened outwards and I caught a glimpse of shelves and bottles, like a wine cellar.' She ate the mushroom, followed it with scrambled egg, bacon. Mac was relieved; he'd expected Fitch's questions to bring on a loss of appetite, but that seemed not to be the case. Miriam was being remarkably calm now they were away from Pinsent and from Frantham. He wondered if the mood would last or if she would suddenly come crashing down.

'When he took me upstairs, he had a blindfold over my eyes and my hands were cuffed. I heard wooden stairs and there was a cold draught, as though the cellar door was close to a window and the window was open. I felt the air on my face. Then tiles on the floor, I think. Echoes. Then a garden. He'd taped my mouth, so I remember thinking there must have been other houses nearby. Someone to hear me if I'd shouted out.'

'A garden?' Bridie asked.

'I could smell wet earth, leaves. Winter honeysuckle – my mum used to grow it – and something else honey-scented; I know it but I can't think what it is. We went down a path and through a gate. I heard the hinges squeak. Then I heard the car boot open and he pushed me inside, and when I tried to fight back, he just gave me this great shove and I lost my balance, fell in.' She poked at the food on her plate and Mac watched anxiously.

'More tea, love?' Bridie asked and glared at Fitch, but Miriam continued to eat.

'Stop watching every mouthful, Mac,' she said at last. 'I'm going to be OK.'

'You've been through a lot,' Mac said cautiously.

'Sure I have and I don't doubt I'm going to have the nightmares to go with it. Right now, the thought of going back to work makes me feel sick. The thought of going back to my sister's place the same. Even talking to her on the phone makes me feel panicky, but I'm OK. I'm going to be sensible and take things slowly, and being here, I feel OK, so thank you, Bridie. I'll get around to the rest a bit at a time if that's all right with everyone, but just now I'm focusing on the relief bit – you know, still being here and the anger bit and all of that . . .' She trailed off lamely, then fetched some more bacon.

Mac opened his mouth to say something, but Bridie frowned him into silence. She leaned over to hand him more tea he didn't really want. 'Leave it,' she murmured. 'Everyone does things their own way. Let her be.'

Mac nodded, bowing to Bridie's judgement which, he figured, usually turned out to be as sound as Rina's. He missed Rina, missed Tim, missed Peverill Lodge. Wondered again if he'd have a job to go back to and if he wanted it anyway.

Later that Thursday, Mac and Fitch, together with a couple of Bridie's other security people, met Igor Vaschinsky at *Patrick's*, the nightclub Bridie had renamed for her dead son. The other had, predictably, been renamed *Jimmy's*. Mac thought it an interesting memorial, not sure if it was in the best of taste, but, as Bridie herself had said, people cope with grief and pain in their own way, and he guessed this was hers.

'Fitch, do you mind if I ask something? Are you and Bridie . . .?'

'No, but I think we may. Joy keeps encouraging me to, you know, move things to the next level, but Bridie's been widowed less than a year and I know it'd just be a rebound thing. I want to be more than that.'

'You seem very close.'

'Always have been, even when Jimmy was still around. Bridie and me, we go back a long way. She fell for Jimmy and I accepted that, but she knows I'm always there for her. Jimmy knew it too.'

'And that never caused any problems?' Mac was intrigued. Fitch had been Jimmy Duggan's right-hand man.

'Jimmy knew us better than that,' Fitch said proudly. 'I don't betray them that trust me, Mac. Never have, never will. Jimmy knew that. Rina knows that. Bridie too.'

Mac nodded. He watched the city pass by from the car window, Fitch not driving for once, but sitting beside him in the very luxurious rear seat. It felt a little surreal. *Patrick's* didn't look much from the outside, but in Mac's experience nightclubs rarely did. This was a converted seed store, Fitch told him, and they had kept the industrial look: red-brick exterior, heavy wooden doors, lots of steel and chrome inside with the old cast-iron pillars taking pride of place in the design. A mezzanine level led to chill-out rooms and another bar, and a private suite that Mac decided to ignore. Fitch took him down into the main area, across the dance floor and into the suite of offices beyond. Bridie's other minders followed and the manager told them that Vaschinsky and his people had already arrived. He had offered drinks but they had all declined.

Fitch opened double doors that would have looked more at home in an operating theatre and revealed a comfortable area beyond. A large polished wooden table, surrounded by matching chairs, took up one half of the room; sofas and easy chairs the rest. Igor Vaschinsky rose to greet them, extending a hand to Mac and then to Fitch.

'So,' Vaschinsky said, 'Thomas Peel is dead.' He looked speculatively at Mac.

'I didn't do it, if that's what interests you,' Mac said.

'No, I know you didn't. Pity, though. Your DCI Wildman

so much wants you to be the one responsible. Don't you feel a duty to make him happy?'

'Not particularly,' Mac said. He wondered where this was leading and glanced at the men with Vaschinsky. They were assiduous in not meeting his eye. Bridie's two were similarly blank when it came to Vaschinsky.

'What do you want, Mr Vaschinsky?'

Igor Vaschinsky nodded slowly, as though Mac had just given the response to some profound question. 'Want?' he said. 'Nothing. But I am curious. My aunt owns a small gallery, down on the south coast. A lovely little pace in a nice location. She enjoys owning it, but feels the time has now come to sell on to someone with more energy. My aunt is not a young woman and, though she looks after herself well, feels the call of retirement, as, I'm sure, I may do one day. As we all will, I'm sure.'

The gallery Karen Parker talked about, Mac thought. He waited.

'A mutual acquaintance of ours showed an interest in buying. She does not, at present, have the capital required, but, in time, would certainly be in the position to make such an investment. I was not unhappy with that option. The young woman in question has been useful, and, well, it is always sensible to invest your wealth, make it grow. It pleased me, I suppose, that this young woman was sensible.'

'Karen Parker,' Mac said.

'The same,' Vaschinsky agreed. 'I knew her father by reputation; not a good reputation, I'm sure you will agree. The daughter, though, she seemed to have more class, more capacity for invention and imagination and discretion.'

'Seemed?' Mac said.

Vaschinsky inclined his head in acknowledgement. 'Seemed,' he agreed. 'When she asked for Peel, I was happy to oblige, as were those who had given him protection and were, shall we say, growing tired of his company. And I was curious. Why did she want this man? What plan did she have? So I watched.'

'She wanted Peel to get at me,' Mac said.

'So it seems. And it was when I realized what she wanted to do, and how she planned to, shall we say, make life difficult for you, that I began to doubt that Karen Parker was really the woman I thought she was.'

'I don't understand,' Mac said.

Vaschinsky spread his hands, as though the facts spoke for themselves. 'It was clumsy, stupid, complicated. If she wanted vengeance, why not just kill you and be done? To play such a childish game. To draw such attention to herself. And to bring the attention of you and your friends upon my family. That, I cannot forgive.'

Mac was genuinely puzzled, but Vaschinsky could really only mean one thing. 'Rina?' he said.

'You look surprised? Your Mrs Martin is a woman to be reckoned with, and your Mr Jackson. It seems they paid my aunt a visit, tried to extract information regarding Karen Parker, or Carolyn Johnson as she had preferred to be known. My aunt called me; I looked into the matter. Be advised, Inspector, I have nothing against Mrs Martin. She has the same instinct to protect her loved ones as do I. I have nothing against you; Karen wished you harm, but I have no reason to do so. She had her chance and failed, so the matter should be closed. But I do not like my family involved in someone else's tale of revenge. You understand me, Inspector?'

Mac nodded. 'I think so, yes. But I think you should know that Karen also acted out of a similar instinct to protect. Most of her life that has been uppermost in her mind.'

'And I wish her brother a happy life,' Vaschinsky said. He rose to leave and his men gathered around him, as though suddenly awakened from their studied inertia.

'What do you make of that?' Fitch asked as Vaschinsky's party left through the double doors.

'I hope Karen has sharp instincts,' Mac said. 'I think trouble is about to call and, as we don't know where she is, there's not a lot that I or any of us can do.'

Karen Parker was truly on her own.

THIRTY-FOUR

Karen was cautious. She had, as yet, only spent the odd few hours in the house Peel had used as his refuge. She knew that she had to put space between her old life and the new, and that the new could not truly begin until she had finished amassing the capital she wanted to make that transition and had gained the respectability she so desired.

She already thought of the house as hers, but Karen had spent her entire life on the move; she was not about to shift her habits until she was completely sure it was safe to do so. George had been the pacesetter here. Had George agreed to go and live with her, then she'd calculated it would take about six months to get through all the hoops Social Services might require her to jump through, and that timescale had been factored in to her plans. By that time she'd have had the gallery, furnished the house, bowed out of her life as Carolyn Johnson and the various other aliases she had acquired. George would never have touched that life, the shadow of that other Karen.

As it was, George's resilience to her persuasion had slowed her plans and, on reflection, she had decided that was no bad thing. Peel was dead, but so far Mac had escaped the fallout from that. He had thrown her schedule. He had changed her direction. He had got in her way.

Karen had been angry with Mac before, but that anger had begun to burn itself out before Peel had fallen into her path. Having Peel available rekindled the sense of betrayal she had felt. She had allowed herself to be drawn back into that mindset that told her Mac had let her down and Mac had let George down. Mac would have to pay. That her careful plans had come to nothing now riled her far more than his original offence.

It had also rekindled her sense of caution. If her plans regarding Mac could go so far astray, then what else could?

So it was that when Vaschinsky's men came to the house where they expected Karen to be residing, she simply wasn't there. Attic to basement searched, but there was no sign of where she might be or when she was likely to return.

With some trepidation, Vaschinsky was informed.

She would come back, Vaschinsky thought. He told his people to keep a discreet watch on the place until she did.

Five miles up the coast, Carolyn Johnson slept in yet another hotel bed, dreamed of a life she had never had and woke knowing that she would wait no longer for either vengeance or for George to be given his last chance to join her.

'I've found the house,' Abe Jackson told Rina. 'Thing is, I don't think I'm the only one taking an interest.

'Oh, how's that?'

'I managed to wangle enough information out of the solicitors to pinpoint what I thought might be it. I texted George, sent him some pictures, and he texted back that it looked right. That was yesterday evening. I did a drive-by this morning, just to take a look, you understand, and there were a couple of big men in big cars not being very discreet. Mac called last night about his meeting with Vaschinsky . . .' He let the question hang.

'Yes, he called me too. You think they're Vaschinsky's people.'

'Well, they look the part. Rina, I can still gain access but . . .'

'No, leave it, Abe. We'll tell Mac you've found the house and then leave the situation to develop, I think. If they're watching, then Karen's not there, which begs the question—'

'Where is she and what is she planning? Next move would seem to be hers, Rina, but you should try and have a word with young George, just give him the heads-up in case she makes contact.'

'He'll be at school by now,' Rina said. 'He's not supposed to leave his phone on. I'll talk to him when he gets back home.'

She hesitated after Abe had rung off. Should she let Cheryl know? Know what? That Karen wasn't at the house she was supposed to own now. Rina shook her head; the feeling that something bad was happening would not go away.

Like most of the kids in the school, George did not actually turn his phone *off*, merely to silent. The essential teenage accessory – in George's case, not a fashion statement, merely a phone – was, in fact, rarely switched off even at night and even more rarely left out of reach.

So it was that George received a text from his sister in the middle of the school afternoon. He felt the phone buzz in his pocket, ignored it while he dealt with the ongoing difficulties associated with quadratic equations, and then sneaked a look while jostling down the corridor to get to the next lesson. It was a message from Karen.

End of the school day and he waited for Ursula to come out of her English class. 'I've sent a text to Cheryl,' he said. 'Told her we're both staying for an after-school thing.'

'Oh? What kind of after-school thing? You know, in case she asks. And what are we actually going to do?'

'Oh, a drama thing. School play. I don't know.'

'School play. Oh, my God. George, that's about the worst excuse you could have made. You hate drama and I can't act. Cheryl knows that. She saw us in that "end of summer term" crap, remember?'

George grimaced. How could he forget? He'd only had two words to say and he'd managed to get those back to front. 'I had to think of something,' he said. He showed her the text.

'*Meet me at Rina's. I'm sorry, George, but I have to leave. Come to say goodbye*.'

'She hates text speak,' he said, as though Ursula had asked.

'You think she's really going away? I mean, just like that?'

George shook his head. 'I don't know,' he said. 'But she's planning something and I don't think I'm going to like it at all.'

They caught the bus to Frantham, got off at the end of the promenade close to the police station. 'You think we should tell someone?' Ursula said.

George shook his head. 'Tell someone what? Maybe she really means it. That she's leaving.'

'If Mac was here, you'd tell him. Text him now, find out what he thinks.'

George hesitated, took the phone from his pocket and stared at it, then slipped it back into his pocket. 'I've got to hear what she has to say,' he told Ursula. 'Rina and Tim will be there; what can she do?'

'Anything she wants,' Ursula said. She sighed. 'OK, whatever. Let's get it over with.' She swung her backpack on to her shoulder and set off towards Peverill Lodge, George, less certain now the decision was made, trailing in her wake.

Rina had been out. Too restless to remain at home, she and Tim had been walking along the promenade and down on the beach, the bracing wind doing Rina a power of good and freezing Tim to the core. Coming back up the steps on to the promenade, they caught sight of George and Ursula walking away, just too far away to hear Rina when she called out to them, her voice snatched back by the bitter wind.

'What are they doing here?' Tim wondered anxiously. 'Rina, they look as though they're heading home – to our home, I mean.'

Rina nodded anxiously. 'I don't like it, Tim. Something's wrong; I can feel it.' She set off at the closest to a run Tim had ever seen her perform, and Tim raced beside her.

She slipped the key into the front door of Peverill Lodge and called out as soon as they were inside. Karen's voice replied from the living room.

Glancing anxiously at Tim, Rina started forward.

'We should get help,' Tim whispered, somewhat belatedly.

'I think it's a little late for that,' Rina said. Shoulders squared, she made her way across the hall, and together they entered the living room. George was there, with Ursula beside him. They both looked shaken and confused. Eliza and Bethany were seated together on the piano stool, and Steven and Matthew sat uneasily side by side on the smaller of the two sofas. Karen held a gun. It sat comfortably in her hand as she turned to greet Rina and Tim and motioned them to sit down.

'I told them to call Mac,' she said. 'They say he's gone.'

'He has,' Rina confirmed. 'He and Miriam have gone to stay with friends.'

'You think I believe that?'

'It happens to be true. Karen, what do you hope to gain from doing this? From bursting into our home, from threatening innocent people?'

'I hope to make him hurt,' Karen said simply. 'Like I hurt when our dad took George. Like it hurt when we were all alone. I want him to feel what it was like.'

'You think Mac doesn't know?' Rina laughed; she couldn't help herself. 'Karen, Mac was one of the loneliest people I ever met. He didn't let you down. He did all he could and you know that full well. Your father was the one to blame, not Mac.'

'Mac would have locked me away.'

'Maybe so. He had a job to do. Karen, you don't want to hurt anyone. Not any of us. Put the gun down and leave. Now.'

'If George goes with me.'

'George doesn't want to go.'

'George needs to go with me. I can't leave him here, not to be poisoned by all of you.'

'Poisoned?'

'Against me! It was always just the two of us. Me and George.'

'And that was then. Not now, Karen. You have to let him be.'

Karen had lowered her weapon, seeming almost to forget it was in her hand, but she raised it now, pointed it straight at Rina's head.

'I don't have to listen to you. George, go and get in the car. We're going now. And tell me, Rina, do you think it would hurt Mac enough if I were to kill you?'

'Probably,' Rina said softly. 'I really wouldn't know.'

She felt Tim move and motioned him to be still. 'It's all right,' she said. 'I'm not afraid.'

'Well, you damn well should be.' Karen's finger tightened on the trigger. Bethany squealed in horror, and Matthew called out for Karen to stop.

George didn't think about it: he stepped between Rina and his sister.

'George, get out of my way.'

'No,' he said. 'Karen, I won't get out of the way. This isn't you, this is something you've made yourself be.'

'No,' she said. 'This is me.'

Ursula moved cautiously, warily, to George's side and took his hand, squeezed it hard.

'Please, Karen,' George said. 'Just go. Do this and you'll hurt Mac, but you'll hurt me more. Karen, please.'

For what seemed like forever no one spoke, no one moved. Karen held the weapon, pointed unflinchingly at Rina's head.

'Karen, please,' George said again. 'I love you, Karen, but you can't do stuff like this.'

Another stretch of time: George unmoving, Rina barely daring to breath.

Karen sighed deeply. 'Oh Georgie.' She shook her head, lowered the weapon. 'But know this, all of you: Mac had better keep looking over his shoulder. One day, I'm going to be there.'

'No,' George said. 'You won't. Not if you still want me to own you as my sister. I love you, Karen. But you've got to go and you've got to let me go too.'

She said nothing, but she nodded briefly, and Rina could see the tears streaming down her cheeks. *Another lost child*, she thought, though, as far as she was concerned now, this one probably couldn't be lost enough.

Karen left, the front door slammed, and Rina collapsed into the nearest chair.

'Are you OK?' George said. 'I'm sorry, Rina. She sent me a message to meet her here, said she was leaving. I never thought . . .'

'George, now hear me,' Rina said firmly. 'None of this is your fault. Get that into your head now. None of this was caused by you.'

Karen drove fast through the little town of Frantham and out on to the main road. Tears still poured down her cheeks and she wiped them away impatiently.

'Oh Georgie,' she said. 'What have we done to ourselves?' She knew she could not go back to the little house she had wanted so much. She knew that soon the alarm would be raised and the police would come looking. Police and probably others too; she had no illusions about there being honour among thieves, or any other variety of criminal, and she had now outlived any usefulness she might have had.

But one thing life had taught Karen was that she should always have a fallback position. Always have her bags packed, money available, identity to exchange.

Her hire car was found in a cliff top car park the following day, but the young woman with the glossy black bobbed hair who boarded the Eurostar was a lifetime away from Karen Parker.

EPILOGUE

Mac returned to Frantham a few days later, but not to work. Internal Affairs were still investigating the killing of Thomas Peel, and Mac was still suspended. He and Miriam drove first to Rina's, to be regaled by first-hand accounts of Karen Parker's threats and Rina's bravery – not to mention the nerve of young George.

'You sure you're all right?' Mac said.

'I'm sure. Mac, what will happen now?'

'I don't know,' he said honestly. 'I imagine I'll be on suspension for a while yet, though even Wildman is having to agree that the evidence against me really isn't there.' He took her hand. 'Do I have you or Tim to thank for that?'

'For what?' Rina asked innocently. 'Mac, let it go. This will all pass, and the less we talk about what should or should not have been done, the better it will be.'

He nodded. 'I'm grateful, Rina,' he said, then added, 'I've been thinking I might resign, but I'm not sure what else I'm cut out for.'

Matthew appeared with tea and fresh biscuits, still warm from the oven.

'Don't rush,' Rina said. 'In time, everything becomes clear; you just have to wait for the fog to lift.'

'I like fog,' Miriam said. 'Fog probably saved my life.' She took a biscuit from the plate and accepted Matthew's tea. Her hand shook and the cup rattled in the saucer, reminding Rina of that day Karen had come to call.

'Miriam?' Mac was suddenly concerned. Miriam was crying. Gently, Matthew took the cup away and Mac wrapped his arms around her, held her while they both, finally, inevitably, broke down and wept away the fear of what might have been.

Several hundred miles to the north on another coast, Alec arrived home. The door opened before he could produce his key and Naomi smiled at him.

'How did you know it was me?'

'Napoleon knew. He's never wrong.' Hearing his name, the large black dog standing beside Naomi woofed happily and snuffled his nose at Alec's hand. Alec stroked the silky ears and then reached for his wife and kissed her, allowed her to lead him inside and into their warm and comfortable front room. He thought of Mac and Wildman, and the mess that others were now clearing up in the wake of Peel's death and the inquest soon to begin.

'I've booked some holiday,' he said.

'Oh, for when?'

'Thought we might start this afternoon.'

She laughed. 'How did you manage that? No, don't tell me. I'm just glad you did. Where shall we go?'

Alec collapsed on to the sofa and pulled Naomi down on to his lap. Napoleon, not to be outdone, pushed his big head against Alec's leg. 'Stick a pin in the map,' he said. 'As long as it's dog-friendly and a long way from Wildman and overtime and anything more complicated than sleeping late and eating too much, and nowhere near a bloody beach.

Ursula and George stood on the headland close to Hill House and gazed out across the grey ocean, watching the seagulls wheel and turn and be blown by the high, gusting wind.

'Where do you think she is?' Ursula asked.

'Far away,' George said. 'I don't think I want to know.' He held tight to Ursula's hand and she moved closer to him, so close he could feel the heat of her body against his and catch the smell of ginger shampoo in her hair. He tried hard to ignore the way that made him feel: a little scared, still more exhilarated.

'We'd better go,' she said. 'It's getting dark. Cheryl will worry and I think we've already got in enough trouble this week.'

George laughed, thinking of the expurgated version of events they had given to their carer. Just the farewell to the sister off on her travels again. No mention of guns or threats or anything more concerning than the fact that George would miss her. 'I guess we have,' he said and, still hand in hand, not caring now who saw or what was said, the two walked slowly back across the lawn.